A DOUBLE DECEPTION

"Miss Mayfield, will you marry me?" Basingstoke demanded. "I know we have not known each other long, but it is long enough that I know my own heart and have reason to believe you know yours."

With a mock curtsy Elizabeth replied, "I am very honored, but I cannot accept your kind offer."

"Kind offer!" Basingstoke exploded. "I am offering you marriage, not a sugared plum or a trip to the theater!"

Elizabeth was sure that this virtual stranger could not be sincere in his sudden proposal. Basingstoke was just as sure that this young lady could not long resist his powers of persuasion.

Who was wrong? The sweet innocent? The worldly aristocrat? Neither? Or both?

D1173069

APRIL KIHLSTROM was born in Buffalo, New York, and graduated from Cornell University with an M.S. in Operations Research. She lives with her husband and their two children in New Jersey.

The Reckless Wager

by
April Kihlstrom

A SIGNET BOOK

SIGNET
Published by the Penguin Group
Penguin Books USA Inc., 375 Hudson Street,
New York, New York, 10014, U.S.A.
Penguin Books Ltd, 27 Wrights Lane, London W8 5TZ, England
Penguin Books Australia Ltd, Ringwood, Victoria, Australia
Penguin Books Canada Ltd, 10 Alcorn Avenue, Toronto, Ontario, Canada M4V 3B2
Penguin Books (N.Z.) Ltd, 182-190 Wairau Road,
Auckland 10, New Zealand

Penguin Books Ltd, Registered Offices:
Harmondsworth, Middlesex, England

First published by Signet, an imprint of New American Library,
a division of Penguin Books USA Inc.

First Printing, November, 1991

10 9 8 7 6 5 4 3 2 1

1

IT WAS A STORMY Cumbria day and the Mayfield manor
house seemed to echo with each clash of thunder. Worse,
it rang with the sounds of a quarrel that had sent its master
and younger daughter in search of refuge, one in his library,
the other to her room. In the drawing room, however, three
persons were unable to escape the quarrel, which matched
the storm outside in its fury. It was, in many respects, a
charming room. The proportions were excellent, the many
windows looked out upon a pleasant garden, and a cheery
fire burned in the grate, casting no smoke into the room.
Blue and silver paper lent an air of distinction to the walls,
and were matched by blue brocade curtains that hung at the
windows. The flowered carpets were straight from Brussels,
ordered some ten years earlier by the first Lady Mayfield.
It was she who had had the furniture set about the room in
such a way as to encourage comfortable *tête-à-têtes* among
those callers fortunate enough to be welcomed here. Indeed,
so successful had her decorating scheme been that when the
second Lady Mayfield dared to broach to her husband the
notion of furbishing up the room and bringing it into the latest
Greek mode, he had roared at her not to touch a thing.

At the moment, however, there were only three persons
in the room and they were not happy with one another. The
youngest was a stout lad of two and a half years who was
delighted with himself for having slipped free of his nurse,
who was suffering terribly from a late-spring cold, and for
having found his way to this room. The eldest was a woman
of no more than five-and-thirty years who was the child's
mother, Lady Beatrix Mayfield. She was dressed in an

5

elegant gown of mauve satin and lace and her hair was
clustered in ringlets about her forehead. Had she not been
engaged in ringing a peal over the head of her elder stepdaughter, Lady Mayfield would have made a most charming
picture.

The third person, Lady Mayfield's stepdaughter, Elizabeth,
sat very still in a brocade chair close to the fireplace. She
did not speak, but looked down at her hands, now clasped
in her lap, and noted, in a detached way, that they held each
other so tightly that the knuckles were white. Her features
were too distinctive for her to be called a beauty, but under
other circumstances she was often held to be a handsome
girl with fine, speaking eyes and blond hair that, if it was
not quite as fair as her sister's tresses, nevertheless shone
in lovely curls about her head. Her height was above average
and her figure well-formed, which gave her a distinguished
appearance, just as her twenty-four years gave her dignity.
If she dressed in somewhat sober colors and not, perhaps,
in the first stare of fashion, her taste was nevertheless
excellent and betrayed a sense of propriety many other
mothers would have wished to see in their own daughters.
Just now she wore a dark blue that set off her coloring to
admiration.

She was not in her best looks, however, though anger had
begun to lend a sparkle to Elizabeth's eyes and an attractive
flush to her cheeks. At her head the tirade continued unabated. She was an unfeeling child. Child? No, she was an
unfeeling spinster, past her last prayers, impossible to please.
It was no wonder a husband could not be found for her.
Between her absurd sense of self-importance, which would
not allow her to look favorably on any gentleman's suit, and
her insufferable ability to exasperate even the most amiable
of persons, she was a veritable antidote. Whatever her fond
papa might say, it was evident that a marriage must be
arranged, whether it suited her or not, or else Elizabeth must
make up her mind to take a position. Only, as what? One
could not countenance the girl taking a servile position, and
her stepmama was dreadfully sorry, but after the way she
had so shamefully abused her dearest half-brother, Elizabeth

could not, in good conscience, be recommended for the post of governess.

It was all jealousy, of course. What else could it be when Willoughby was such an amiable child? Heaven knew Beatrix could understand Elizabeth's natural unhappiness at being thrust out of the spotlight by a new and prettier stepmama, but must she take revenge upon a poor, helpless child?

Meanwhile the half-brother in question, Willoughby, had captured her notebook, his pursuit of which had started this uproar. Helplessly Elizabeth watched as the child tore the pages of her notebook out, one by one, and proceeded to shred them. Pointless to try to retrieve it, of course. Even if she succeeded in doing so, her stepmama would only seize it from her and toss it into the fire to teach her a lesson for being so mean-spirited toward her stepbrother, as she had done once before. So Elizabeth watched, hands clenched in her lap, as six months of work was destroyed. Work! That was a fine name to give to her scribblings. And yet it was work, though no one in this household save herself might know it. It was to have been the fourth and most successful of Mrs. Bethfrey's lurid romances, but to say so would be to draw upon her head another and far worse peal as well as the certain end of Mrs. Bethfrey's short career.

Beatrix Mayfield noticed, to her chagrin, that her charming gestures were wasted on her stepdaughter. The impossible girl was staring at dear Willoughby as if she wished to strangle the poor child. Edmund must be made to realize that the situation could not go on as it was. The girl must be sent away if she could not be married off. The trouble was, where would Edmund agree to send her? Not London, they had had that discussion once before. Edmund seemed to believe the girl ought to be a comfort to her, especially now that she was finally breeding again. Beatrix could not bring him to comprehend that such a thing was impossible. He was convinced that if only the two females—three if one counted Annabelle—he loved best in the world would only put their minds to it, they would get along famously. And indeed, Beatrix thought with a sniff, there was no difficulty with Edmund's younger daughter. Annabelle understood perfectly

Willoughby's charm and never exchanged cross words with
her stepmama as Elizabeth was always doing.

It did not occur to Lady Mayfield to wonder if perhaps
a difference in her behavior in any way accounted for the
difference in the behavior of the two girls. And even if it
had, Lady Mayfield could no more have altered her behavior than Elizabeth could have altered hers. The battle
lines had been drawn from almost the first moment they
met, and nothing at this late juncture was likely to alter
them.

Elizabeth was also conscious of the disparity between her
behavior and Annabelle's toward the second Lady Mayfield.
There were unkind moments when the word "traitor"
crossed her mind, but even as she thought it, Elizabeth knew
she was being unfair. It was not Annabelle's fault that Lady
Mayfield should have conceived an affection for Annabelle
and not for Elizabeth. Or that Annabelle should have such
an equable temper that nothing her stepmama said put her
out of countenance. Indeed, Elizabeth would have given
much to be so calm. With a sigh she admitted that the root
of the trouble lay as much with her as with her stepmother.
She had been close to her mother and had taken her death
hard. Then, for four years before her father had remarried,
Elizabeth had held the reins of the household in her hands,
trying to fill the void her mother's death had left. It did not
help now that for those four years she had been freed from
the constraints of girlhood, for everyone agreed that a girl
old enough to manage a household might be allowed a trifle
more freedom than was usual for a chit straight from the
schoolroom. The darker colors she wore had succeeded in
their purpose, which was to convince the world that Elizabeth
Mayfield was a sensible girl, older than her years, and one
who might be allowed a trifle leeway in such matters as
chaperones. For, indeed, there was a wild streak beneath
the sober facade that had always found it hard to submit to
the dictates of propriety and authority. Had she not been able
to run free, at times, those first years after her mother's
death, Elizabeth had more than once thought she might go
mad. And then her father had married Beatrix.

It had been hard, too hard, to relinquish that freedom when her stepmama took the reins into her own hands. Had those hands been as capable as the first Lady Mayfield's, it might have been possible, and there the trouble might have ended. Had the new Lady Mayfield been understanding and tolerant of a girl still feeling the loss of her mother, Elizabeth might soon have accustomed herself to the situation. But the trouble was that the new Lady Mayfield was neither. She had immediately sought to return Elizabeth to the status of a school-room miss, hemmed about with rules on deportment and propriety, and no say in the day-to-day management of the household. Close upon that maneuver, the new Lady Mayfield had managed to ruffle the sensibilities of every member of the household staff. They had turned to Elizabeth, and feeling vindicated, she had tried to remedy matters. This had been a fatal error, since it had not unnaturally led the new Lady Mayfield to assume that the trouble between herself and the servants was due to her stepdaughter's interference. She had said as much, and Elizabeth had responded hotly. The gauntlet had been thrown down between them and a war begun that had not yet ended.

It had not taken Elizabeth long to realize the impropriety of her behavior and the unhappiness it was causing her father. Much mortified, Elizabeth had approached her stepmama to apologize for her part in the fray. Beatrix, however, had chosen to treat this overture as some sort of trick and redoubled her efforts to bring the girl to heel, with what effect might well be imagined. Briefly Elizabeth had considered looking to her father to support her. But as Lady Mayfield had, in short order, presented to Sir Edmund a long-wished-for heir, in his eyes she could do no wrong. Nor could Elizabeth bring herself to wish to spoil his happiness. So she held her peace and sought solace in her pen instead, but days like today tried her sorely.

Lady Mayfield paused and studied her stepdaughter. The girl was far too quiet, far too meek, for Beatrix to trust this mood. Surely this hid a plot for revenge. Still, it were best, perhaps, not to press the point. "You may go to your room," she told Elizabeth austerely.

Elizabeth regarded her stepmama a moment, then quietly retrieved her notebook from the floor where Willoughby had just abandoned it. Then, without a word, she sought the refuge of her bedchamber, grateful that Beatrix had never realized what a sanctuary it had become for her. Still, Elizabeth was not a poor-spirited creature, one to give herself over to a fit of tears. If the notebook had been all but destroyed, her first task, nevertheless, must be to go through it and determine if any part might be salvaged. Then she would turn to the painstaking task of recreating a manuscript that had been three-fourths complete. Linley and Collier's Publishing House had been promised a manuscript, and a manuscript they must have. Resolutely she set to work.

At that moment, just south of London, the Earl of Basingstoke was riding across a field in the general direction of the country home of Lady Sophia, daughter of the Marquess of Wey. Anyone watching would have known at once that the earl was a notable horseman, for his seat was remarkably steady and he never checked at any hazard he came across, but let his horse have his head and leapt them all. His manner of neck-or-nothing riding might have led such an observer to suppose the earl to be on his way to a meeting of some importance, perhaps involving a lady and love, and such an observer would not have been far wrong. The earl was expected to present himself to Lord Wey on Thursday, for the purpose of requesting the Lady Sophia's hand in marriage. Not being possessed of a strong sense of patience, however, Basingstoke had decided, on a whim, to ride out to Wey to visit Sophia and discover what had called her away from London in the midst of the Season. He had no expectation of discovering trouble. The Lady Sophia had made it very clear that she found his suit quite welcome and that, in her opinion, although neither he nor she might feel a grand passion for each other, they would deal extremely well together. Indeed, most of the *ton*, scenting a match in the air, had declared the two made for each other. It was not a compliment.

At the moment, however, the Earl of Basingstoke was untroubled by what the *ton* or anyone else might think. He simply wished to see Sophia, and knew her too well to suppose that an impromptu visit would offend her. He was still some distance from the house when he drew his horse up short, recognizing, in the distance, a particularly lively mare and a neatish bay hack tethered to a tree. A little beyond, hidden almost completely by a very large bush, Basingstoke thought he could see the top of a head he had cause to know well, and it was close, too close for his comfort, to that of some unknown man. On impulse, Basingstoke slid off his horse and tethered it where he stood. Then, softly, he crept closer to the bush in question, meaning to surprise her. He could no longer see the top of Lady Sophia's head, but as he drew closer, he could begin to hear their voices. There was, as the saying goes, an odd kick to her gallop, and that suited him, for so did he. But what Basingstoke now heard went beyond even what he had come to expect of her.

"Ah, but I shall tell Basingstoke I wish to bring you with me when he and I are married. It will not seem unusual, for you are well-known to be my favorite groom. And after a year or two, when I have presented Basingstoke with the requisite heir, we may enjoy each other as we wish," said Sophia's teasing voice.

"It's not right," the male voice countered stubbornly.

Sophia laughed the laugh Basingstoke had heard so often and that had first drawn her to his attention. "Ah, but surely you must see that I cannot and will not marry you?"

"I know it," the voice replied in the same way as before. "It wouldn't be fitting. This ain't fitting. But all the same, I don't like you marrying him."

Now Sophia's voice turned hard as she said with words that seemed to cut through him, "You are not to say whom I should and should not marry. Basingstoke is an earl and I will wed him."

"Aye, him and his twenty thousand pounds a year," the groom scoffed. Sophia replied something that Basingstoke could not overhear and then the groom spoke again. "I'm a toy for you, no more, my lady, and well I know it; but you needn't rub my face in it."

Sophia murmured some soft reply and Basingstoke drew back, able to guess only too well what was taking place on the other side of the bush. His first impulse was to confront her. His second to escape, to be away from her as quickly as possible. To confront her now would lead to his thrashing the groom, if not Sophia as well, and both or either action could only lead to scandal. In disgust Basingstoke chose retreat.

As he moved swiftly but silently back to where his horse stood still tethered, Basingstoke could not help remembering all the times he had heard Sophia compared to Lady Caro Lamb and heard it said she had a taste for low company. He had always put the first down to spite and liked her the better for not being too high in the instep to chat with a groom or footman who had performed an unusual service for her. Now the comparison seemed all too apt and the friendly condescension took on sinister undertones.

To be sure, the Earl of Basingstoke had not reached his thirtieth year without acquiring a certain cynicism. He knew all too well that it was his wealth and title that made him the target of so many young females and their matchmaking mamas. Indeed, he would have said that the notion of marrying for love was falderol and that one might as well marry with a clear head as not at all. But somehow what he had seen touched his vanity far more than he had thought possible. It was not that the Lady Sophia was cold-headed in her acceptance of his suit. He had expected no more, nor offered more himself. It was rather, Basingstoke thought with a frown as he rode, that she was so warmhearted toward someone else. That was what galled him beyond measure, that she appeared to care for, to desire, her groom so much more than she cared for or desired himself, the man she meant to marry. And that she meant not simply to cuckold him once they were married, but to cuckold him with a mere groom. How cheaply she valued his person, Basingstoke thought acidly, and how highly she valued what marriage to him would bring.

With bitterness at his heels, Basingstoke rode back to London, determined to search out his friends and drink himself into oblivion.

2

THE COCK AND GULL had not always catered to quality.
Indeed, until quite recently it was more the sort of place that
men from the docks or warehouses frequented on their way
home from work. But then the proprietor had had the happy
notion of turning a room in the rear into a place where cock-
fights might be held from time to time, and that accounted
for the presence of the two young lords now drinking the
landlord's best ale. Well, that was one of the reasons, at any
rate. The other was that, due to a particularly notorious prank
involving a certain rather stiff-necked duke, they were,
at the moment, unwelcome at places such as White's and
Brooks's, where their friends had retired, some hours earlier,
at the end of the entertainment here at the Cock and Gull.
To be sure, the elder of the two had another reason for
choosing to imbibe as deeply and as quickly as he was able,
but he was not yet ready to divulge that reason to his
companion. It had been more than twenty-four hours since
he had overheard the encounter between a lady and her
groom, but he had been able neither to forget it nor to forgive
her nor to speak of it to anyone else.

Anyone observing the two gentlemen would have known
at once that they were quality, and of the sort who pursued
physical pleasures rather than aspiring to the dandy set. Both
wore coats of the finest Bath cloth, tailored to fit their figures
and yet allow movement in the shoulders should it become
necessary to demonstrate a boxing stance or draw a bow or
run an impromptu race. To be sure, any sane gentleman
would remove his coat before entering into such sport, but
there were times when one did not have the luxury of doing

so, and these two gentlemen preferred to be prepared for such contingencies. Their cravats were tied neatly, but not in so high a style as to prevent them from lowering their chins to study a handful of cards. And while their pantaloons were knit and of flattering cut, again they bore evidence that the two gentlemen had not been averse to pressing close to the front of the crowd in observing the cockfighting earlier.

There was, moreover, a careless ease about the two men that proclaimed they were accustomed to go where and when they willed. A habit of tossing orders over their shoulder without looking to see if they had been heard argued a lifetime of being surrounded by persons whose job it was to fulfill one's wishes. There was also, however, a downward turn to the mouth, a mocking glimmer in the eye, a cynical way of speaking that marked the elder of the two as a man to be avoided. Perhaps that was why the other patrons of the Cock and Gull gave the two gentlemen such a wide berth and consequently did not overhear the wager that was shortly to be exchanged.

The Earl of Basingstoke was a handsome man, but as has been said, one with a cynical, arrogant, dangerous air. At thirty he had already been banned from Almack's as well as a good many households. And yet there were those who said his faults sprang more from his upbringing than from any innate flaw in his character. Such persons felt that the lack of a mother's gentling hand, combined with a father who had had no time to spare for the boy as he was growing up, had contributed to matters coming to this pass.

His companion, Lord Trahern, was also the black sheep of his family, but at twenty-eight he was considered a much milder case than Basingstoke. Indeed, he was still admitted at Almack's, or rather he had been until this prank with the duke. It remained to be seen whether the patronesses would admit him the next time he tried to gain entry. Since he had come into his inheritance less than six months past and thus was suddenly a very eligible *parti*, it was generally held that they would.

Right now it was this unlikely topic of marriage that was under consideration. "A fool's paradise," Basingstoke proclaimed contemptuously in reply to some comment of Trahern's.

Somewhat astonished, Trahern replied, "But aren't you about to be married?"

"Who says so?" Basingstoke demanded with a frown.

"Everyone," Trahern replied. "The betting at White's is that you will make Wey's daughter an offer before the Season is out."

"Well, everyone is wrong," Basingstoke retorted harshly.

Trahern made an effort to focus on his companion. "But didn't you tell me that your advisers have urged you to marry? To provide an heir?"

"Do you think I do everything my advisers tell me to do?" Basingstoke countered, a dangerous edge to his voice.

"No," Trahern replied frankly, "I thought you'd taken a fancy to the Lady Sophia."

"I had thought we might deal together," Basingstoke agreed, "but I have come to change my mind." He paused, then added cynically, "I discovered she cared more for my wealth and position than my person."

"Is that all?" Trahern demanded incredulously. Then, pointing a nicely tapered finger at Basingstoke, he said rather drunkenly, "I tell you what it is, Hugh, you are spoiled. The Lady Sophia is no different from any other young lady. I don't doubt that if it were not for your title and fortune and family connections, there is not a mother in England who would accept you as a prospective son-in-law. Besides, I cannot conceive of you marrying any lady unless she met your strict requirements of lineage either, Hugh."

Basingstoke frowned. "It is not the mothers I should be concerned with," he countered, ignoring, as usual, what Trahern had said that he did not wish to hear. Basingstoke spoke carefully so as not to slur his words as he went on. "It is the daughters who interest me, and they, I think, would not reject me, whatever my fortunes." He paused, then added meditatively. "I have it on the best of authority that my very wildness adds an edge of interest." Trahern gave a short, sharp laugh and Basingstoke frowned. "I have never had trouble finding comfort and companionship when and where

I willed, not even when I'll swear my identity was unknown.''

Trahern waved his hand again. "Oh, seduction! That is
another matter entirely. But one must not confuse an entertaining dalliance with something so serious as marriage.''
He leaned forward and spoke as though imparting a great
secret. "You have always known you would inherit your title
and fortune. Indeed, you came into it some years ago, and
so you have never been in the position of a younger son.
You have always enjoyed the favored status of a desirable
partner and so cannot comprehend precisely how mercenary
our ladies of the *ton* may be. Now I, on the other hand, until
four months and three weeks ago was merely a younger son.
One with a hale and handsome older brother who stood in
line before me. Those mothers and daughters who most welcome me into their parlors today are the ones who most
disdained me before. And I was not half so notorious as
you.''

"Perhaps you were not half so charming, either," Basingstoke suggested with a cynical smile. Very deliberately he
added, his voice turning harsh, "With or without my name
and fortune, I could wed any woman I chose. Short of
royalty, of course.''

For a moment matters hung in the balance and Basingstoke
wondered idly if Trahern was about to call him out. It would
be a shame if he did so, because Basingstoke would be honor-
bound to accept and he had not found a more congenial companion in some time. He was astonished, therefore, to see
Trahern begin to smile at him. The fellow was foxed, of
course, but surely not so deep in his cups that he would find
the insult amusing. Trahern's next words enlightened Basingstoke.

"I have a wager for you," Trahern said, steepling his
fingers under his chin.

"Done," Basingstoke answered with a careless wave of
his hand.

"Not until you have heard the wager," Trahern countered
with a laugh. "You may not wish to accept.''

"I have never run from a wager in my life," Basingstoke

retorted with a frown. "State your wager and be done with it."

Trahern smiled foolishly at his friend. "The wager is simply this: you must meet and court a gentlewoman without her knowing who you are, who your family is, or what your fortune might be. She is to think you are the younger son of an undistinguished family who is frequently a trifle short in the pocket. You are to get her to agree to marry you. The amount of the wager is to be one thousand pounds."

"The devil you say!" Basingstoke replied, stunned. "But suppose I do not choose to be married to the girl? I am not in the least desirous of losing my freedom and becoming leg-shackled to some unknown creature merely for a wager. A thousand pounds is far too paltry a sum for that."

"Ah, but you do not need to wed the lady," Trahern said softly. "We must obviously leave London to find one who does not know you, and I propose we choose some out-of-the-way town and that you court her under some name other than your own. You must do so, in any event, for the wager to be proved, and once she has agreed, and I have heard her, you may simply disappear." Basingstoke hesitated and Trahern said, laying one finger alongside his nose, "Of course, if you do not think you are sufficiently charming, we may call off the wager before it is begun."

His voice like steel and his eyes glittering dangerously from the effects of anger and the ale, Basingstoke replied, "On the contrary, you may be sure I accept the wager. But how do we choose the town and how do we choose the lady?"

Trahern rose to his feet, swaying slightly as he did so. "I have," he said, "a map. At least I think I have a map, in my library. We may choose the town from that."

Basingstoke also rose to his feet. "And the lady?" he demanded.

That took somewhat more thought. Finally Trahern looked directly at Basingstoke. "The lady shall be the first unmarried gentlewoman we encounter once we reach whatever town we have chosen."

"Done!" Basingstoke agreed curtly, and together they

made their way out of the inn and headed toward Trahern's town house and the map.

The footman who opened the door to the pair betrayed neither surprise nor disapproval at their appearance. Though belowstairs the servants might generally regret the careless habits of the current viscount after years of a far steadier hand at the helm, Brent was nevertheless a favorite due to his good nature and willingness to be pleased. As for Lord Basingstoke, he was no stranger to the staff, and if his influence on the new viscount was to be deprecated, his openhandedness in rewarding any petty service made him welcome.

In any event, the two went directly to the viscount's library, where after a few minutes of searching Trahern found the map of England that he was looking for. He unrolled it and braced each corner with a book, then he looked at Basingstoke unsteadily and said, "I think we must go to the north of England if we want to be sure we're unknown. I shall let you pick the spot."

"Any spot I choose?" Basingstoke asked.

Trahern frowned. "No," he said cautiously, "for you might find that too easy. I have it! Close your eyes and choose," he concluded triumphantly. "I'll tell you if it's not far north enough and you can try again."

With something perilously close to a sigh, Basingstoke did as he was bidden, his forefinger landing on a small village called Ravenstonedale. "Will that do?" he asked, opening his eyes.

Trahern peered closely at the map. "It ought to do," he agreed cautiously. "But we'll have a devil of a time getting there."

"If you choose to withdraw the wager . . ." Basingstoke offered softly.

"No, no," Trahern said, straightening immediately. "You'll not get out of it that easily! I'll go pack my bags and we leave tonight."

"As you wish," Basingstoke agreed lazily. "I shall wait for you down here."

Ten minutes later, Trahern reappeared in the library dressed in more suitable clothes for traveling, with a packed bag in hand and an irate valet right behind. ''Please, your lordship,'' the fellow pleaded, ''you must take me. Who will look after your things?''

Trahern turned to him and said in exasperation, ''I shall look after me. And you are not coming.''

Basingstoke set aside the book he had been perusing and lazily got to his feet. He addressed the valet in his soft voice, a wry smile upon his face. ''I shall look after his lordship,'' he said with an unsteadiness that betrayed the depths of his intoxication, ''and I promise he shall return to you with no harm and his and your reputations unmarred.''

The poor fellow did not look convinced, but confronted with two resolute lords, he had no alternative save retreat. He did so, muttering to himself that if his lordship's shirts were torn and his boots left unpolished, he would only be coming by his just deserts.

When they were again alone, Basingstoke regarded Trahern wearily. ''So we travel lightly,'' he observed. ''Is it really necessary to leave your valet behind?''

''I hope you don't mean to bring yours,'' Trahern retorted roundly. ''Not unless you wish the gossip of our wager to make the rounds of London within the fortnight. You know how servants are. Better to inscribe the bet in the book at White's.''

Basingstoke bowed unsteadily. ''You are right, of course. I stand corrected,'' he said with a smile that disarmed Trahern. ''Let us away to my town house and I shall pack my bag.''

Arm in arm they headed out the door. This time the footman could not forbear to ask, ''You are going on a trip, my lord?''

''I am,'' Trahern replied curtly.

''When do you mean to return?'' the fellow asked.

Trahern did not bother to answer.

As they walked the short distance to Basingstoke's residence, the earl said unexpectedly, ''Did you leave directions for your business affairs to be taken care of while we are gone?''

Trahern stopped dead still in the street, then turned to retrace his steps. Basingstoke put a firm hand on his shoulder and urged him forward instead. ''Come along, Brent. You can write your agent a letter while I pack, and my man will deliver it. At this rate we shall miss the stage going north.''

Basingstoke's servants displayed even less curiosity than Trahern's at their appearance. Nor did Basingstoke's valet remonstrate when told his lordship would be gone for an indefinite period and would not require his services. Had he been the sort to object, he would not still have been in the earl's service. Instead, he swiftly and silently packed the requisite articles of clothing and other necessaries while Basingstoke changed into traveling clothes and both lords wrote their men of business with the necessary instructions to take care of that which might arise in their absence.

Privately Basingstoke gave his secretary, the younger son of a fine family, additional instructions regarding certain visitors who might call in the earl's absence. He also left a note to be delivered to his latest mistress, regretfully breaking matters off. It was a step Basingstoke had been meaning to take for some time but had not, out of a sense of lethargy and because she did still occasionally amuse him. He must have done so, of course, as soon as his engagement to the Lady Sophia had been published. Now he would do so anyway. His secretary could be trusted to handle the matter with the utmost delicacy, not only delivering the note by hand but also soothing her inevitable outburst with appropriately tactful statements that nevertheless committed his master to nothing.

As he received the notes, instructions, and assorted comments from the obviously inebriated earl, the secretary became more and more distressed. ''M'lord,'' he finally ventured timidly, ''I see no difficulty in sending your regrets concerning invitations you have previously accepted. I must point out, however, that you have an appointment for this coming Thursday, and that you have indicated to me that you consider the matter important in the extreme. Do you mean to return by then?"

Basingstoke hesitated. He had dipped into his cups rather heavily and might have wished a clearer head at this moment. But if his head were clearer, he knew he would not be embarking on this foolish quest in the first place. Or would he? he wondered. It was more than drink that had made him reckless enough to accept Trahern's wager, it was what he had seen at Wey. To escape that memory or Thursday's appointment he might have taken steps far more drastic than these. Some part of his mind told Basingstoke that to cry off when all of London appeared to be in hourly expectation of hearing the announcement of his engagement to the Lady Sophia would be accounted the action of a blackguard. Another part of his mind retorted that with so many black marks against his name already, one more could scarcely signify. "I shall give you another note to deliver at the time of my appointment," he told his unhappy secretary at last. "I doubt very much I shall have returned by then. In fact, I think it impossible."

"But, m'lord," the secretary started to protest. A fiercely unhappy look from the earl silenced him. And when Basingstoke had finally sealed the missive and handed it to him, the secretary's face was perfectly expressionless as he took it and said, "I shall have it delivered at precisely eleven A.M. on Thursday."

"You will also deliver any communications Lord Trahern shall have ready when we go downstairs. He is in his cups as thoroughly as I, and I am not sure how coherent you may find his directions. You will do your best, however, to carry them out," the earl informed his secretary.

"Yes, m'lord," was the impassive reply.

Five minutes later, the two lords were on their way to the inn called the Swan with Two Necks to catch the northbound stage.

3

BASINGSTOKE came awake abruptly, jolted by the rocking of the coach as it took a corner a trifle too sharply. His first thought was that he ought to have the springs of his carriage inspected, for the ride was much rougher than he was accustomed to. His second thought was the realization that he was not in his own coach. For some inexplicable reason, it seemed that he was riding in a public conveyance. And that the coachman, judging by the way he handled the reins, was somewhat foxed. His third was to wonder just what the devil he was doing riding in any carriage at what seemed to be a disagreeably early hour of the morning. It was not an hour when the earl would have chosen to be awake at all, or anywhere save in his own bed.

Slowly Basingstoke looked around, trying to remember the events of the night before. Two of his traveling companions were solid citizens of the commercial sort and both avoided his eyes with a distinct sniff of disapproval. Basingstoke smiled grimly. But then his eye fell upon Trahern, still snoring in the seat facing his. A prank. He and Trahern must have pulled another prank, Basingstoke concluded with satisfaction. Now, if he could just remember what it was. And why they had chosen to depart from London in such discomfort. And where they were headed. To his or Trahern's estate perhaps? A quick glance out the window informed Basingstoke that rather than heading south, they were heading north. Suddenly the memory of the wager he had made with Trahern flooded back to Basingstoke and he turned a jaundiced eye on his friend.

Lazily Trahern opened first one eye, then the other, and

Basingstoke watched as he went through several moments of confusion. Finally he regarded Basingstoke warily. "I don't suppose you know where we are?" he asked hopefully.

Basingstoke started to shake his head, then changed his mind as the effect of the night's drinking made itself felt. Instead, he replied quietly, "Only that we are traveling north and appear to be stopping here."

Even as Basingstoke spoke, the coach lurched to a halt in the courtyard of a busy inn and loud voices could be heard calling for someone to change the horses. A moment later the door was wrenched open and the driver stuck in his head to say, "Half an hour for breakfast, gents. Then we'll be on our way."

Along with four other men, two of whom had been riding on the top of the coach, Basingstoke and Trahern descended upon the inn. The proprietor was hastily taking orders from the passengers and hurrying to fill them. Basingstoke and Trahern placed their orders as well, though if the truth were known, both were lacking in appetite.

Looking around the room, Basingstoke said casually, "We seem to have no dearth of traveling companions this morning."

Trahern shrugged. "P'rhaps they'll get off at Birmingham," he replied offhandedly. "At any rate, I hope so, I've no desire to be crammed in with a crowd of strangers."

"Our traveling companions do not seem overeager for our company," Basingstoke observed dryly.

"Well, of course not," Trahern snorted. "They are scarcely our sort."

"Remind me, then," Basingstoke said softly, "why we are traveling with them?"

Trahern looked at Basingstoke in astonishment. "Well, if that ain't the daftest thing I've ever heard! As though one can pick one's companions on a public coach."

"Ah, but I was asking you to remind me why we are on a public coach at all," Basingstoke said, twirling lazily the elegant eyepiece that hung from a cord about his neck.

"I say, don't you recall our wager?" Trahern demanded

with a frown. "We're to travel to the north of England and you're to find a lady to agree to marry you."

"Softly," Basingstoke warned in a voice that chilled his listener. "I do not choose to share the nature of that wager with every fellow in this room. And, yes, I do recall the wager. What I do not recall is why we are traveling in this absurd manner."

Trahern shook his head and said with some asperity, "Well, if that ain't the second daftest thing I've ever heard! How would it look if we showed up in your coach and then tried to claim you hadn't any money? Or family connections?"

"I understand that," Basingstoke conceded, "but why did we not take yours? As I recall, you've not bothered to have the family crest put on the door as yet."

If the truth be told, Trahern didn't quite remember the answer to that one. Since he was, however, a fairly clever fellow, he was not long at a loss for words. "Well, that was for your protection, Hugh," he pointed out magnanimously.

"Oh?"

The simple word spoken in precisely that tone of voice warned Trahern to be careful. He knew Basingstoke too well to disregard it. He leaned toward his friend and expanded upon the theme. "Well, of course it was. My cattle are so well-known and my high-perch phaeton so remarkable that I feared they might be recognized on the road. One wouldn't wish to have anyone in London get wind of our destination, since one wouldn't want the lady, whoever she turns out to be, to get wind of how to track you down later. Besides, we can't travel all that way in an open carriage, and to take my coach would mean taking a driver. Servants do gossip, you know."

"I see."

Basingstoke's tone was grim, but not so grim as before, and Trahern felt as though his cravat were suddenly a trifle less tight about his neck. "You could, of course, simply concede the wager," Trahern suggested offhandedly.

"I could?" Basingstoke asked, his voice giving nothing away.

Emboldened, Trahern warmed to the subject. "Yes. After all, a thousand pounds is but a trifle to you, and I could certainly put the money to good use. We could be back in London in time to attend the auction in Tattersall's. There is a lovely gelding I've had my eye on and a pair of grays, and while I daresay they won't come to above seven or eight hundred pounds, that's more than I have free at the moment."

Basingstoke's eyes darkened. He regarded his highly polished boots for what seemed to Trahern a dangerously long time before he drawled, "I shouldn't count on that gelding just yet. Or the pair of grays. Alvanley's grays, I presume. I have never walked away from a wager and I do not mean to do so now. To the contrary, I mean to win this one."

Trahern swallowed hard and turned to the food the innkeeper was just now setting before them. It must be said that nourishment greatly heartened both gentlemen, and there was a determined swagger to their steps as they returned to the stagecoach a quarter of an hour later. As before, their companions were the four men from London, clearly tradesmen, two of whom again chose to ride inside the coach, although they did not seem enamored of the scapegrace pair before them. Once the coach had negotiated the narrow street that ran through the middle of town and reached the clear road northward, one of the tradesmen addressed Basingstoke and Trahern. "Rusticating, are you?" he asked with a sneer of disapproval.

Trahern immediately turned to Basingstoke and said excitedly, "That's it! We shall explain that you are on a repairing lease and must avoid your creditors until the next quarter at the very least."

Basingstoke regarded his erstwhile friend with something akin to dislike. "How kind of you to remind me," he said dryly.

Trahern colored. He turned to the trademan who had addressed the pair and replied stiffly, "I cannot see that it is any of your affair, my good man, and I find your question most impertinent!"

"Do you now?" the dour fellow retorted. "I don't doubt

it. Quality, you call yourselves? Niffy-naffy ne'er-do-wells is a better name for you, I don't doubt.''

"I think,'' Basingstoke said, his voice dangerously quiet, "that you forget yourself.''

The tradesman started to disagree, but something in Basingstoke's expression stopped him. Instead he contented himself with clearing his throat pointedly and turning his attention to the other fellow of his own sort.

Basingstoke leaned back in his seat and closed his eyes as though resting. In truth, however, his mind was as active as ever. Why had he agreed to continue with this absurd wager? he asked himself silently. Was it because of what he had overheard Sophia saying to her groom? A desire to somehow spite her? Absurd! Surely he had outgrown such folly? Certainly there were no rational reasons that would justify such a rash course, one that might ruin both himself and Trahern, as well as the yet-to-be-discovered young woman. But determined to pursue this course, Basingstoke undeniably found himself.

Had anyone thought to ask him, Basingstoke's valet might have provided the answer that the earl could not. For some time Foster had watched his master fall into a state of discontent that was not one whit diminished by the furious pursuit of pleasure to which the earl gave himself over. Nor did the attentions of various birds of paradise or the welcome afforded in the homes of ambitious mothers of eligible young ladies serve to raise his spirits. Indeed, upon more than one occasion when the earl had returned home well into his cups and allowed Foster to help him undress, the earl had been heard to voice the very accusation that had been the source of last night's preposterous wager. Was it only his title and wealth and family connections that made him acceptable to the ladies of the *ton*?

Foster had coughed and discreetly reminded the earl that any number of married ladies had shown themselves not to be averse to his attentions. But that had not done the trick, for Basingstoke could not help remembering that it had been his gifts of various baubles and his expertise in bed that they had admired. More than one had said quite frankly that she preferred not to have his company in public because he was often so infernally rude. It was a charge Basingstoke could not deny. Of late he had found it increasingly difficult not to be rude. As no one had ever taken his feelings into consideration, he saw no need to consider anyone else's. He was dissatisfied with his life as it stood and found his discontent an exquisite irony, knowing how many in England would gladly have stood in his place.

And that, Foster would have said, was precisely the reason the earl was bent on pursuing the wager. Not to prove anything to his lordship, Trahern, but to himself. If Foster's suspicions were correct, moreover, the earl would wish to do so before the appointment that had been set for Thursday morning. The one the earl now meant to break. After all, any man might feel trepidation before committing himself to matrimony, even matrimony with so lovely a lady as the Marquess of Wey's daughter. Any man might embark upon a bizarre wager at such a point. And once bent upon a course, nothing would turn his lordship aside.

Of course, Foster had no way of knowing what his lordship had seen and overheard, but he otherwise knew his master's state of mind. Basingstoke had decided to offer for her ladyship because he had decided it was time that he was married and had thought they would suit. She was as wild as he, and not likely, his lordship had thought, to object to his nature or desire him to change it. Nor had he thought himself or her to have conceived a passion, one for the other. But neither had he thought she took such a cavalier attitude toward their proposed marriage.

Trahern, watching from his seat as the stage jolted its way along, was wishing he had never proposed this absurd wager. Its consequences would be severe if anyone ever discovered what they were about to do, for the *ton* would consider it far more than an innocent prank. And yet Basingstoke had befriended him before he inherited his title, at a time when most of the *ton* dismissed him as a mere younger son, despite his connections. For some time now he had danced to Basingstoke's tune, though far more temperately, and he had learned to recognize the mood that now seized the earl. He would not turn back from the wager, and Trahern had but one of two choices: to allow Basingstoke to pursue the matter alone or to continue with him. And since the dances Basingstoke led were never dull, Trahern found himself unwilling to withdraw from this one either. Come what may, Trahern would witness this dance to the end.

4

ELIZABETH MAYFIELD brushed a curl away from her face. It was only nine o'clock in the morning and the day was already promising to be uncharacteristically warm, for spring had come early to Cumbria this year. On such a sunny day it was impossible not to be happy, and indeed Miss Mayfield was, for there were few things she enjoyed more than working in the garden as she did this morning. To that purpose she wore a dark green gown protected by a practical apron borrowed from one of the maids, a circumstance that would have earned her censure had anyone been about to see. But no one was.

Lady Pickworth and the first Lady Mayfield had for years carried on a friendly rivalry in the matter of their gardens, and after her mother's death, Elizabeth had kept up her mother's roses. The second Lady Mayfield had come to her marriage caring nothing about roses. Indeed she had been heard to remark that the garden took up far too much of her elder stepdaughter's time. That was before someone made the mistake, however, of assuming the second Lady Mayfield had grown the roses herself and complimented her on her skill. To be sure, the fellow had been a stranger who had not visited Ravenstonedale again, nevertheless his compliments had given Lady Mayfield pause. And after that day, she had never again been heard to rail against Elizabeth's desire to tend to the gardens. Indeed, she positively encouraged her to do so. If Elizabeth realized that it was because her stepmother wished to take credit for the flowers herself, she did not protest. It was enough to be allowed to pursue their care unobstructed, for the gardens were the one place where she still could feel close to her mother's memory.

Yesterday Lady Mayfield had noticed that one of the finer rosebushes had come into bloom and she wished to show off the blossoms to Lady Pickworth, for she supposed correctly that nothing else she could do would so successfully annoy the woman. Unfortunately, due to an accident while out riding, Lady Pickworth was temporarily confined to her parlor, so Lady Mayfield had decided to call on her with some of the roses.

With a sigh, Elizabeth chose the last perfect rose and slipped the gardening shears into her basket. A dozen blossoms ought to do, and, provided the worst of the heat held off until after they had made their courtesy call to Lady Pickworth, these ought to assure Lady Mayfield of her neighbor's envy. If only she were not caught in the middle. And yet Elizabeth could not regret the chance to visit Lady Pickworth. The woman had been kind to her after her mother's death, and if Elizabeth had let her, she would have entered into Elizabeth's sentiments exactly concerning her stepmother. But Elizabeth would not allow it, feeling that would be too disloyal to her father. Still, she would have looked forward to this visit with pleasure were it not for Giles.

It was a pity, Elizabeth thought as she walked back to the large gray limestone house, that the two families had not promoted an alliance between Annabelle and Giles. The pair might have suited one another as she and Giles had not. To be sure, in earlier years they had been fast friends, but that friendship had never ripened into anything more.

In fairness, it must be said that both Sir Edmund and Lady Pickworth would have ceased to press the match at once had Elizabeth only shown signs of forming an attachment to any other eligible male or Giles to any other eligible female. But so far she had not. Though her dance card was filled at any country ball or party she attended, and any number of young gentlemen had paid court to her as soon as she had been of age for them to do so, none had asked for her hand in marriage. This was due not to a lack of desire on their part, but to skill on hers in preventing matters from reaching such a point. And though Sir Edmund was an indulgent parent, Elizabeth's persistence in remaining thus far aloof was sorely trying his patience, while Lady Mayfield made no secret of her dislike of Elizabeth's maiden state. As for Giles, Elizabeth had reason to know his parents were distressed at the current object of his interest, and they hoped she could capture it instead.

"Well, well, well, woolgathering again, my dear?" Sir Edmund's voice broke into Elizabeth's thoughts as she entered into the back hallway, having carefully stripped off the offending apron first.

"Papa, I didn't see you!"

"Evidently," he retorted dryly, but there was something of a twinkle in his eye. "Dreaming about some young man, I hope?"

Elizabeth colored, making her, in her father's eyes, prettier than before. "Papa!" she said reprovingly. "I was thinking about these roses and the best way to prepare them for the drive to see Lady Pickworth."

"Giles will no doubt be pleased to see you," Sir Edmund suggested mildly. Then, his voice growing a trifle stern, he added, "I do not mean to force you into any alliance distasteful to you, Elizabeth, but you are four-and-twenty. Upon the shelf, to put no finer point upon the matter. Do you mean to stay a spinster all your life? I tell you bluntly I do not like ths notion and do not mean to countenance it."

"Perhaps a trip to London, a Season, would do the trick," Annabelle suggested, coming into the hallway behind her father.

Sir Edmund rounded on his younger daughter. "You are not going to London," he thundered, "and neither is your sister! I will not have the pair of you wasting yourselves on some scoundrel there, or worse."

Then, before either daughter could argue with him, Sir Edmund turned on his heel and strode from the room. Annabelle turned to Elizabeth, her face stricken. "Why was he so angry?" she asked. "I know such a trip would be expensive, but Papa has never given us reason to think he could not afford such a thing. Quite the contrary. He is for-

ever encouraging us to indulge ourselves. It is only upon the
issue of a trip to London that he is so unreasonable.''

Elizabeth hesitated. It was, she felt, her father's place, or
her stepmother's, to explain matters to Annabelle. Indeed,
it could only sound churlish for her to say what she thought.
But there was no need, for Annabelle went on pettishly, ''It
is not fair that Papa should be so clutch-fisted! Or be so afraid
that we should have to see his sister. What does he fear?
That she shall somehow turn us against him? It is their feud,
not ours, and I cannot see why anyone should feel we must
take sides. Anyway, he cannot have always held his sister
in such dislike or he would not have named you after her.
It is not fair,'' Annabelle repeated.

''Fair or not,'' Elizabeth said reasonably, ''it is pointless
to pine for what we cannot have. I, for one, have no patience
for it. I must get these blooms into water until it is time to
call upon Lady Pickworth.''

Annabelle made a face, but let her sister pass.

Lady Pickworth held court from the plush divan in her
parlor, seeing callers who came to commiserate with her
upon her mishap. This particular afternoon, however, Lady
Mayfield and her stepdaughter were her only visitors. After
the flowers had been duly admired, Lady Pickworth turned
her attention to Elizabeth. ''My dear,'' she said with all
apparent affability, ''Giles will be delighted to see you. He
is out riding, but I expect him back at any moment. He must
show you the garden. I have one or two interesting blooms
of my own.''

This last was directed at Lady Mayfield, who affected not
to hear. In any event, she did not ask to be shown the blooms.
If Lady Pickworth had surpassed her stepdaughter's efforts,
she did not wish to know it. And if Lady Pickworth had not
and this was merely a pretext to throw Giles and Elizabeth
together, she had no desire to thrust a spoke in the wheel
of Lady Pickworth's plans.

Elizabeth was too well-bred to show her dismay. Were
Lady Pickworth and her stepmother prepared to show their

hands so openly in thrusting her into the company of Giles? Did they not realize that if Giles were as fond of her company as they supposed, he would have sought her out? Guiltily she realized that perhaps it looked as if he did. And yet she dared not explain that he came to see her because he was a partner to her writing, a circumstance that would have brought down a diatribe on both their heads. Still, Elizabeth was uneasy. Lady Pickworth seemed too sure of herself. Surely Giles had not decided to bend to his family's wishes and offer for her hand? Surely he was too good a friend to press her when he knew she did not wish it? Only the sight of his carefree face, a few minutes later when he strolled lazily into the room, allayed Elizabeth's qualms. He greeted her with the same indifferent ease that he always had. And his mother's command to show Elizabeth the garden appeared to be a complete surprise to him.

Impudently Giles grinned at his mother. "All right," he agreed, "but you needn't think you are playing at Cupid, because it is no such thing! Elizabeth and I are doing this only to please you."

"Giles!" his mother remonstrated, turning scarlet at such impertinence.

Elizabeth recognized only too well the mutinous look that now graced her friend's face. Hastily she rose to her feet and put a hand on his arm to gently restrain him. "I should be glad of a turn about the garden, Giles," she said softly.

"Very well," he said with poor grace.

It did not help his mood that as the two left the room he could hear his mother telling Lady Mayfield with a sigh, "I shall be so glad when Giles has settled down with a wife. He needs someone like Elizabeth to steady him."

Elizabeth heard the exchange as well and could not but sympathize with Giles. When they had reached the garden she told him, "I shall understand if you wish to leave me to my own devices and go off on your own."

He shook his head impatiently. "No, that would not be kind to you and it is not you I am angry with."

As they walked down the path, Elizabeth chose her words

carefully. "It is vexing, I own, to listen to our mothers make such plans for us, and yet surely it would be wiser not to answer so rashly?"

Giles paused in the path and took both of Elizabeth's hands in his own. He looked so young, she thought, a mere boy instead of the man he was, with one year more to his credit than she had to hers. "You know my mother," Giles told her with patent frustration, "she will listen to nothing I say unless it is outrageous, and rarely even then. She will have it that I am a mere boy, not a man, and incapable of knowing my own mind even on something so important as whom I will wed. Not worthy, indeed!"

It had been patent, ever since she had seen Lady Pickworth at church two weeks before, that that lady had been concerned about Giles and afraid that he had developed a *tendre* for someone unsuitable. But in that time she had not seen Giles. Now his words confirmed what Lady Pickworth had feared. And it was evident that this was the circumstance which had forced Lady Pickworth's hand so sharply. With some trepidation Elizabeth asked, "Who is unworthy, Giles?"

"Leala!" he flung at her.

He need say no more. Elizabeth stared at Giles with no little astonishment. "But you have known her forever and not shown the slightest partiality!" she blurted out.

"What has that to say to the matter?" he asked irritably. "To be sure, if my mother hadn't warned me I must not see her again because such a connection would be sure to ruin me, I might not have thought of her in those terms, but—"

He broke off, as though overcome by emotions too strong to speak of. Elizabeth continued to regard him with dismay. It was just like Lady Pickworth, who was the kindest woman imaginable to other people's children, to make such a muddle of matters with her own son. To have spoken to Giles in such a way was just the sort of thing to make a chivalrous young man look at Leala romantically. And Giles would have been too desirous of protecting Elizabeth to explain that he visited Leala on her account. For it had been the triangle of three— Elizabeth, Leala, and Giles—who had launched the career of Mrs. Bethfrey, authoress of, by now, three successful romances. To be sure, they had been written by Elizabeth alone, but had it not been for the persistence of Giles and Leala in helping her overcome the obstacles of sending a manuscript to London and arranging for an answer where her family would not discover what was afoot. *The Trials of Magdalena* must still be languishing at the bottom of a pile of petticoats in Elizabeth's room. Neither of them would have betrayed her, for both were fiercely proud of their friend's success and felt it an unfair world that Elizabeth could not openly enjoy her success. They knew that one word leaking to Sir Edmund or Lady Mayfield would result in the instant demise of Mrs. Bethfrey's career, and they were determined to prevent such a catastrophe. But never had Elizabeth supposed that such a conspiracy would lead to romance between Leala and Giles.

"How long . . . ? How far . . . ?" Elizabeth began, not very coherently.

Immediately Giles looked over his shoulder toward the house, as if afraid they might be overheard. Then he let go of one of Elizabeth's hands. With the other he pulled her toward the far end of the garden. Only when they stood under the shade of the old apple tree did Giles halt and let go of Elizabeth's hand completely. "I have seen her once or twice alone," Giles answered honestly. "Leala is afraid for more." As though guessing what Elizabeth must be thinking, he added, "And don't tell me it is too soon to know my own mind. One may know it in a day, an hour, a moment!" Elizabeth was silent and he went on, doggedly now, "You may laugh at me, but my mind is made up. I made the mistake of saying so to my mother. Of saying that, in time, I might ask Leala to marry me." He paused and then went on, a sliver of anger in his voice as he said, "She said that I might marry only where she and my father approved, and forbade me to see Leala. They've told me they want me to offer for you this summer."

Elizabeth's eyes widened in dismay. It was useless to ask if Giles had refused to do so. In spite of his words in the parlor, he was not the sort to stand up for himself. He would stand buff for Mrs. Bethfrey, but when it came to his own case, it was a far different matter. And Elizabeth knew Sir John and Lady Pickworth too well to believe they would accept a refusal from Giles in any event. They would be more inclined to treat such behavior more in the way of a child's temper tantrum than as a decision made thoughtfully by a young man. "I will not accept an offer from you," Elizabeth told him frankly.

"Yes, but if you don't say so to our parents, they will continue to encourage us to see each other and I can take you out riding and that way I will be able to see Leala in your company," Giles told her naively. "They will not object to that, for if they find out, I shall tell them I was only escorting you to see *your* friend."

"Giles," Elizabeth began, "I cannot like this way of doing things. You will give our families hope, and in the end it will not be any easier to convince them to let you marry Leala."

Giles looked at her with burning eyes. "I will not give her up," he said. "It is not as though Leala were someone to be ashamed of. I thought you, at least, would understand that. You are, after all, her best friend. So what if her father died under a cloud of scandal? What has that to say to Leala? It is not her crime, after all. Her birth is as good as mine, and I cannot believe that you would say I should care that she had no fortune. As for objecting because her mother is encouraging the advances of a . . . a merchant, there is no certainty she will marry him. And even if she does, what has that to do with Leala?"

Elizabeth placed a hand on his arm. "I do understand," she said gently, "and I do agree it is not fair to Leala. But I am not your friend if I do not warn you of the grief I foresee."

Giles put his hand over hers. "Of course," he said. "And I am a brute not to think of the distress my plan would cause you. It is one thing for Leala and me to choose to defy the tattlemongers, another to involve you. But I thought, perhaps, it would be easier for you, as well, if you did not have to spend the summer with everyone reminding you that you are all but on the shelf. If there is someone you have formed an attachment for, you need only tell me and I shall not ask again. But if not, why, then, your apparent complacence will keep the fingers from being pointed at you and your stepmother from persecuting you. Yes, I know you will say it is not my affair, but I cannot bear to see how she treats you.''

''She will not treat me any better when I am jilted for Leala,'' Elizabeth pointed out dryly. ''Not that I should mind,'' she added hastily, ''if I were sure it would mean your happiness.''

Troubled, Giles looked at her. ''It has been difficult for you since your father remarried, hasn't it?'' he asked quietly. ''There is no one hereabouts to suit, and your father refuses to send you to London for a Season. I cannot think you were meant for spinsterhood, Elizabeth. Or to share a household with such a stepmother.''

Elizabeth pulled her hand free and turned away. After a long moment she said over her shoulder, ''It is not the notion of spinsterhood I find so difficult to accept, it is the thought that I might never leave Ravenstonedale. That I shall spend my life here without ever seeing all the places and people I have read about. When I first began *The Trials of Magdalena*, I told myself that if I could launch a career, I could leave. But it will not serve, will it? Mr. Linley and Mr. Collier have been all that is kind, but what I have earned, what I can earn, with my pen will not support me in an establishment of my own.''

Giles regarded her with sympathy and clenched fists as he replied, flushing, ''My parents refuse to countenance the notion of letting me travel either. They will not consider purchasing a commission for me or letting me go to London or anywhere. They treat me as though I were still a child, wild to a fault, who cannot be trusted out on his own.''

In spite of her own distress, Elizabeth felt a smile tug at the corners of her mouth. There was, she owned, some justice in the Pickworths' fears. And yet, how would Giles ever come to manhood if he were not given the chance to do so? ''We make a sorry pair,'' she told him frankly, "hemmed about by our parents and forever chafing at our bonds."

"Well, I do not mean to be hemmed in for much longer," Giles warned angrily.

"Nor I," Elizabeth agreed. "But I do not see how we shall escape."

"Give me time," Giles promised darkly, "and I shall show us both the way."

Elizabeth laid a gentling hand on his arm. "Perhaps you will," she said, "but for the moment I think we had best go in before your mother and my stepmother begin to misunderstand our continued absence."

"By Jupiter, yes!" Giles said, thunderstruck. "It would be just like them to fancy I am making love to you out here. Let's go in at once."

5

NEITHER BASINGSTOKE nor Trahern was in a pleasant mood when they finally approached Ravenstonedale. There had been no choice of horses and only two possible carriages, a shabby curricle and a battered gig, to hire for the last leg of their journey. Basingstoke had chosen the curricle. The weather had favored them with a brief windy downpour, and while the road was now dry again, Trahern insisted he could have bettered their pace on foot. Basingstoke, not pleased to have to drive a team he described witheringly as "touched in the wind," countered that it had been Trahern who had thought up the wager and agreed to this abominable destination, and therefore it was his fault they were in this situation. Trahern had countered that Basingstoke was free to concede the wager at any moment that he chose. And after a few more such choice charges had been exchanged, the two had traveled in silence, which, under the circumstances, was no doubt a fortunate solution.

Abruptly Basingstoke jerked on the reins, causing Trahern to exclaim bitterly, "Dash it all, Hugh! The horses are in poor enough shape as it is. There's no need for you to damage them further."

To which Basingstoke replied dryly, "My apologies, Brent, but I think I finally see something of interest on this appalling journey. Possibly, in fact, the solution to our wager."

Immediately Trahern looked about him and realized that at the side of the road ahead two young ladies were standing beside a pony cart that had lost its wheel. Basingstoke drew up at the site of the mishap and jumped down, tossing the reins to Trahern as he did so. With his most charming smile he said, "I hope you will pardon my impertinence, but I should like to be of assistance if I may."

Up close it was evident that the two were ladies. The cut of their gowns and the quality of the pelisses they wore proclaimed their status, as did the delightful high-crown bonnets that framed their faces. But even had Basingstoke not been an expert in ladies' clothing, the calm, composed way in which the elder of the two young ladies addressed him would have been sufficient to confirm her as quality. "I thank you, sir, and wonder if perhaps you might inform the blacksmith in town that we have need of his services," Elizabeth Mayfield replied with a politely distant air. Then, unbending a trifle, she added, "I confess I should be grateful to be saved the walk."

Instinctively, and to her consternation, his eyes immediately went to her feet. "To be sure," he agreed, "your sandals do not seem best suited for such a purpose."

If Elizabeth was aloof, Annabelle was quite the contrary. She leaned toward the strangers, her light blue eyes dancing with excitement. She was too well-bred to ask the questions that filled her curious mind, or even to address these gentlemen without having been introduced. But perhaps it is understandable that she was not in the least disappointed that the younger of the two very handsome, very smartly dressed gentlemen also descended from the carriage and addressed her. To be sure, his words were for Elizabeth as well, but that did not stop Annabelle from fancying that his eyes were on her. "I hope you do not think us too forward, but I am"—he paused so briefly the ladies scarcely noticed—"Brent Holden and this is my friend Percival Wythe." If Trahern felt Basingstoke stiffen beside him, he affected not to notice, but continued to smile charmingly at the ladies as he said to Elizabeth, "Percival and I should be delighted to come to your aid. Perhaps you would like to ride with Percival to locate the blacksmith. I should be glad to wait here with the other young lady until you both return."

Basingstoke gritted his teeth in grim appraisal as he listened to Trahern. This was not lost on Elizabeth, and she was amused. It was not the first time two gentlemen had tried to outmaneuver each other to monopolize Annabelle. The child was bidding fair to be a beauty.

Elizabeth regarded first one gentleman and then the other as she considered Trahern's suggestion. There was a natural elegance about their attire and an easy courtesy that marked them as gentlemen. She supposed there could be no harm in what Mr. Holden proposed, but a natural caution made her hesitate. Annabelle, however, had no such reserve. "Elizabeth, why don't you ride with Mr. Wythe in his curricle? I shan't mind staying here with the cart," she suggested. And when her sister directed a speaking look at her, Annabelle added innocently, "It might be difficult for him to find the smithy."

"It's a small village," Elizabeth countered dryly. Still, her sister regarded her so beseechingly that Elizabeth allowed her natural caution to be overruled. Besides, it would be amusing to observe Mr. Wythe's reaction to being outdone. She had a lively sense of humor and there was something about his rigidly indignant posture that awoke in her a desire to deflate his air of self-importance. "Very well," she said to Trahern. "Perhaps it would be simpler that way. If, of course, the plan meets with your approval, Mr. Wythe?" she added innocently.

Coolly he bowed. "I should be delighted," he said politely. He paused, then turned to Trahern and added, "I think, however, that my friend Mr. Holden should be the one to accompany you. He is a far better hand at the whip than I."

Trahern all but gasped at this outrageous untruth. Instead, his eyes narrowed as he replied quickly, "Yes, but you have forgotten that injury to my wrist which prevents me from handling the reins. Which is, after all, why you were driving in the first place."

"Point and counterpoint," Basingstoke said softly to his friend. "But I am not done up yet." He bowed. "Very well, then I shall drive this young lady," he said curtly as he indicated Annabelle.

"Oh, no, I couldn't," she objected instantly. Then, blushing, she said hastily, "That is, it wouldn't be proper. Elizabeth would be the better choice to go!"

Again Basingstoke gritted his teeth. "Very well, Elizabeth it is," he said, turning to offer the lady in question a hand up into the rented curricle.

Elizabeth allowed herself to be settled in his carriage and pretended not to notice the ironic glance that passed between the two men. As they drew away from the pony cart, Elizabeth felt rather than saw Mr. Wythe's hostility and she said coolly, "I suppose I had best introduce myself if I do not wish to have you continue to make free with my Christian name. I am Miss Mayfield."

If there was one thing Basingstoke detested, it was dowdy starched-up spinsters and he judged Miss Mayfield to be both. "Miss Elizabeth Mayfield," Basingstoke could not resist adding churlishly.

"Quite true," Elizabeth agreed cordially. "And you are Mr. Percival Wythe."

Basingstoke winced. "Yes, but I am more generally known as Hugh."

"I quite understand," Elizabeth replied amiably.

Basingstoke looked at her sharply, but there was nothing to be seen save a pleasant vacuousness to her expression. The earl permitted himself to relax slightly as he asked, "Is the young lady you were with your sister?"

"Yes. That was my sister, Annabelle," Elizabeth answered reluctantly.

"I thought so," Basingstoke told her curtly. "There is a marked resemblance between the pair of you. Has she many suitors?"

Elizabeth frowned. The question itself was impertinent, the manner in which it was asked insulting, and the cause behind it intriguing, for she sensed something other than an ordinary attraction between this man and her sister. Indeed, he had looked at Annabelle more as a man assessing a prime bit of horseflesh than a possible suitor. Her curiosity piqued, Elizabeth could not resist saying tartly, "Far more than are good for her. Annabelle has received three proposals of marriage in the past year alone.''

''And yet she is not married? Or betrothed?'' he asked swiftly.

''No, my father is a most difficult person to please,'' Elizabeth replied repressively.

''I see,'' Basingstoke said thoughtfully.

Elizabeth had the distinct impression he was pleased to hear it. Again the impish part of her could not resist adding in an innocent voice, ''So is my sister, Annabelle.''

They had, by now, reached the edge of the town and Basingstoke could not turn on her the piercing gaze he would have liked, for it required all of his attention to keep those horses from colliding with people on the street. Ravenstonedale might, as Miss Mayfield had told him, be a small village, but there were farmers' carts aplenty to block the way, and any number of persons carrying out their midday errands. Miss Mayfield directed Mr. Wythe to the blacksmith's forge. It was a moment's work to get the blacksmith's agreement to follow him in his wagon. ''Soon as I collect my tools,'' he promised. '' 'Twon't take but a shake or two afore I'll have that wheel back on, Miss Mayfield.''

Elizabeth thanked him. As they waited, Basingstoke asked abruptly, ''Is there an inn here in Ravenstonedale, Miss Mayfield, where I and my friend might put up?''

''Oh? Do you mean to stay here, then?'' she asked with some astonishment.

Basingstoke was amused. ''You seem surprised,'' he said. ''Why? Don't you get many visitors in Ravenstonedale?''

Elizabeth shook her head. ''No. No, not gentlemen like yourselves, unless they come on visits to one of the families hereabouts. I suppose you could stay at the Black Swan,'' she told him doubtfully. ''Do you mean to make a long stay?''

''I don't know,'' he answered honestly.

''What—?'' she started to ask, then stopped, coloring under his amused gaze.

''What am I doing here?'' Basingstoke asked. She hesitated, then nodded. "Rusticating," he replied airily. Then, elaborating on the theme, he added, "We thought we might find the north a trifle less expensive than London just now."

"Under the hatches, I suppose," Elizabeth said, nodding thoughtfully. "You were undoubtedly wise to put yourself so far out of the reach of your creditors."

Impatience at her impertinence warred with the knowledge that it was he himself who had given her such an impression. It nettled Basingstoke beyond measure, he discovered, to have her think he was the sort of scapegrace fellow she obviously envisioned. Finally he said, frowning and with dignity, "It's not as bad as all that, Miss Mayfield. I may have chosen to be prudent in my expenditures, but I assure you my debts were all paid before I left London."

"I beg your pardon," Elizabeth said contritely, "I should not have said that." She chuckled. "It is my wretched tongue, I'm afraid. My stepmother tells me I am forever saying things I ought not to say."

"She's right!" Basingstoke said irritably. Elizabeth looked at him, so taken aback that it abruptly occurred to him that to make an enemy of Miss Annabelle Mayfield's sister was not the way to further his cause. A rueful look entered his eyes and he said to her meekly, "I'm afraid, Miss Mayfield, that I suffer from the same complaint."

Elizabeth was not deceived. "Don't worry," she told him kindly. "I shan't throw a rub in your way. And as soon as you have returned me to my sister, you need suffer my company no further. I have no doubt my father and stepmother will be happy to welcome you at the house, once they hear the service you and your friend have performed for us. And you shall be free to pursue my sister's acquaintance with their blessing."

This time when Basingstoke turned his startled gaze on Miss Mayfield's face he searched it for some clue to what she meant. Elizabeth returned his gaze calmly, meeting his eyes without evasion, and he was surprised to see a lively intelligence and even a twinkle of humor in her fine eyes. She was still dowdy, but Basingstoke realized he had erred in calling her starched-up. That Miss Mayfield meant what she said and meant it kindly was unmistakable, and Basingstoke felt abruptly abashed by his own rude behavior. Taking her hand in his, he surprised even himself by saying, "Miss Mayfield, forgive me. Fatigue has made me rude, and I pray you will forgive my atrocious manners."

Elizabeth gently tried to free her hand, but he would not let it go. She wanted to reply tartly, but there was something so appealing, so honest in the dark eyes that rested on her face, that Elizabeth found she could not. "There is nothing to forgive," she replied more gently than she had intended.

The earl held her hand a moment longer, then, as if suddenly realizing he still held it, abruptly let go. "You evidently have a far better temper than I," he said briskly. "The smith appears ready. Shall we go?"

"What the devil were you about?" Basingstoke demanded of his friend some time later, when they had arranged for rooms and been shown into a private parlor at the Black Swan Inn.

"I?" Trahern asked indignantly. "I merely effected an introduction for us with the Mayfield girls. I assume you agree with me that they meet the criterion of our wager?"

"Oh, granted," Basingstoke agreed, smiling thinly. "Which is why I take exception to your attempt to prevent me from fulfilling it."

"I?" Trahern repeated, astonished. "I thought I made every effort to aid you in fixing your interests with Miss Elizabeth Mayfield."

"Miss Elizabeth Mayfield?" Basingstoke echoed, thunderstruck. "I thought to court the younger sister."

Trahern seated himself and carelessly braced a well-shod foot on another chair. He leaned back, clasped his hands behind his head, smiled sweetly up at his friend, and said, "Did you? But I thought the elder more appropriate. After all, you did say you could court any woman successfully. Come, Hugh, what difference does it make, anyway?" he asked, bringing his chair back down with a thud. "It is not as if you were really planning to marry the girl. Simply win her over and we can be out of here." He paused, then added slyly, "I should think the elder sister would be easier game, anyway. At her age she should be almost upon the shelf and will welcome your attentions."

"All the more reason not to serve her with such a trick," Basingstoke retorted irritably.

Trahern leaned forward. "What? A conscience? You? I don't believe it! Particularly as you have no such compunctions about the younger girl."

Basingstoke shrugged. "She would find a handsome fellow to console her in no time."

"And you think Miss Elizabeth will not?" Trahern replied. "Come, Hugh, you cannot have lost your eyesight. Miss Elizabeth might be older, I have said so myself, and I'll grant you that she could stand better dressing, and I don't deny that the younger is the beauty. But even in London and even at her age, Miss Elizabeth Mayfield is handsome enough to enjoy a ready success. Particularly as her sister tells me she stands to inherit quite a tidy sum when her aunt dies." He paused, then snapped his fingers. "I have it! You fear Miss Mayfield's common sense and good intelligence will cause her to reject you. I'll admit her sister assures me she possesses both qualities in abundance. The more I think of it, Hugh, the shabbier a trick it seems to me that it would be for you to ensnare such a little innocent as Miss Annabelle Mayfield."

"No, I am to leave that to you, I suppose," Basingstoke retorted ironically.

Trahern shrugged. "If you wish to call off our wager, I stand ready to accept your thousand pounds at any time," he said carelessly.

Basingstoke gritted his teeth. "Miss Elizabeth Mayfield it shall be," he countered, flinging his driving gloves onto the table between them.

6

As HAS BEEN said before, the drawing room at Mayfield Manor was a charming one, and so comfortably furnished that it was the place where most of the family was generally to be found. Particularly when there were callers, as there were this morning. Lady Pickworth had come to visit, bringing her latest floral triumphs and a desire to gossip about the new arrivals in town. It was her first expedition out-of-doors since her riding accident, and she was at Mayfield Manor to discover the truth of the gossip concerning the arrival of strangers in town, with one of them driving Elizabeth about in his curricle. Was it true the two gentlemen were from London? And that they were exceedingly handsome? Did Elizabeth think either of them was handsome?

Miss Mayfield was not deceived. She answered lightly, well aware that Lady Pickworth wished to gauge the threat to her own plans for Giles and Elizabeth. So she turned the account into an amusing story of two gentlemen vying for Annabelle's attention. This tactic answered amazingly well, and Lady Pickworth was able to relax in her chair and laugh over the whole event. Elizabeth herself was not so easily satisfied.

Miss Mayfield was neither foolish nor overly vain. She did not discount her own charms, but was well aware that her sister had the advantage of youth, classical features that everyone agreed were beautiful, and an amiability of disposition that could not help but please. To be sure, Elizabeth was not lacking for suitors herself, but she was honest enough to acknowledge that she was no match for Annabelle. Her temper was not so equable or her tongue so gentle, particularly when her lively sense of humor had been engaged, or her sense of injustice. As for her intelligence, it was a vivid one and her father had more than once described it as indecently strong for a female. In short, while not an antidote, Elizabeth had long since resigned herself to the possibility of spinsterhood, thinking it preferable to pretending to be the sort of creature most men admired. Or to being leg-shackled to someone for whom she could not feel a decided preference. Therefore, when the footman announced that Mr. Holden and Mr. Wythe had come to call, she assumed that Annabelle was the one they had come to see.

Indeed, Elizabeth admired the grasp of strategy the gentlemen displayed by allowing two full days to pass between their encounter and this social call. While she might feel a pang of envy, she would also enjoy the diversion in watching these two compete for Annabelle's attention. Elizabeth refused to admit, even to herself, that she had anticipated their arrival with any other emotion. Just as she refused to admit there might be any meaning to the fact that both yesterday and today she had spent an inordinate amount of time choosing which gown to wear.

Lady Pickworth observed with great interest Elizabeth's heightened color. What had begun as mere curiosity to discover the circumstances of the girl's encounter with the new arrivals now became a grim desire to meet the gentleman who had managed to disturb Elizabeth's composure; something no local beau, including Giles, had ever managed to achieve. To be sure, Elizabeth had spoken of the interest shown by both gentlemen toward Annabelle, not herself. For that reason, Lady Pickworth was prepared to dislike whichever gentleman it was who had slighted the girl, for however much she might wish to see Elizabeth and Giles make a match of it, she did not like to see the child unhappy.

Lady Pickworth was impressed, as was Lady Mayfield, by the two gentlemen who entered the parlor. As she studied them openly, Annabelle introduced the pair. "Beatrix, this is Mr. Holden and his friend Mr. Wythe. Gentlemen, my stepmother, Lady Mayfield, and her friend Lady Pick-worth.''

Holden bowed to her first, but it was Mr. Wythe who caught Lady Pickworth's attention, for she could not help but see the way Elizabeth looked at him. And she was sure it was no wonder, for his manners as well as his person were exquisitely neat. He bowed to Lady Mayfield and murmured, ''Your servant.''

Indeed, Lady Pickworth could not deny that she liked what she saw. Mr. Wythe met one's eyes frankly, and while dressed in what must be considered high fashion in this remote corner of England, she did not think either gentleman would be considered a dandy. The boots were polished, the coats well-tailored and of the finest cloth, as were the shirts and trousers. But the cravats were not extravagantly tied, nor were the shirt points excessively high. And neither gentleman so much as glanced in the looking glass near the door. A telling point, since, in Lady Pickworth's experience, a dandy could not bear to pass one without assessing his appearance. There was, moreover, an openness, a politeness, an air of consideration that could not help but be pleasing. Mr. Holden seated himself beside Annabelle and immediately began to monopolize her attention. Mr. Wythe, on the other hand, seated himself beside Elizabeth with an air of being pleased by her company. He did not show in any way his chagrin that Mr. Holden had once more outmaneuvered him, though if Elizabeth's account of their adventure with the pony cart was correct, the fellow must be disappointed. Mr. Wythe, moreover, chose to discuss with Elizabeth, Lady Mayfield, and Lady Pickworth the events in Europe and the weather and the local activities hereabouts, as though nothing could have interested him more.

As for Lady Mayfield, she was no less astute than Lady Pickworth. She, too, had noted Elizabeth's heightened color and allowed herself a moment's satisfaction, for she thought Mr. Wythe a suitable *parti* and yet he appeared not to be such a remarkable catch as to arouse envy in her breast. She therefore exerted herself to encourage Mr. Wythe's interest in Elizabeth. For the first time she was able to think it possible that someone might take the dratted child off her hands. Lady Pickworth watched this gambit with a mixture of approval and alarm.

Elizabeth found herself profoundly puzzled. Mr. Wythe must be disappointed that his friend had once again taken precedence with Annabelle, and yet he acted for all the world as though he wished to talk with her instead. His air of frankness did not entirely fool her, however. She noticed how neatly he evaded all questions her stepmother asked about his background and Mr. Holden's. Not that he refused to answer; he merely was somewhat vague. To be sure, he had pleaded fatigue the other day, and perhaps this was his habitual manner. Nevertheless, Elizabeth was stunned when he asked her if she would show him the gardens.

"Elizabeth?" her stepmother prodded briskly when she merely blinked in dazed surprise. "Wouldn't you like to show Mr. Wythe the roses? My stepdaughter has been a great deal of help to me in growing them," Lady Mayfield added blithely to the gentleman in question.

Hastily Elizabeth collected her wits and suppressed the stirrings of outrage at her stepmother's words. "I should be delighted to show Mr. Wythe the garden," she agreed, rising to her feet.

Basingstoke turned to Elizabeth and offered her his arm with a smile so unexpected that it threatened to overset her composure completely.

It was a beautiful day, once more unexpectedly sunny, and Elizabeth found that it matched her mood. At first she and Mr. Wythe exchanged such civil commonplaces as to the weather and its effect upon the roses. Then Elizabeth thrust caution to the winds and spoke bluntly. "You are very amiable to walk in the garden with me when I know it is Annabelle's company you would prefer," she said.

"On the contrary," he countered, "it is you I came to see. Not your sister."

Elizabeth came to an abrupt halt on the path and looked at the earl speculatively. "Now you have surprised me," she told him frankly.

"Why? Do you so badly underrate your charms?" Basing-stoke asked with a frown.

"I? Oh, no, Mr. Wythe!" Elizabeth said with a musical laugh, shaking her head as she did so. "In point of fact, I think I rate my charms rather highly."

"But you don't rate so highly the perception of my sex, perhaps?" Basingstoke persisted.

Since this was close to the mark, Elizabeth did not deny it. Instead she turned her attention to the roses. Basingstoke displayed not the slightest indication of impatience as Elizabeth traced the lineage of various roses her mother had created. To her surprise, not only did he listen courteously, but he asked a number of shrewd questions. He even guessed that it was she and not her stepmother who was responsible for the current state of the garden. In the end he requested a favor of her.

"A favor?" Elizabeth asked warily.

Did his eyes really dance or was it only an illusion as Mr. Wythe replied, "A rose for my buttonhole."

Now, why should such a simple request fluster her so? Elizabeth wondered. And yet, undeniably it did. She made a show of selecting a prize blossom and presenting it to him. Basingstoke took it and kissed her hand, watching the color rise in her cheeks and thinking it made her more attractive than ever. Just as he was congratulating himself on the success of his strategy, however, a young man strode confidently into the garden and headed in their direction.

Basingstoke frowned. "Your brother?" he hazarded a guess.

"Elizabeth!" the young man called before she could answer. "I must talk with you, at once!"

Basingstoke's frown deepened. "Not your brother?" he murmured to Elizabeth.

She smiled distractedly at the earl before stepping forward to greet the newcomer. "Giles, may I present Mr. Wythe? Mr. Wythe, this is Mr. Pickworth, a good friend and neighbor," she said.

Pickworth had, by now, reached the pair, and grasping Elizabeth's hand, he chided theatrically, "Friend and neighbor? When we have been so much more to each other than that?''

"Indeed?" Basingstoke said icily.

Giles Pickworth regarded the earl quizzically, thinking the fellow resembled nothing so much as a bulldog guarding a bone. A very handsome and well-dressed bulldog, and one, moreover, who had an air of being accustomed to getting his way. But what on earth could the fellow think he had a right to guard here? According to Lady Mayfield, he had met Elizabeth only two days before. Finally mischief won out and Giles bowed sketchily in the earl's direction. "Hello, Mr. Wythe," he said amiably as he put a proprietary arm about Elizabeth's shoulders.

Miss Mayfield had watched the two men square off, a mixture of exasperation and amusement in her eyes. That neither gentleman had any claims upon her only added to both emotions. "Mr. Wythe," she said impatiently, "Giles has been a friend since childhood. We have often depended upon each other's counsel."

"Yes, but you've forgotten to tell him that our families also intend our betrothal," Giles teased.

Basingstoke's brows now seemed to meet in the center of his forehead as he listened to this latest piece of information. Trahern had assured him that neither Miss Mayfield was attached. Basingstoke was going to have a most interesting discussion with him when they returned to the Black Swan. So intent was he on his thoughts that Basingstoke did not notice the look of very real vexation on Elizabeth's face. "I see," he said irritably. "I shall leave you to your discussion, then."

Elizabeth turned to Giles Pickworth. "Now that you have effectively chased away my latest beau," she told him shortly, "do you mean to tell me why you are here?"

Giles had the grace to look abashed. "Well, I'm sorry about that, but I didn't like the looks of him, you know. He's come straight from London and no doubt thinks us all rustics."

"Well, we are, aren't we?" Elizabeth asked reasonably.

"I suppose so," Pickworth grumbled.

"Well, you'd best have a care what you say, even to Mr. Wythe, or it will be all over Ravenstonedale in a flash that you and I are betrothed, and I can't think you want that," Elizabeth said crossly.

"By Jove, no," Pickworth agreed. But even that was not enough to deflect him from his own concerns. "I didn't come to talk about Mr. Wythe, Elizabeth," he said. "I came to ask a favor."

"What favor?" Elizabeth asked warily.

Giles took her hands in his. "You know that I have been seeing Leala and I have told you how my parents feel. Well, now Leala tells me she is not good enough for me, that we must not see each other when there is no hope for it. You must talk with her, persuade her to see me again. Arrange for her to meet us one morning when I shall take you out for a drive. Promise her you will act as chaperone and I know she will come."

Elizabeth pulled her hands free. Reluctantly she said, "Giles, I am not at all certain I ought to encourage you in this folly. If Leala does not wish you to court her—"

"You know Leala!" Giles cut her short impatiently. "It is her absurd sense of honor that is speaking. She is as much in love with me as I am with her, but she will not say so. She is afraid my family will disown me or some such nonsense."

For a long moment Elizabeth was silent. What Giles said was possible. Certainly, when they had been schoolgirls together, Leala had had a *tendre* for Giles Pickworth, a boy who had entirely ignored her at the time. And it was possible that her sense of shame over her changed fortune would make her refuse to see him now. When the scandal had broken over Leala's father two years ago, Elizabeth's stepmother had forbidden her to continue any connection with her friend. This command Elizabeth had instantly defied. But Leala herself had turned Elizabeth away, saying that she must become accustomed to her new circumstances and that if Elizabeth's stepmother did not wish her to see Leala, then she must accept such a decree. Fortunately, Sir Edmund had taken a kinder view of matters and said that he would dislike it very much, thank you, if his daughter turned out to be the sort of girl who spurned her former friends so easily. And because he had relented, so had Leala, though she would still not come to Mayfield Manor, no matter how kindly Elizabeth coaxed her to do so. Elizabeth had long admired her strength of character and wondered if she herself would have been so quick to adapt had it been her fortune that had so changed. Perhaps it was guilt, perhaps it was admiration, perhaps it was still the tug of friendship. Perhaps it was the thought of a certain pair of dark eyes that made her realize Giles had told the truth when he said that one could know in a day, an hour, a moment that one was in love, but whatever the reason, Elizabeth found herself promising to talk with Leala straightaway.

"Bless you!" Giles exclaimed, kissing her on the forehead. "You won't regret it."

"I hope I may not," Elizabeth retorted dryly, "but I have no dependence upon that. And I still do not think it will help you!" she warned him frankly.

"Just persuade Leala to see me and I shall do the rest," Giles retorted confidently.

"Well, I shall try my best," Elizabeth promised, her voice softening. "And I do wish you luck. But now," she added briskly, "we'd best go back inside. You will have set your mother and my stepmother's tongues wagging as it is by routing Mr. Wythe so quickly."

And with an ache that was all the stronger for being, she thought, absurd, Elizabeth turned to lead Pickworth back inside. It was foolish beyond permission, she told herself sternly, to wish so greatly that Mr. Wythe would still be there. To wish that she might somehow tell him the truth about herself and Giles. It was even more foolish, she told herself, to feel such devastation when she learned that Mr. Wythe had already gone. Even if one could not take Mr. Wythe's pretty compliments seriously, there would surely be another time to set matters straight. And yet, somehow all the sensible things she could think of to say to herself did not serve. Elizabeth still found herself missing Mr. Wythe.

Elizabeth managed all the necessary polite words as Lady Pickworth and her son took their leave, and then entertained with an equally polite smile Annabelle's raptures over Mr. Holden's visit. But finally she fled to her room with a plea of letters to write, there to daydream of a cynical, sardonic smile, dark eyes full of intelligence and smoldering danger, and arms that had touched her but briefly and yet threatened to set her carefully banked emotions on fire.

7

BASINGSTOKE drove the curricle back to the Black Swan in silence, Trahern seated cheerfully beside him. He ought to be pleased, the earl told himself, that Miss Elizabeth Mayfield appeared to be attached. Surely Brent would agree the wager must be set aside or a new lady chosen for the venture. He need no longer pay court to Miss Mayfield, who looked at him with eyes that seemed to see far too much. So why did he perversely feel so disappointed? It was not as if he had meant to actually marry the girl.

But Basingstoke found himself haunted by a pair of fine hazel eyes and the startling possibility that the intelligence behind them might match his own. He wanted to see Miss Mayfield again, he realized. He wanted to erase the look of half-contemptuous amusement she wore when she looked at him, and replace it with desire. Desire for his company, desire for his embrace.

He certainly hadn't seen anything of desire in the way she had looked at that young puppy who had routed him. Nor, come to think of it, had he seen anything of desire in the young puppy's face. What, then, was the meaning of this talk of betrothal? Not that the earl had any illusions. He knew as well as anyone that most people did not marry for love, certainly not among the *ton*. And he had rarely questioned the matter. What point wedding for love, if such a thing even existed, when it was so much more rational to wed for reasons of common sense? After all, one need only fulfill one's obligation to produce heirs in the wedding bed, and then seek one's pleasures elsewhere. Certainly that was the sort of marriage the earl had always envisioned for himself.

And the one that had gone awry before it had begun when he realized that his bride-to-be meant to do just that, he thought ruefully. And now a face with hazel eyes had shaken that assumption even further. Not, he told himself irritably, because he was so green as to imagine himself developing a *tendre* for the chit. No, it was more the thought of what she would say of his notion of marriage. He rather fancied she would laugh and think him a fool, and that thought stung.

Basingstoke was in such a foul mood that he didn't even notice the close attention with which Trahern was watching him. Not, at any rate, until the viscount said softly, "What ho? Bad fortune with Miss Mayfield, perchance?"

The earl drew the horses to a halt and turned to stare at Trahern. "You forgot to tell me," he said, biting off each word, "that Miss Mayfield was all but betrothed to some puppy named Pickworth."

Brent carefully hid a smile. He shrugged carelessly as he replied, "Annabelle told me her parents wished for the match but that she was certain her sister would refuse. Does it matter? This only means she will have someone to console her when you disappear."

Basingstoke, to his dismay, realized that he did not want to think about some young sprig consoling Miss Mayfield. But he could not say so to Trahern.

"I had not thought to prevent a betrothal," Basingstoke retorted irritably. "It is one thing to court a young lady who has not settled on a husband, quite another to ruin a choice already made." He paused, then added, "Suppose the young man chooses not to console her after I, as you put it, disappear?"

"Well, what has that to do with me?" Trahern demanded irritably. "I acted in good faith and I'll be damned if I thought you'd ever develop a conscience. You can choose to forfeit the wager if you wish." Basingstoke shot him a warning look and Trahern immediately added, "Or we could choose another young lady for you to lay siege to, if that's what you prefer."

Basingstoke started to agree and then stopped. Did he really want to, as Tahern put it, lay siege to some other young lady? Some insipid miss who would bore him to tears as the young females in London had? Three days ago he would have said yes without hesitation. But today, well, today he had seen again a pair of hazel eyes that met his frankly and whose owner had met his repartee, wit for wit. As for simpering, Hugh could not imagine Elizabeth Mayfield ever doing so. A smile tugged at the corners of his mouth as he tried to picture such an event. Trahern brought him back to the present by demanding impatiently, "Well? Do you mean to cry off the wager or do you mean to choose another young lady to court?"

"Neither," Basingstoke said curtly as he started up the horses once again. "I intend to continue to court Miss Mayfield."

Brent Trahern blinked. He stared at the earl for a long moment before he asked suspiciously, "Are you foxed, Hugh? At this hour of the day?"

"Percival," Basingstoke corrected him cheerfully. "I am Percival Wythe, remember? And no, I am not foxed."

"Well, I'll be dashed if I understand what's wrong with you if you're not!" Trahern retorted roundly. "And I'm dashed if I understand why you were so angry with me. First you're complaining that I chose Miss Mayfield for the wager, and then you're saying you don't want to change the choice after all."

"Oh, I'm not angry with you, now that I think about it," Basingstoke informed him kindly. "A certain Mr. Pickworth, however, may not be so fortunate."

And with that the earl effectively ended the conversation. It did not stop Lord Trahern from speculating on the matter. Or Basingstoke himself. The earl discovered that quite aside from the wager he had exchanged with Trahern, he wished to prevent Miss Mayfield from making the mistake of wedding young Pickworth.

It was not that he underestimated the difficulties facing a young lady of Miss Mayfield's years who had not yet found a husband. Or that he failed to understand the amiability between the pair. He could think of a number of unions that had been successfully formed on just such a foundation. It was simply that he could not imagine Miss Mayfield being happy with the youth. Never mind that the earl had never properly met the boy or gotten to know him. Never mind that most of the *ton* would have been quick to say that Miss Mayfield was better off with the rustic swain than with Basingstoke. Right now the earl found himself determined to convince Miss Mayfield that she deserved better. And if there was not a great deal of sense to the decision, well, the earl simply did not let himself think about that part of it.

As he watched the emotions chasing across Basingstoke's face, Trahern coughed gently. "If it comes to that," he told the earl mildly, "it occurs to me, Hugh, that you are pledged to escort Sophia to a ball tonight. Did you, er, remember to cry off?"

Basingstoke regarded his companion grimly. "Oh, I think Sophia will understand," he replied curtly. "I sent round a note that ought to make things plain."

Now Trahern stared openly at the earl. "I may be a slow-top," he said, offended, "but even I know you are on the point of offering for her. Disappearing for a few weeks ain't going to help you."

"I told you I had changed my mind," Basingstoke replied carelessly.

"Yes, but you were in your cups," Trahern retorted roundly. "For that matter, so was I. We're sober now and I tell you frankly, I don't understand."

"I repeat, I have changed my mind," Basingstoke answered grimly.

"The Marquess of Wey won't be pleased if you sheer off now after making such a point of courting his daughter this Season," Trahern warned.

Basingstoke drew the horses to a halt again and turned to face Trahern. "You are remarkably concerned about the matter," he said bluntly, "for someone who encouraged me to race to the north on a foolish wager."

"Foolish or not," Trahern countered instantly, "I stand

your friend. And the more I think on it, the more I think we ought to call off this wager.''

"Call it off?" Basingstoke said silkily. "Do you concede the matter? The thousand pounds?''

Under the earl's piercing gaze, Trahern shrugged uncomfortably. "You know my pockets aren't as deep as yours. I meant we could simply forget the wager.''

"Forget the wager?" Basingstoke echoed. "After we have come so far just to carry it out?''

"I did suggest we abandon it at the first inn we stopped at,'' Trahern reminded his friend.

"So you did,'' the earl agreed. "My answer is the same. I have never yet walked away from a wager and I do not mean to begin now.''

"Sometimes I think you're half-mad!'' Trahern said, shaking his head.

As Basingstoke started up the horses once again, he cocked his head to the side and asked, "Only half-mad?''

Trahern shook his head in disgust.

Back at the Black Swan, Basingstoke found a message waiting for him. The earl accepted the message calmly and directed the innkeeper to serve them a neat luncheon in their private parlor before he sauntered out of the common room and into that same private parlor. Only when the door was safely shut did he begin to open the sealed letter. This nonchalance was too much for his friend's composure. "What the devil?'' Trahern said, blinking in astonishment. "How did anyone know you were here?'' he demanded suspiciously.

The earl glanced at Trahern. "I assume,'' he said coolly, "that your servants are as efficient as mine. Which means that one of them will have listened at the keyhole and overheard our discussion of where to travel. Having discovered that, it cannot have been a great matter for the messenger to find out which inn we were staying at here in Ravenstonedale, since there is but one in question.''

Basingstoke did not add that he had, as a matter of precaution, informed his secretary of the name of the town where he could be found in an emergency. That discreet fellow had not addressed the message by name or title, but merely informed the messenger how to describe the earl so that he might be found.

Trahern, however, did not question the matter. He nodded, with a scowl, and said, "Well, what the devil is so important that your man must needs send someone all the way here to tell it to you? Particularly as he must have done so soon after we left."

For a long moment Basingstoke stared out the mullioned windows, not answering his friend. At last he turned and said, "It seems you were right that the Marquess of Wey was not pleased when he received my message saying I would not call on him, after all, to ask for his daughter's hand in marriage. I am, it seems, to be an outcast for some time in London."

"The devil you say!" Trahern exclaimed. "Then you mean you were supposed to offer for the Lady Sophia? It was a fixed thing?"

Basingstoke shrugged and turned back to the window. "Not precisely a fixed thing, perhaps," he said, placing one immaculate hand on the side edge of the window, "but certainly expected. I had arranged to call upon the marquess on Thursday and I did not. Not unnaturally, he took exception to the note I sent round saying I would not offer for Sophia, after all. Now Wey has branded me a hardened rake whose capricious behavior is beyond the line and who ought to be given the cut direct by every proper member of the *ton*." Basingstoke paused and a bitter smile twitched at the corners of his mouth before he went on. "Not satisfied with merely scorching myself in that quarter, I also sent round a note to my mistress telling her I wished to sever the connection. *She* is outraged and spreads the tale that it is not at all certain with which gender my interests lie."

Stunned, Trahern could think of nothing to reply. There was a long silence and finally he ventured hesitantly to say, "In a few weeks it will, it must, blow over and be forgotten."

Basingstoke shrugged again. "Perhaps," he said. Then,

with an indifference that chilled Trahern, Basingstoke added, "Go back to London whenever you wish, Brent, but I have no reason to be there. Indeed, more than ever I find myself wondering if what you said at the Cock and Gull is true. I think I shall stay and find out."

"If you stay, then I shall certainly stay," Trahern said quietly, his mind wandering to the vision of Annabelle's lovely face. He was, he realized, in no hurry to return to London. He was only amusing himself, of course. He would never really think of marrying the girl, of course. But Trahern nevertheless found himself very reluctant to think of leaving her.

Basingstoke noted the expressions that flitted across Trahern's face, and among the many unexpected things the earl found himself regretting was having led Trahern into so many reprehensible pranks. It was one thing to blacken his own name, another to hurt this young man's. Before he could find himself entirely sunk into a depression, however, the innkeeper brought in their luncheon.

"You might be interested, sirs," he said, "to know there's a squire hereabouts with some horses for sale. It's a bit of a ride, near on twenty-five miles, but they do say his horses are prime bits of flesh. Good hunters too, they say."

Trahern's interest was piqued and he asked for more particulars. The innkeeper left the room promising to bring back with him the fellow who had brought the news into the taproom.

"With luck," Basingstoke said lightly as he took a slice of ham for his plate, "you'll find just the thing and save yourself some blunt. Alvanley's gelding is certainly well-bred, but if I know the man, he wants a hefty price for the creature. Out here, depend upon it, you'll find the squire ready to deal a fair price for his cattle."

Trahern's eyes gleamed in anticipation. "You may have the right of it," he agreed. "Lord, how I should laugh to bring back a chestnut gelding. Chatham had it that no chestnut could beat his, and I have sworn to race him the moment I find a suitable one. I should love to see his face if I appeared without warning and challenged him to a race. He has said publicly that he thinks I will not, and every time he hears that I am interested in a chestnut gelding, he makes haste to persuade someone else to bid for the creature first.''

''What else can he do?'' Basingstoke asked derisively. ''Even he must realize that you are by far the better horseman, and he cannot expect the horse to make up for his deficiencies. I am surprised he has not gone even further.''

Trahern laughed, and a short time later the innkeeper returned as promised with a local farmer. A few minutes of conversation served to confirm their interest in the squire's horses, and precise directions were obtained as well. An hour later, in surprisingly good spirits, Basingstoke and Trahern left the Black Swan to go and see the squire's horses.

8

IF BASINGSTOKE AND TRAHERN did not call at Mayfield Manor every day, it was almost as often. Trahern continued to pursue a lighthearted flirtation with Annabelle, which neither took altogether seriously, while Basingstoke tried hard to fix his interest with Elizabeth. If he was not bringing her some posy of flowers picked at the side of the road, he was charming them all with tales of London or running errands for her stepmother. He was not above amusing Willoughby whenever Lady Mayfield saddled Elizabeth with his care, for Nurse was unaccountably long in regaining her feet after her latest spring cold, and it was best, Lady Mayfield would say imperatively, not to expose Willoughby more than necessary to Nurse's company. Another man might have caviled at such an odd chaperone to his *tête-à-tête* with Elizabeth, but Basingstoke displayed not the least impatience or distress. A sight Elizabeth thought she would never forget was that of Mr. Wythe seated on the ground, oblivious of the damage to his biscuit-colored pantaloons, playing spillikins with Willoughby. In short, there was everything to admire and nothing to dislike in Mr. Wythe's behavior. And yet Lady Mayfield was troubled.

She had welcomed her stepdaughter Elizabeth's interest in Mr. Wythe since it had provided the hope that she would finally have the girl off her hands. But Lady Mayfield was too shrewd a woman to let such hopes cloud her better judgment. If she promoted a match that later turned out to have been a mistake, Edmund would never forgive her and the tattlemongers hereabouts would say that it was because she disliked Elizabeth and had wanted the girl off her hands at all cost. Which was true, but Lady Mayfield had no wish for others to say so.

She lost no time in writing to her sister-in-law, Lady Elizabeth Salvage, who lived in London, to discover what could be learned of Mr. Wythe and his friend Mr. Holden.

Lady Mayfield had no doubt that her husband, Sir Edmund, would be displeased if he found out what she had done. He would not hesitate to ring a peal over her head, inform her that such behavior could not be tolerated, call her disloyal, declare that any information from such a source was not to be trusted, and then seize the letter to discover just what his sister, Elizabeth, knew. The trouble was that Lady Salvage had written to say that she knew precisely nothing concerning Mr. Wythe and Mr. Holden.

To be sure, Lady Salvage would be the first to say, and indeed she had in her letter, that she no longer went about much and that both gentlemen might be well-known to others. But Lady Mayfield knew that Sir Edmund had great respect for his sister's judgment and common sense, whatever he might say to the contrary. If Lady Salvage had been unable to discover any word about either fellow, then perhaps there was none to be found. And that made Lady Mayfield profoundly uneasy. Mr. Holden might pass unnoticed in London, but she could not believe it to be true that Mr. Wythe would do so. If his broad shoulders and generally fine features did not cause remark among the ladies, his shrewd insight would mark him out among the men. To be sure, that sort of notice might not reach her sister-in-law's ears, and perhaps Lady Mayfield ought to be reassured by the absence of gossip about the man. And she might have been if it were not for the cynical gleam that from time to time lit his eyes or caused the corner of his mouth to curl in contempt, and the bleak look that crossed his face once when Lady Mayfield asked about his family or when another caller joked about what a desirable *parti* he must be. Lady Mayfield found herself thinking that Mr. Wythe was a man who had seen a great deal and done a great deal, not all of it admirable. This was scarcely the sort of thing, however, she would have ventured to suggest to Edmund, who would not hear a word against the man. He would have laughed at her suspicions, pinched her cheek, and assured her that she was a silly puss for talking of things she knew nothing about, he was happy to say! Though if they later proved true, he would be the first to say she ought to have scotched the romance. It was grossly unfair, Lady Mayfield concluded irritably.

Lady Mayfield soothed herself by noting that Elizabeth kept the fellow at arm's length. Therefore, Lady Mayfield told herself, she need not speak of her suspicions to Elizabeth or forbid the man permission to call at the manor. That was a step she was loath to take, for she was convinced that nothing could be more certain to drive a stepdaughter into the arms of an unsuitable fellow than for a stepparent, no matter how reasonable the objection, to attempt to thrust a spoke between the pair. Depend upon it, if Elizabeth eloped with him, that would be laid at her door as well. But oh how delightful it would be to have the girl off her hands.

And so Lady Mayfield held her counsel and watched with a mixture of spiteful pleasure and uneasiness as Elizabeth fell more and more under Mr. Wythe's spell. At the same time, on those occasions when Giles Pickworth arrived to take Elizabeth out for a drive, Lady Mayfield readily encouraged her to go. After all, there was no certainty that Elizabeth would succeed in bringing Mr. Wythe to the point of offering for her, and one must allow for the possibility that she would not. Indeed, Giles Pickworth would be a most suitable match, and one without the worries of an unknown gentleman from London. Besides, she told herself virtuously, jealousy was a very useful emotion to rouse in the breast of a gentleman. Unaccountably, however, after one such drive, Elizabeth returned to the house vowing never to accompany Giles again.

Aghast, Lady Mayfield demanded to know why. "Beatrix," Elizabeth said, pausing in the act of tossing her chipstraw hat onto the sofa, "you must know it is pointless for me to encourage Giles. Neither he nor I wish for a match between us, so why should I continue to drive out with him?"

"If Giles Pickworth were so set against a match between the pair of you, he would not call so often to see you," Lady

Mayfield replied tartly. "I've no doubt he has managed to somehow offend you, for that is plain as a pikestaff by your face. But you must recollect that men are forever doing so and that it is pointless to take offense at something they cannot help."

Elizabeth hesitated. It was not in her nature to lie, and yet neither was it in her nature to betray a confidence. Giles might lack common sense and be courting trouble, but if he paid heed to her words, he might yet come about. If she, however, betrayed his confidence concerning Leala, she would bring down upon all their heads precisely the sort of trouble she most wished to avoid. So Elizabeth merely shook her head at her stepmother and said mildly, "Pray don't press me to go where my inclinations must protest."

"I must say that if they have not protested until today, I do not see why they must do so now!" Lady Mayfield told her obstinate stepdaughter. "I suppose you will tell me you prefer the company of Mr. Wythe?"

An odd smile lit Elizabeth's eyes as she replied, "Why, yes, I suppose I do. Why? Do you dislike him?"

Now it was Lady Mayfield's turn to prevaricate. She busied herself with rearranging a vase of flowers that was already arranged precisely to her liking. Over her shoulder she said, "Oh, as to that, I have nothing to say against the man. But after all, we know so little about him. Who is to say he is eligible?"

"Who is to say he is not?" Elizabeth countered mischievously. At her stepmother's sharp look, however, Elizabeth moved closer. In a more sensible voice she said, "I am fond of Mr. Wythe's company, but I do not look for anything more than that of him."

She spoke lightly, but there was something in her voice that made Lady Mayfield turn swiftly and eye her step-daughter in an appraising way. "Is he trifling with you? Has he said anything to mean he is ineligible or does not think of marriage?" she asked sharply.

Now Elizabeth turned away. "No," she said with a shrug.

"Then I have never seen a greater piece of foolishness," Lady Mayfield said impatiently. "From what I have seen,

Mr. Wythe seems to be quite set on fixing his interest with you. Or have you done something to discourage him?''

"No, I have not!" Elizabeth said wearily. "As for what Mr. Wythe's intentions are, I suppose we must wait and see." Then, unable to bear her stepmother's catechism anymore, Elizabeth said, "Pray excuse me, for I have some things I must do upstairs."

Lady Mayfield made no demur. Before she could reach the safety of the second floor, however, Elizabeth had to cross the foyer, and it was there that Mr. Wythe found her, her hat in her hand, when he and Mr. Holden were admitted to the house. Elizabeth directed Mr. Holden to the garden, where she felt certain he would find Annabelle, then turned her attention to Mr. Wythe. She felt a tremor at the sight of his handsome face and the confident set of his broad shoulders beneath the mulberry jacket he wore. Nor was she immune to his smile as he greeted her with unabashed pleasure and an exaggerated bow. "Miss Mayfield, I count myself fortunate to find you in," he said, taking her hand and lifting it to his lips.

Elizabeth felt another tremor run through her, and the color rose in her cheeks. Every day made her more eager to see him, to share some absurd story he had to tell, some thought she had had since the last time she had seen him, to have him look at her with approval and dangerous desire. Elizabeth felt the familiar longing to stroke the dark curls on his head and tell him softly that he was both wonderful and absurd. She was too well-bred to do either, however, and nothing showed in her voice as she pulled her hand free and greeted her guest coolly. "Mr. Wythe, how do you do this morning?"

Swiftly he raised his eyes to hers, and a wicked gleam seemed to dance in them as he put his hand over his heart and said, "Miss Mayfield, you wound me to the quick. This coolness, this lack of regard for my most fervent emotions. How shall I bear it?"

In spite of herself, Elizabeth's lively sense of humor was touched and she began to chuckle. "Oh, do give over your nonsense!" she said, trying to sound severe.

"Only if you promise to come out for a walk with me," he countered, possessing himself of her hand again and smiling in a way that he must have known no female could resist. "Or if not a walk, then a drive about the countryside. I am a great lover of nature, you must know."

"Are you indeed?" Elizabeth replied, eyeing him speculatively. "Now why, I wonder, do I find that so hard to believe? Never mind, if you are hoaxing me, it will serve you right to have to endure a lecture on the properties of the plants we pass, for I promise you I mean to further your education on that score."

Again Basingstoke bowed. "I should be delighted," he told her grandly.

Her eyes sparkling, her spirits unaccountably lighter, Elizabeth tied the ribbons of her chip-straw hat under her chin, the bow rakishly at an angle, then took Mr. Wythe's arm as the footman held open the door for them.

"Shall it be on foot or in my carriage?" Basingstoke asked when the door had closed again behind them.

Elizabeth regarded the vehicle in question and her lips twitched as she replied tartly, "You have far more patience than I in putting up with those nags you have hired. I think I should prefer to depend on my own two feet. It seems the safer course."

Basingstoke's own eyes danced as he replied, "I certainly shan't protest. Though I do think you are cruel to my horses."

"The only cruelty is harnessing them when they are so far past their prime," Elizabeth retorted frankly.

"Now you have put me on my mettle to prove they are not as hopeless as you say, and we shall have to go for that drive," Basingstoke countered, stopping where he was and holding out his hand to help her up into the carriage.

Elizabeth hesitated but made no real demur. Upon reflection she had decided that sitting beside Mr. Wythe in a curricle while his attention must be claimed by the horses was likely to be more comfortable than to have him watching her as closely as he often did when they walked. She allowed him to help her into the curricle and watched as he directed the horses down the drive back toward the main road. Her quick eyes noted how shrewdly he handled the horses, prizing out of them a far better performance than she would have thought possible. "Now, why, I wonder, do I find myself thinking that you are accustomed to far better?" she asked aloud.

Startled, Basingstoke looked down at wide hazel eyes that stared up at him with a mixture of amusement and shrewdness. For a moment he couldn't answer her, so unexpected was the response of his own heart. This was to be a light flirtation, the winning of a wager; anything more surely spelled disaster. Why, then, could he not tear his eyes away?

But abruptly Basingstoke had to, his attention drawn by the two horses veering off the road. Miss Mayfield laughed and Basingstoke felt his own spirits lift at the musical sound. He risked glancing down at her for the merest fraction of a moment, his brows quizzing her as he directed the horses back onto the road. "If you have been wishing to convince me that you are not such a nonpareil with the reins after all, you have succeeded admirably," Elizabeth explained.

"And if I tell you that it was your beautiful self which distracted me?" he countered lightly.

"Why, then, I shall know you are dealing in Spanish coin," she answered placidly.

"Are you so certain?" he asked, his voice unaccountably serious.

Because his voice had been serious, Elizabeth did not at once answer. Without knowing she did so, she clasped her hands tightly together in her lap. That she wanted Mr. Wythe to be telling the truth could not be denied, and yet she could not, would not, allow herself to believe it. At last, turning her head away from him, she said as lightly as she could, "I think you an expert in Spanish coin, sir."

"You seem very sure of that," Basingstoke observed, amused in spite of himself.

Carefully Elizabeth smoothed her skirt before she replied, "Well, sir, you are ready with your compliments, and if you did not deal in Spanish coin but something more sincere, then I cannot believe you would still be unwedded."

"Perhaps I am difficult to please," Basingstoke retorted coolly. "Or perhaps," he added, recollecting what had led to the wager, "it is simply that I have not the lineage or fortune necessary to procure myself a wife."

"Now, why," Elizabeth said thoughtfully, as though to herself, "do I find that difficult to believe?"

"What? That I lack the lineage or fortune?" Basingstoke asked, pleased that his true qualities had shown through his disguise.

His bubble of pleasure was promptly burst, however, as Elizabeth replied with a gurgle of laughter, "No, that you would let such disadvantage stop you from obtaining a wife. If you wanted one, that is," she added conscientiously.

"Perhaps it is not I, but protective parents who would hold my status a bar," Basingstoke suggested, nettled.

"Is that why you have come so far afield?" Elizabeth asked, looking at him wide-eyed again. "Because you think that we will not prove so strict in our notions? You dash all my romantic hopes! Somehow I had thought you would be the sort to ride off with your intended bride in the teeth of her parents' opposition if need be. And it is that rather than your lack of fortune or name that would put parents on their guard, I should think."

"A pretty notion of my character you have," he retorted, as though offended.

Elizabeth laughed. "Well, would you not do it?" He had no answer to that, and after a moment she laughed again. "The only thing I cannot decide," she added thoughtfully, "is if the girl's own objections would weigh with you."

"Oh, not in the least," Basingstoke said airily, having decided the tone he wished to take. "I should be so confident, you see, of bringing her round to my point of view once I had her away from her, er, so protective parents."

The difficulty was, Elizabeth had no trouble believing him. He might speak in jest, but there was something in his manner that made her feel that beneath the jest he spoke the truth. No trace of her thoughts showed on her face, however, as she replied with apparent tranquillity, "Why, then, I must take care never to give you cause to desire to abduct me, I see.''

''And I should think you would be the devil to abduct if you did not come willingly,'' Basingstoke countered frankly.

She met his eyes steadily as she replied merrily, ''You are a superb judge of character, Mr. Wythe!''

He was amused. The thought of what Brent would say were he to extract an agreement of marriage after abducting Miss Mayfield made him smile. Noticing the smile, Elizabeth mistrusted it. And yet she could not say that she felt unsafe with him. She had meant it when she said she could imagine him ruthlessly abducting a female over her objections. His past, she felt sure, held things that would be judged shocking. And yet Elizabeth could not but feel that it was as if an angry boy were trying to shout at the world to take account of him. Sunnily she smiled back at Mr. Wythe. Glancing down at her, Basingstoke leered lightly and said, ''Perhaps one day we shall put it to the test.''

Still Elizabeth smiled up at him. ''No,'' she said, shaking her head, ''you won't. As you say, I should be the devil to abduct against my will.''

''But what if it were not against your will?'' Basingstoke countered swiftly.

Again she shook her head. ''I have not the temperament to wish for such an uncomfortable proposition,'' she replied tranquilly. ''I can imagine nothing more unpleasant than to be seized and have a hand clamped over one's mouth. That is what happens, isn't it?'' she asked uncertainly.

''It is,'' he agreed promptly.

''Well, then, seized, a hand clamped over one's mouth, and a jolting carriage traveling at shocking speed that threatens to overturn at any moment, stopping, no doubt, at dreadfully uncomfortable inns,'' Elizabeth continued, relishing the tale.

''Most uncomfortable, I should think,'' Basingstoke agreed, amused. ''I hadn't thought in those terms before, but I assure you, now that you have brought it to my attention, when next I abduct a female I shall take great care to moderate my speed, seize her as gently as possible, and choose my stopping points with an eye to comfort.''

''But I don't think you could,'' Elizabeth protested.

Nonplussed, Basingstoke was startled into exclaiming, ''What?''

''Well,'' Elizabeth said reasonably, her brow furrowing as she thought the matter through, ''you would have to travel speedily, for fear of pursuit, and you couldn't stop at the best inns for fear of encountering an acquaintance, so the whole business would have to be uncomfortable, wouldn't it? Unless, of course, you could manage to give everyone the slip and delay anyone's realization of your flight for some time.''

''You seem,'' Basingstoke said severely, ''to have given the matter a remarkable degree of thought!''

Elizabeth colored instantly, thinking that as all three of her novels thus far had involved abductions, she had indeed considered the matter quite in depth. But she could not tell Mr. Wythe so. Upon the one occasion that Beatrix had caught Elizabeth at her writing, she had impressed most emphatically upon her that while she might amuse herself composing stories, on no account was she to allow any gentleman to know that she did so.

It was too much to hope that Mr. Wythe would overlook her confusion. His own face creased into a frown as he realized that his retort had so discomposed the girl. What ailed her? Did she, in fact, contemplate such an experience? With whom? Young Pickworth? The Scottish border was far too close for comfort, Basingstoke reflected, and it occurred to him that someone had best halt any such plans before they went further. Repressively Basingstoke said, ''You are quite right in thinking an abduction or even an elopement is not a romantic matter, Miss Mayfield. I trust you have no such notion in mind?''

''Me? No! How absurd an idea!'' Elizabeth replied a trifle breathlessly, looking everywhere but at Mr. Wythe.

Which could only, she told herself later in severe reproof, have convinced him that of course you did! If you will write novels, you must learn to control your countenance far better than that, she scolded herself sternly.

But now Basingstoke grimly pressed his lips together. He would have to keep an eye on the chit. Not only did he not wish her to ruin herself, there was the wager with Trahern. With an effort he set aside his ill humor and exerted himself to charm Miss Mayfield into laughing again, as though he had noticed nothing odd in her manner. To his surprise, he found it a pleasant task, and it would have been hard to say who was more pleased. Unlike the young women who had populated the salons during the past Season, Miss Mayfield did not respond with foolish coyness or vacuous comments to things he said. Her mind was well-formed and it was evident she had had excellent tutoring as well as access to a well-stocked library, for her reading had ranged farther and wider than was usual for a female. Nor was Miss May-field afraid to contradict him, a circumstance which first startled and then delighted Basingstoke. With relish he pressed her to stand behind her own opinions and found her both willing and able to do battle with her wits.

There were advantages in being simple Mr. Wythe rather than the Earl of Basingstoke, he reflected as he finally turned the carriage down the drive to Miss Mayfield's home some time later. And yet, he admitted to himself wryly, he had little doubt that Miss Mayfield would have disagreed with the Earl of Basingstoke as readily as she did with plain Mr. Wythe. And as Basingstoke handed her down from the carriage, he found himself acknowledging what his heart already knew: he was beginning to care a great deal about Miss Mayfield.

Absurd! his dignity cried. What would the *ton* think to know the Earl of Basingstoke had been captured by a mere baronet's daughter? What Basingstoke found most frightening was the realization that he simply didn't care.

So intent was his gaze on her that Elizabeth shivered. Even the touch of his hand on hers made her blood take fire. She found herself all but swaying against him, wondering what it would be like for him to make love to her. That she had no notion who he was or that she was certain there was a mystery about his courtship of her didn't matter. Not now, not when he looked at her as though his hunger to hold her equaled her own.

"Miss Mayfield," he began.

And then, abruptly, the spell was broken as an alert servant opened the front door for them. Mr. Wythe was his remote self once again, bowing and saying politely that he hoped to see her on the morrow. And she was blushing again as she replied breathlessly that that would be delightful, but why didn't he come in and see if his friend Mr. Holden was still there? Politely he agreed.

9

As Basingstoke stepped into the drawing room with Elizabeth Mayfield, he saw that Trahern was bending his head toward Annabelle's, a teasing laughter in the fellow's eyes. At their entrance, the viscount immediately stood up and greeted Elizabeth politely before turning to Basingstoke and saying, "Miss Annabelle has been telling me about the little people to be found hereabouts!"

"Little people?" Basingstoke asked, confused.

"Little people," Elizabeth told him, as though he hadn't heard. "Pixies. Fairies. Elves and goblins. Surely you've heard of those?"

"Oh, surely," he agreed wearily.

"Well, it seems they are exceedingly active hereabouts," Trahern told him with relish.

Basingstoke cast a withering eye on his friend. Undaunted, however, Trahern pressed on, saying, "Have a care, Percival! They have been known to lead the disrespectful straight into horse ponds and such, in the dead of night."

"And far worse!" Elizabeth added darkly.

Basingstoke looked at her suspiciously, but she merely smiled innocently back at him. Irritably he asked, "Is there some point to this nonsense?"

"Please don't call it nonsense," Annabelle begged him earnestly. "It is far more than that."

"The point of all this," Trahern broke in to say, "is that we are to make an expedition of it to Long Meg's Circle near Great Salkeld. We shall count her daughters," he concluded solemnly.

"Yes, for if we count them correctly, they shall all come

to life again,'' Elizabeth added, for all the world as if she believed the tale.

"I see," Basingstoke replied politely. "And when do we go on this, er, exciting expedition?"

At this point Lady Mayfield, who had been sitting quietly observing the byplay, told him dryly, "You need not go, sir, if you do not wish to do so. I am quite certain Giles Pickworth would be happy to accompany Elizabeth instead."

Basingstoke regarded Lady Mayfield with a strong sense of dislike. It was not that he was unaccustomed to such tactics; rather he was far too well acquainted with them. He was about to serve her a sharp setdown when he realized that Elizabeth was regarding him anxiously. He had already noted that matters were strained between the two and he had no wish to add to Elizabeth's discomfort. Therefore he contented himself with bowing to Lady Mayfield and saying smoothly, "Why, of course Mr. Pickworth would be welcome to join us."

It was evident that this reply was not to her liking, for Lady Mayfield retorted coolly, "That is for Elizabeth to decide, is it not?"

Helplessly Elizabeth watched the two wrangle. After this morning's drive she had no wish to invite Giles Pickworth anywhere, and yet it looked as though she would, in a few moments, have no choice. The two would contrive to make it impossible for her to refuse to do so.

Abruptly she realized that Mr. Wythe was addressing her. There was concern in his eyes and a gentleness in his voice that almost undid her countenance. "Do you wish to invite Mr. Pickworth?" he asked quietly. And then, more softly, so that her stepmother could not hear, "Are you all right, Miss Mayfield?"

Mortified that she had so far betrayed herself, Elizabeth forced herself to smile at him and say lightly, "Yes, of course, thank you, Mr. Wythe. As for Giles, I should be happy to have him along."

Basingstoke pressed his lips together but did not argue. Instead he replied carelessly, "As you wish. When is this expedition to be set for?"

"The day after tomorrow," Annabelle answered excitedly. "Mr. Holden tells me it will take a day to arrange for extra carriages," she added, blushing delightfully.

Basingstoke cast an ironic eye upon his friend, who shrugged all but imperceptibly. "I shall look forward to it," Basingstoke said lazily, "particularly if I do not need to arrange the matter."

"I doubt your purse could stand the expense," Trahern said with an air of frankness. Then, as Basingstoke's eyes snapped with anger, he added kindly to the assembled group, "I keep assuring Mr. Wythe that he need not apologize for not being plump in the pocket, but he will insist upon feeling badly about the matter. I keep telling him that he need only marry well."

The effect of this pronouncement upon Lady Mayfield was comical. First she was helpless to suppress the look of dismay that crossed her face, but it was shortly replaced by one of mean-spirited satisfaction. Finally it was succeeded by one of politic politeness.

Basingstoke ground his teeth together in impotent rage. By the terms of their wager, he had no recourse to Trahern's pronouncement. He could not deny the assertion, nor Trahern's mastery in making it.

It was left to Annabelle to make a total shambles of things. "Is that why Mr. Wythe has been dangling after Elizabeth?" she asked artlessly. "Because I told Mr. Holden about Aunt Elizabeth's will?"

Silence filled the small room, oppressive in its significance. It was Basingstoke who finally broke the silence by asking coolly, "Who is Aunt Elizabeth?"

It was Lady Mayfield who finally answered. In a voice calculated to depress pretensions she said, "Elizabeth's aunt, Sir Edmund's sister, Lady Salvage, lives in London. Regrettably, she chose to marry a Frenchman, an *émigré*, and my husband chose to sever the connection."

The effect of this pronouncement on Basingstoke was as comical as the earlier one had been with regard to Lady Mayfield. He sat as if transfixed. "Lady Elizabeth Salvage?" he repeated in a strangled tone of voice.

"Yes. Do you know her?" Lady Mayfield asked, her voice conveying that she considered it most unlikely.

Nevertheless Basingstoke replied, as offhandedly as he was able, "I believe I may have met her a time or two."

"How odd, then, that she does not recall having met you," Lady Mayfield said thinly.

But Basingstoke had recovered himself and, flicking an imaginary piece of lint from his sleeve, replied coolly, "Oh, well, you know what a crush these London affairs are. We may not actually have spoken, perhaps she was merely pointed out to me, or some such thing."

"Then you should have said so," Lady Mayfield said tartly, "instead of pretending to be well-acquainted with my sister-in-law."

"Yes, ma'am," Basingstoke said meekly. "Perhaps Mr. Holden and I had best take our leave now."

Trahern glared at his friend in outrage, but there was nothing to be done, as the ladies rose to their feet and he was forced to do so as well. A few minutes later the two men were outside the front door and climbing into the hired carriage. When they were well down the drive, Trahern turned to Basingstoke and asked in exasperation, "What the devil was that all about?"

"I know Lady Salvage," Basingstoke said through clenched teeth.

"So? She appears not to have betrayed you," Trahern replied with a shrug.

"Only because Lady Mayfield must have written asking about Mr. Percival Wythe," Basingstoke retorted scathingly. "I have no doubt that the name meant nothing to her when she wrote her answer, but if I know Lady Salvage, her mind will nag at her until she resolves the mystery, and how long can it be before she recollects that Wythe is the family name of the Earl of Basingstoke?"

"How long do you think we have? Long enough for you to resolve the wager and be gone?" Trahern asked uneasily.

"Perhaps, but I cannot like the odds," Basingstoke replied grimly.

Trahern was silent a moment; then he said, "Why? I mean, why should she trouble to recollect your family name? Isn't it possible she won't?"

That gave him pause. Finally Basingstoke replied, "You have not been long in London."

"Three years!" Trahern broke in indignantly.

Basingstoke smiled as he deftly guided the horses past a hole in the road. "Yes, but this story began twenty years ago. It was a time of terror in France. My father helped organize the rescue of a number of French noblemen and others felt to be in danger of the guillotine. The Comte de Salvage was one of them. His heritage was illustrious, if a trifle irregular, and with my father's help he arrived in England safely and with a large quantity of jewels, which he proceeded to translate into mercantile interests in the city. Investments that were extremely successful. He met and married Elizabeth Mayfield, and by all accounts that, too, was a success. She, in turn, interested herself in my affairs after my mother's death. So, you see, I find it unlikely that she will not sort out the matter of my name, particularly when she realizes that I am not in London or my home estate."

"Well, how the devil will she find that out?" Trahern demanded.

"The lady is remarkably astute," Basingstoke retorted dryly. "I did not see her often, but whenever I did, she put me in a quake because it seemed as if she could read my mind."

"I know just what you mean," Trahern said sourly. "I've a Cousin Mathilde who's the same. Avoid them like the plague, that's what we've got to do." He paused, then added hopefully, "Y'know, p'rhaps it's just as well. I have been thinking that we ought to call off this wager. If we did, you'd have nothing to fear from the woman."

"Call off this wager?" Basingstoke asked, looking at Trahern sharply.

"Yes. You could go back to London and we could pretend this never happened," Trahern replied earnestly.

"I could go back to London?" Basingstoke echoed.

Trahern turned in his seat to stare at the earl. "Do you have to repeat everything I say?" he demanded. "It's a damned annoying habit."

Basingstoke merely smiled thinly, his attention on his horses. "Now, I wonder why you should want to call off the wager," he said thoughtfully. "And why you wish me to disappear. It couldn't, by chance, have to do with a certain Annabelle Mayfield, could it?"

"You're devilish acute yourself, Basingstoke!" Trahern retorted waspishly. Then, changing his tactics, he said wheedlingly, "Wouldn't you like to go back to London? I could tell the Mayfields that urgent business called you away."

"And Miss Mayfield?" Basingstoke asked, considering the matter.

"Let her think she overestimated your interest in her," Trahern replied airily. "It would not be the first time a young lady has done so. The important thing is that I am releasing you from the wager."

"But suppose I do not choose to be released from the wager?" Basingstoke asked softly. Then, meditatively he added, "I think I shall ask Miss Mayfield to marry me on the excursion to Long Meg's Circle. That ought to be a sufficiently romantic spot, don't you think?"

"Here, no, you can't!" Trahern said in alarm.

Basingstoke glanced at his friend with raised eyebrow. "Why not?" he asked succinctly.

"Well, you just can't," Trahern answered hotly. "It's the outside of enough for you to ruin my chances with Annabelle for some absurd wager. And it *will* put paid to my chances if you jilt her sister."

"But suppose I don't mean to jilt her sister?" Basingstoke countered, as softly as before.

Trahern blinked. He stared. He tried and failed to muster words with which to reply. Finally he croaked, "You mean to marry the girl?"

"Why not?" Basingstoke asked coolly. "She is, after all, an heiress."

"Humbug!" Trahern said decisively. "As if you cared
for that! You could marry a pauper and be well enough to
do for the pair of you."

"But one ought to always have an eye to enriching the
family coffers," Basingstoke replied meekly.

Trahern turned a decidedly jaundiced face on his friend.
"Do you mean to tell me you believe Miss Mayfield to be
heiress to a greater fortune than the Marquess of Wey's
daughter would bring to marriage as a dowry?" he
demanded. "No, I tell you what it is! You've been caught.
Ensnared. Developed a *tendre* for a creature you'd not have
looked at twice in London!"

A wry, slightly sad smile crossed Basingstoke's face. "No,
I probably wouldn't have," he agreed.

"Bedeviled, that's what you are," Trahern continued,
encouraged by the absence of a sharp setdown from his
friend. "And I tell you what, it's good for you! Not that I'm
all fired certain you ought to marry this girl," he added,
suddenly sobered. "She's only a baronet's daughter."

"Do you think I would care for that?" Basingstoke
demanded.

"Yes," Trahern retorted bluntly.

"Well, perhaps," Basingstoke agreed with a shaky laugh,
"if she were a mere baronet's daughter, but she is also the
granddaughter of a baron on her mother's side, and even you
must have been able to perceive her good breeding."

"Now you are bamming me," Trahern said severely, "and
I don't think it kind of you."

Basingstoke's voice turned serious as he replied, "I have
often said, you have often heard me say, that I am too well
aware of what was due my lineage to marry any female whose
father was not a peer of the realm. And perhaps I have even
meant it. Or perhaps," he added with a shrug, "it was a
convenient means of cutting short the number of eligible
females who would throw their cups at me. Since I thought
to marry out of duty, not affection, one reason served as well
as another."

"Good God," Trahern said, shocked, "surely you were

not as shockingly cynical as that? Didn't you think there was even the slightest chance you would find someone you cared about?''

A ghost of a bitter smile crossed Basingstoke's face as he replied, "Someone I cared about? Only in the lightest, most comfortable of ways, and I assure you I didn't think that would include marriage."

"B-but that's appalling," Trahern objected.

"Don't stammer and don't act as though all of this comes as such a surprise to you. I must have told you any number of times that I thought this way," Basingstoke replied shortly.

"Yes, but I didn't think you really meant it," Trahern said frankly. "I thought it just one more of your affectations. You have been known to play the role of cynical earl with devastating effectiveness and then turned around and done something kind or good or in direct contradiction of some outrageous idea you have expressed. I thought this one more pronouncement of the sort. It's positively shocking to realize you meant it."

"I don't see why," Basingstoke countered, affronted. "People are forever making marriages based more on convenience than affection. I simply accept the notion more readily than usual." He paused, then added with a frown, "The trouble is, I didn't reckon on Miss Mayfield. I can't tell you, even now, what it is that makes me care. Her figure is neat; her face is fine and shows great character. Her eyes are steady, her manner well-bred, and her intelligence superior. But what there is that sets her apart from a hundred other such females, I cannot say. I only know that I have gone from treating this as a lark to meaning to ask her to marry me in earnest."

"Do you mean to tell her who you are?" Trahern asked, alarm once more tingeing his voice.

Basingstoke shook his head. "Not until after she has agreed," he said. Again there was the bitter smile as he added, "I am foolish enough to wish to know she would marry me for myself and not for my title or fortune."

"After today she is more likely to think you wish to marry her for hers," Trahern said bluntly.

"Yes, thanks to you," Basingstoke retorted, turning his wrath on Trahern. "I could wish you at Jericho for that!"

"Well, if she does agree to wed you after that, you will certainly know it is for yourself," Trahern offered weakly.

An angry snort was the earl's only reply.

10

THE DAY DAWNED warm and fair, a much-welcome favor
from the heavens. Elizabeth rose early and then made sure
that Annabelle was out of bed before she returned to her own
room and dressed. It was a journey of a couple of hours to
Long Meg's Circle and it was best to set out in good time
if one wished to get there and back before afternoon tea. And
yet, once she was dressed, Elizabeth found herself lost in
thought for some time before she went down to breakfast.
She was remembering her meeting with Giles Pickworth the
day before and the step she had agreed to take.

"I didn't mean to distress you yesterday," he had said,
standing in the garden with her. "But I still mean to run away
with Leala. I came to ask, one more time, if you will help
us. I realized, when I had your note inviting me on your
expedition, that if I brought Leala with us when we go to
Long Meg's Circle tomorrow, she and I could leave from
there."

"Oh, Giles, why?" Elizabeth had asked again. "Surely
you must know how bad it will look? To fly to the border
must be held the outside of enough!"

"I don't mean to go to Scotland," he had answered with
dignity. "I mean to take Leala to London."

"But how does that help you?" Elizabeth said, troubled.
"Why do you wish to go north if you mean to take her
south?"

Pickworth scuffed the path with the tip of his boot. "If
my parents believe me merely to be on an expedition with
you, and headed north, they will not miss me until the end

of the day, and by then Leala and I shall be well on our way. And if they do try to follow, they'll start out in the wrong direction, for they will believe we've gone to Scotland.''

''And I shall be left to explain how we, you, deceived them?'' Elizabeth asked dryly. Reluctantly Pickworth nodded. ''Oh, Giles!'' she said in exasperation. ''How can you think such a plan would work? You could not be more than halfway to London before your father caught up with you! You would only have succeeded in landing all of us in the briars.''

''Perhaps,'' Pickworth agreed grudgingly, ''but I cannot bear to have things go on as they are.'' Turning to face Elizabeth, he went on urgently, ''You must know what I mean! You have said yourself that you wish to travel, to see other places. Come with us. We shall all escape and then you need not face my father.''

''No, but you would face mine. And the cleric, for my father would eventually track us down and insist that you had compromised my reputation and ought to marry me to set matters right,'' Elizabeth pointed out impatiently.

''No, he couldn't,'' Giles replied defiantly, ''for I would already be married to Leala!''

Elizabeth turned and paced. ''Giles,'' she said at last, ''I do understand how you feel about Leala, but surely this is not the answer. I have told you so before.''

''Have I a choice?'' he demanded defiantly. ''My family will not countenance the match. And to be married under Mrs. Comfrey's auspices, even if she would agree, would only have everyone saying she ensnared me for her daughter, which is not true. And ten to one my father would try to have the marriage set aside,'' he said heatedly.

''But such a thing as this will ruin the pair of you! I said so yesterday and I have not changed my mind,'' Elizabeth replied stubbornly.

''If we do not, Leala is ruined anyway,'' Pickworth said bluntly.

Elizabeth stared at him, eyes wide with dismay. ''Oh, Giles!''

''No, no, not that way!'' Pickworth exclaimed hastily

before she could say more. Now he began to pace about distractedly. Finally he seemed to make up his mind. He turned to her and said, "You must know about the fellow who's been dangling after Leala's mother?"

"Yes, of course, everyone does," Elizabeth said doubtfully. "He's some sort of merchant, I collect. And Papa said he was a rum touch, not the sort of person he would want to see either of his daughters encourage even if he were well-born."

"Well, Leala's mother means to marry him," Giles said grimly. "As for being a rum touch, your father doesn't know the half of it!" He paused, paced a bit, then said, "It is not my secret and perhaps I should not be telling you, but the fellow has been behaving in the most damnable way to Leala. He—" Pickworth broke off, then forced himself to continue. "To put no finer point upon the matter, he has made it clear he desires Leala as much as he does her mother."

"Surely not," Elizabeth protested, horrified. "Surely if Leala told her mother, then Mrs. Comfrey would refuse to marry the man?"

Pickworth's voice was bitter as he replied, "Leala's mother has come full under the fellow's thumb. She will protest and protect nothing. Either I remove Leala from under her roof or he will—" This time Giles could not bring himself to finish the sentence.

"What of her relatives?" Elizabeth asked. "Will none of them help her?"

"Leala said that her father's family cast him off when the scandal broke and that her mother's family did so as soon as she began encouraging the fellow from Kendal. Mrs. Comfrey has applied to them more than once and they have all said that they will have nothing to do with her or Leala," Giles explained quietly.

Elizabeth did not at once answer. Finally she said, "I agree you must not abandon Leala, but what if you tell your parents? Perhaps they would understand, and if you married her beneath their roof and with their blessing, her position would be far easier."

Giles shook his head. "No!" he said decisively. "My

parents have made their position clear more than once. My father would say it was only one more reason I must pull myself free of the entanglement and he would undertake to find her a position in some household. As frightened as she is, she would have little choice but to agree. I'll not have her faced with that.''

Elizabeth bit her lower lip. She had known that Leala's position was a difficult one ever since the scandal surrounding her father's behavior had broken, only to be followed, shortly, by his death and then her mother's encouragement of such an ineligible suitor. That Leala's position was now suddenly unbearable was evident, nor did Elizabeth discount the truth of what Giles had said about his parents. However sympathetic the Pickworths might feel toward Leala's predicament, they would welcome the match even less, knowing this latest scandal was brewing. Had her father not died under such shocking circumstances and her mother turned out to be so precipitate, no one would have doubted that Leala was a suitable bride for Giles. She was a pretty young woman with a kind heart and a natural grace and dignity. If she was not as quick-witted as Elizabeth, that was nothing to say against the matter. Giles had failed his exams far too often for Elizabeth to think he wanted a bluestocking for a wife. It seemed bitterly unfair to Elizabeth that the folly of Leala's father must keep the two lovers apart. She had to own, moreover, that what she had first thought would be a short-lived romance had spawned changes in Giles that she would not have expected. The determination he now showed to shoulder the responsibility of caring for Leala was not something anyone who knew him well would have expected of the boy.

"I'll stand your friend," Elizabeth told Giles quietly. "Indeed, I'll come with you. I know Leala well enough to know how such a step will distress her. And with me along, at least you will have given the nod to propriety and it will not look so bad."

"It cannot help but look bad," Giles retorted bluntly. "And if I could see any other way out, I should take it. But I cannot and will not leave Leala in Mrs. Comfrey's house any longer. Already the man grows too particular in his attentions to Leala, and her mother will only scold and tell her to be nice to her papa-to-be!''

"Well, that is a great deal too bad of Mrs. Comfrey," Elizabeth said hotly. Then, more temperately, she said, "Must you run off to London with Leala? Is there not somewhere else you could take her? Somewhere both safe and respectable? Some relative, perhaps, who might look after the pair of you, so that later you may say you were married with at least some semblance of propriety?"

Pickworth pondered the matter. "Perhaps my aunt and uncle in Inglewhite might help me. Lord, Elizabeth, I shall have to think about this and talk with Leala. But it will lift her spirits greatly to know you mean to help us."

"Well, you have not much time to decide," she answered, troubled.

"I know it," he said quietly. "I must assume we shall leave from Long Meg's Circle. And you as well, if you can find a way to detach yourself from Mr. Wythe's side, for I collect he means to come on the expedition?"

"Leave that to me," Elizabeth said, resolutely suppressing the pang of regret she felt. "I shall contrive to quarrel with him and ask you to take me up in your carriage." She paused and thought for a moment before she went on, "I shall have to come in the clothes I stand in. I see no way to contrive to bring so much as a bandbox with me."

Pickworth gripped her hand and said, "I shall undertake to buy you whatever you need. And to have you home again as soon as possible, if you wish it. If my aunt and uncle will help me, you need be gone only one night."

Elizabeth shook her head. "Don't worry about me," she said. "I do not fail easily. But will Leala be allowed to accompany you tomorrow to Long Meg's Circle? And won't her mother guess something is amiss when you do not return?"

There was a hint of bitterness in Pickworth's voice as he replied, "By hedge or stile, I'll contrive to bring Leala with me. And I do not think Mrs. Comfrey will follow us. The fellow from Kendal might be tempted, but even he cannot have the effrontery to think he has a right to interfere." He paused, then added earnestly, "We have no right to ask your help, but we'll be devilish glad to have it, Elizabeth."

He kissed her on the cheek and then bounded down the path back toward the house, leaving Elizabeth to watch him go, as troubled as ever. How could her family or his ever think they were well-matched? she wondered helplessly. To be sure, she could not help but admire his determination to protect and take care of Leala, but this current start appalled her. When, if, she ever wedded, Elizabeth wanted to marry someone whose head was as level as hers, whose intelligence was as great as hers, and whose understanding was superior and leavened with a sense of humor. That it had begun to seem as if she would never meet such a person had dismayed Elizabeth as much as her intransigence upset her parents. And now that she had finally met such a person, she must leave on this absurd journey with Giles and Leala. But they had stood her friend when she needed them most, and she could not, would not, fail them now. Time enough, later, to sort matters out with Mr. Wythe.

Abruptly Elizabeth shook her head. Useless to go over and over again in her mind the step she meant to take. The decision was made, and having been made, would be kept. With a gurgle of laughter Elizabeth reminded herself that none of her heroines would be so fainthearted as to protest such a simple step as this, not when one considered the terrors they had faced. What would her heroines have done? Camelia Fanesworth, perhaps? Elizabeth wondered. Camelia would have accepted the inevitable, she decided, and gone down to breakfast instead of wasting a perfectly good morning. Still smiling to herself, Elizabeth headed downstairs to the breakfast room, for she was not, she decided, going to be outdone by one of her own creations.

Belowstairs, the cook hummed happily to herself as she made up a large hamper with food for six. It was time and past that Miss Elizabeth had a treat such as this picnic. It was precisely the sort of pointless adventure the girl would have delighted in before her mother died, and precisely the sort of thing she had avoided since, becoming, in the cook's view, far too serious. Not that one could wonder at such a thing. First to lose one's mother and then to have a One Such As That put in her place!

The cook and the present Lady Mayfield were not on good terms. Her first week in the house, Lady Mayfield had managed to put up the good woman's back by informing her that if she did not know how to make scones properly, Lady Mayfield would undertake to teach her.

Now, it was not as if the cook were saying the scones were her best. Indeed, an unfortunate series of kitchen crises had distracted her attention at the most unfortunate of moments. But they were not that horrid. And there had been no need for her ladyship to make her pronouncement in front of the entire staff. She might just as well have called Cook in to see her in private and expressed her just concerns. But things were as they were, and a quiet war had been fought between the pair ever since, with Cook saying that were it not for her loyalty to the family, she would have been long gone. Particularly her loyalty to that poor motherless child, Miss Elizabeth, who was so shamefully mistreated in this house.

And that was why Cook put in her very best treats for the picnic party. If her ladyship should happen to demand to know what had happened to that jar of special preserves sent up from London, why, the cook would be quite happy to tell her.

Fortunately Elizabeth knew none of this, for although it would not have surprised her, it would have dismayed her quite a bit. As it was, she was able to retrieve the hamper from the cook, though to be sure, a footman carried it to the front door, with very pretty thanks, and be ready to leave the moment Mr. Holden and Mr. Wythe arrived in two separate conveyances.

It was immediately evident to Elizabeth's shrewd eyes that somehow the two had managed to acquire vehicles and horses vastly superior to those they had been tooling about in the past week or more. It seemed to Elizabeth that her heart skipped a beat as Mr. Wythe jumped lightly down and came toward her, a smile on his face that played havoc with her composure. He was dressed neatly in a coat of brown Bath cloth and his pantaloons were of a light shade of biscuit. But it was the way the coat sat upon his shoulders and the pantaloons clung to the muscular shape of his thighs that set her pulse racing. He paused before her and bowed, sweeping the hat from his head as he did so. "Good morning, Miss Mayfield."

Vaguely, out of the corner of her eye, Elizabeth could see Mr. Holden greeting Annabelle in a similar manner. "Good morning, Mr. Wythe," she managed to say, coloring prettily. "The hamper is on the top step," she added hastily, to cover her confusion.

Basingstoke thought, as he looked down at her, that he had never seen Miss Mayfield in finer looks. The jaconet muslin dress she wore was of a prettier shade of blue than she usually wore, and her straw bonnet was tied at a jaunty angle at the side of her face by a ribbon of satin that matched the color of her dress. His own pulse was not entirely steady as she looked up at him with a light in her eyes that matched the one in his heart. But the awareness of all the eyes on them made him speak carelessly as he replied over his shoulder, "Holden, the picnic basket is on the top step."

A gurgle of laughter bubbled up out of Miss Mayfield's throat as she said, "Ought you not to get it yourself, Mr. Wythe?"

Basingstoke looked down at her, a lazy smile in his eyes as he replied, "On the contrary, it will do him good to exert himself."

A few moments later he was handing her into his carriage and Trahern was handing Miss Annabelle into the other. "Does Mr. Pickworth join us?" Basingstoke asked easily as he turned the horses down the lane.

"Upon the road, just north of here," Elizabeth agreed. "He is not always punctual, but he has promised to be waiting for us these ten minutes past."

Indeed, Pickworth was waiting in his carriage, newly purchased for him by his father just this past spring. Beside him sat Leala Comfrey. At the sight of her Annabelle gasped, but Elizabeth leaned forward and greeted her warmly. "Leala, how are you? Mr. Wythe, this is Miss Comfrey, who has been my dearest friend for many years. Leala, this is Mr. Wythe."

Shyly Leala greeted him, shrinking a little from the cool eyes that swept over her faded dress and then dismissed her as someone of no consequence. Basingstoke's voice was friendly, however, as he said, "I trust you know the way, Pickworth? Holden and I have equipped ourselves with directions, but somehow I should prefer not to have to rely upon them."

Pickworth shrugged easily as he replied, "Oh, I have been there two or three times so I daresay I shall have no trouble recalling the way."

"Lead on, then," Basingstoke said lightly.

Carefully Pickworth avoided Elizabeth's gaze, and her own shifted swiftly to another direction as well. As the two carriages drew apart, Mr. Wythe addressed a polite question in her direction. "The hamper?" Elizabeth echoed blankly. "Oh. Yes, well, I'm not certain what Cook has put in the hamper, only that it is sure to be something in the nature of a feast. You are a prime favorite with her, you know."

"I am?" Basingstoke said, startled. "But I've never met your cook."

"That has nothing to say to the matter," Elizabeth replied primly, avoiding his eyes. "You are a favorite simply because you make me laugh."

Basingstoke looked at Miss Mayfield incredulously. "Now you are bamming me," he said severely a moment later, just before he had to turn his attention back to the road.

"Upon my honor I am not," Elizabeth assured him earnestly, though it was to be seen that a dimple emerged in her cheek and her lips quivered slightly in spite of her best efforts to control them. "I have it upon excellent authority—my former nurse's, you know—that ever since Cook heard me laughing with you she has decided you are just the person to rescue me from the melancholy I was headed for."

"And were you headed for melancholy?" Basingstoke asked, hazarding a glance at her.

"I hope I am not such a poor creature as that," Elizabeth replied stoutly. "It is simply that I have not had a great deal to laugh about since my mother died."

"No," Basingstoke agreed thoughtfully, "it cannot have been a laughing matter to discover yourself saddled with a stepmother not far older than yourself and one, moreover, whose temper is not very compatible with yours."

Elizabeth blinked in surprise. "I have said nothing to make you feel I am unhappy with Lady Mayfield, have I?" she asked with some concern.

"You need not," Basingstoke replied bluntly. "It is evident in the way in which the pair of you look at one another. And in the way you are both always so carefully civil, with none of the easy bantering that marks the speech your stepmother and your sister share."

"You are far too perceptive, Mr. Wythe," Elizabeth said severely. "And I pray you will not tell anyone else of this."

Basingstoke looked down at her and his eyes softened at the distress evident upon her face. "Miss Mayfield, I should do nothing to upset you," he said gently. "Indeed, if I could, I should like to lift some of the burden from your shoulders."

Miss Mayfield blinked, staring straight ahead and trying very hard not to let the tears that sprang to her eyes have their way. She replied with some asperity to Mr. Wythe by saying, "I am not such a fool as to think my situation a tragedy, sir. I am well aware that many would consider me most fortunate, and so I see it as well. If . . . if upon occasion my stepmother and I disagree, well, so it is in many households. I do not see that I have any great burdens that need lifting, Mr. Wythe."

"Save that you do not laugh so often as your cook thinks you ought," Basingstoke pointed out in an innocent voice.

Elizabeth looked at him sharply. And then, in spite of herself, she did laugh. "You are impossible!" she said.

"Yes, Miss Mayfield," he replied meekly.

"Now, why," Elizabeth asked thoughtfully, "do I find

myself thinking that meekness is not something with which you are familiar?"

Basingstoke glanced at her, a twinkle in his eyes. "What am I familiar with, then?" he demanded playfully.

"Oh, authority, I should think," Elizabeth replied carelessly. But then her eyes narrowed as she went on, "You have the air of one accustomed to issuing orders and having them obeyed. Far from having to consider the wishes of others, I should say you are accustomed to having others consider your wishes. I must say that for someone with no fortune or title, you certainly behave as though you possessed both," she concluded a trifle waspishly.

Startled, Basingstoke did not at once reply. He was too taken aback at having his character so neatly read, nor did he, he discovered, particularly like the portrait she had drawn of him. "You do not make me seem a very admirable fellow," he said at last.

It was, Elizabeth reflected crossly, grossly unfair of Mr. Wythe to look at her like that, for it made her want to stroke away the frown and assure him that she did not in the least mean what she had said. It was all the fault of her wretched tongue! But to apologize would not do, particularly as Elizabeth could not have said, in good conscience, anything of the sort. Instead she said softly, "I think you most probably spoiled, sir." As he looked at her, startled and not in the least pleased, she went on, a smile twitching up the corners of her mouth, "For all that, however, I think you have a kind heart, a good intelligence when you choose to use it, and . . ." she paused, casting about for what to say, then added as inspiration struck, "you've a good hand on the reins."

For a moment matters hung in the balance; then Basingstoke threw back his head and laughed. Turning a mock-severe look upon Elizabeth, he said, "Let me tell you, Miss Mayfield, that I am overwhelmed by your kind words!" He paused, then added with a smile, "And you may tell your cook that if I have made you laugh, so too have you taught me to laugh again."

Elizabeth regarded him quizzically but forbore to ask the questions that tumbled through her head. Instead she found herself wondering how she would describe him were he in one of her stories. Not as a mere ordinary fellow, that was for certain. He would be a nobleman, arrogant and spoiled. Briefly she also found herself wondering how he had come by his manner if he were not one. Perhaps he had been considered the heir to some estate and title and then been displaced by the unexpected birth of a son to the current possessor of the property. She said none of this aloud, of course. Instead she turned the talk to London and asked Mr. Wythe to tell her about his life there. It was a subject he had heretofore neatly avoided and she found herself amused, now, by the evident effort he put forth to tell her only what he thought she ought to know without her realizing he was doing so. In that way the time was quickly passed until they reached the inn where Pickworth had advised the party they should stop for a short rest before going on.

11

ALL THREE COUPLES descended from their carriages with patent relief, and Trahern went inside with Annabelle to bespeak refreshments for their party. Leala shyly tried to talk with Basingstoke. "Has Elizabeth told you any of our local legends, Mr. Wythe?" she asked. "We are known for our tales of pixies and elves and fairies. We shall even pass a fairy ring on our way, Mr. Pickworth tells me."

Basingstoke looked at Elizabeth with raised eyebrows. "Miss Mayfield, you have neglected my education shamefully," he told her, a gleam of laughter in his eyes.

"Perhaps I thought you too sensible to listen to such nonsense," she retorted, avoiding his eyes as she smoothed down her skirt, "or so you said."

"I said, I think, that I thought the notion that anyone might take such things seriously was nonsense," Basingstoke countered thoughtfully. "I do not recall saying that the notion of having you tell me such tales was nonsense."

"Very prettily said," Elizabeth told him tartly. "One might actually suppose you had not been rude two days ago when I tried to do so."

Basingstoke had the grace to wince. "Shall I promise not to be rude today?" he asked meekly.

"I shouldn't think you could keep that promise," Elizabeth told him frankly.

"Now you see why our Elizabeth still stands a spinster," Pickworth told Basingstoke with a crow of laughter. "She is far too honest."

"So she is," Basingstoke agreed levelly, with only the tight look to the corner of his mouth to indicate his true feelings.

"But do you know, I think I prefer it to the insipid amiability of most of the usual crop of aspiring damsels who grace London ballrooms every Season."

"If you are indeed without a feather to fly with, as Mr. Holden has said, I wonder that any matchmaking mother would allow her daughter to look twice at you," Elizabeth said demurely.

"I am amazed then that you care to allow my company," Basingstoke told her, a gleam in his eye. "But at least you have now explained the reason you treat me with such comfortable contempt."

"Oh, no, Elizabeth treats everyone that way," Pickworth broke in cheerfully.

Elizabeth shot a darkling look at her old friend and playmate, then told Basingstoke primly, "I have no matchmaking mama to warn me away from you."

Again Pickworth broke in to say, "Aye, that's true enough. She has a matchmaking stepmama. And Lady Mayfield is so eager to see Elizabeth wedded, she would not care about such a trivial matter as to whether the suitor had a fortune or whether his pockets were all to let."

Basingstoke glanced shrewdly at Elizabeth as he said in a different voice altogether, "You, I suppose, do care about such things? After all, you are such a sensible young woman."

Elizabeth did not answer for a moment and Pickworth surprisingly held his tongue. Leala was silent and moved away, as though to look at the small garden near the wall. Elizabeth's eyes followed her, and when at last she replied, her voice was thoughtful as she said, "I should think the world well lost for love, Mr. Wythe. And no, I am not so foolish as to think it would be romantic to live in a hovel or to be forced to wonder whether there would be food on the table tomorrow. I have seen, in the experience of one of my dearest friends, the difficulties that can encompass one when one has lost one's fortune. Nor would I wish to wed someone addicted to cruelty or drink, however much my heart reached out to him. But I cannot think it better to marry for a title or fortune someone whom one dislikes or even merely respects. Had I thought that,'' Elizabeth said with a wry smile, ''I should have been married a long time since. Far better to have a companion at one's side who can share one's sentiments, life's joys, and life's sorrows, where there is a mutual affection, even though the world may disapprove.''

There Elizabeth stopped, her face flushed with the sense of having made a fool of herself. But Pickworth's voice came low and full of approval as he said, ''Bravo, Elizabeth!''

Basingstoke's reply came a moment later. It was not, for once, sardonic or taunting. Indeed, how could he contradict her? Not when he meant to ask her to marry someone whom she must suppose to be all but penniless. Her words had touched a chord, moreover, within himself, and Basingstoke was left with the unaccustomed sensation of being unable to feel superior to anyone. Still, his tone was light as he replied, ''I should think a great many people would disagree with you, but I shan't. Indeed, I like you better for not being a young woman on the lookout for a rich husband.''

''Yes, you would, wouldn't you?'' Giles Pickworth said pointedly.

Basingstoke flushed. He looked up at Pickworth, a glint in his eye that those acquainted with him would have recognized as distinctly dangerous. ''I don't recall addressing my remark to you,'' he said icily.

His voice had risen, and now Leala moved back toward the three as if intending to ward off danger. Pickworth was undaunted, however. He replied through clenched teeth, ''Someone must look after Elizabeth's interests, since Lady Mayfield and Sir Edmund obviously do not.''

What Basingstoke would have replied is unknown, for Elizabeth placed a hand on his arm, and when he looked at her he found her wide eyes pleading with him. Her voice, however, was surprisingly calm as she said coolly, ''Odd, I had not thought myself so young or so green a girl as to need someone looking after my affairs, Giles.''

''You're green enough when it comes to a man like

Wythe," Pickworth told her roundly. "Have you never asked yourself why he is here in Ravenstonedale dangling after you?"

"I should assume," Elizabeth replied with quiet amusement, "that he is here upon a repairing lease."

"Aye, and the fortune you are due to inherit from your aunt has nothing to say to the matter, I suppose?" Pickworth went on heatedly.

"Perhaps it does," Elizabeth said calmly, "but I did not think to be so rude as to ask him directly."

"Why not?" Basingstoke demanded, an unholy gleam in his eye. "You have not hesitated to be frank with me before."

"Are we to have the gloves off, then?" Elizabeth asked tranquilly. "Very well, though I would not have thought you would wish us to bramble in front of Giles."

"Oh, I shall happily retreat, so long as I know you are going to demand of the fellow proper answers," Pickworth said at once. "Come, Leala, let us see if those refreshments are soon to be served."

When they had disappeared inside, Elizabeth turned to look at Mr. Wythe, who had turned his attention pointedly to the horses, standing restlessly as a groom gave them water. A frown creased his brow and Elizabeth waited patiently for him to look at her again. She was well aware that between them, she and Giles had placed Mr. Wythe in an untenable position. Was the charge concerning her supposed inheritance from Aunt Elizabeth true? It would account for his odd behavior since arriving in Ravenstonedale. He had most certainly been more interested in Annabelle that first day, but no doubt Mr. Holden had told him what Annabelle had said about her inheritance. Then, having decided to marry an heiress, Mr. Wythe had been single-minded in his pursuit of her ever since. Elizabeth wished it were not so painful to face the possibility it was true. She had meant what she said about the world well lost for love, but not when that love was unreturned. Oh, Mr. Wythe was an excellent actor, and one might be pardoned for almost believing that he had fallen for her charms. But the important word was "almost."

Elizabeth could not, whatever her treacherous heart might say, give herself to one who was such an unscrupulous creature as he might prove to be.

For his part, Basingstoke's brow was creased with a sense of dismay. Impossible to tell Miss Mayfield the truth, especially since he had so stubbornly decided that if she were to agree to marry him, she must do so thinking him all but a pauper. Time enough to tell her father the truth when he formally asked permission to wed her. But first he would know she meant to accept him. And yet, what was he to say if she did ask him the truth of his circumstances? Was he to lie or was he to tell her that he had come to Ravenstonedale upon a wager? And the nature of the wager? It was the devil of a coil, and Basingstoke could not see a way out.

They were both relieved when Trahern appeared to impatiently summon them inside for something to drink.

It was almost noon when the party of six reached Long Meg's Circle, and Elizabeth had still not pressed Mr. Wythe for an accounting. There had been something too forbidding in the set of his lips and the challenge in his eyes when he at last had looked at her again. That alone might not have stopped Elizabeth, for she was no coward, but behind the arrogance she had glimpsed a trace of fear, and suddenly Elizabeth had seen the small boy behind the man, the small boy who was forever being scolded for things he could not help. She knew she was supposed to force a quarrel on him, but not yet, not in this way, she told herself. Surely there would be time at Long Meg's Circle.

So she had pushed away the questions Giles had raised and told Mr. Wythe, instead, all of the local legends she could remember concerning pixies and fairies. He had listened gravely, as though aware of what she had seen on his face and grateful for her restraint, though that was no doubt, she thought wistfully, only her fanciful imagination. Now, as he handed her out of the carriage, she looked up at him mischievously and said, "Well, Mr. Wythe, do you mean to try your hand at counting Long Meg and her daughters? Though what you would do with dozens and dozens of village maidens appearing before your eyes, I can't imagine. I think it would be most uncomfortable, particularly if they should chance to be hungry and expect you to feed them, as I should imagine they would be after having been turned to stone for hundreds and hundreds of years!''

Basingstoke looked down at Elizabeth, his fear gone and a lively sense of humor lighting his own eyes as he replied in kind, ''I shouldn't dream of risking it, Miss Mayfield. Let your sister and Mr. Holden or even Mr. Pickworth and Miss Comfrey attempt to count them correctly, if they dare. I should much prefer to walk about and admire them, one by one, with you to tell me if there is anything particular I ought to know about any of them.''

Elizabeth felt an unaccountable wave of shyness steal over her. Absurd to be so shaken now, when she ought to be preparing to quarrel with the man, she told herself sternly. Absurd at any time, a part of her whispered in return. But it was no use. When they walked about the circle and Mr. Wythe gathered a posy of wildflowers, only to present them to her with a flourish and a bow, Elizabeth found she preferred it to anything she had elsewhere received. When Mr. Wythe bent close to whisper some complimentary nonsense in her ear, she found herself pleasantly aflutter and hard put to recall her own self-warnings. He was kind, he was gentle, he even looked at her with a warmth in his eyes that Elizabeth found difficult to deny.

Giles and Leala watched from where they, too, strolled, wondering if they were doing Elizabeth Mayfield a service or the worst possible disservice. Pickworth did not trust Mr. Wythe, but if he were mistaken and the man meant honorably by Elizabeth and truly cared for her and she for him, then it was no service to take her away from here just when the man might come up to scratch. And yet there was Leala, and he could not desert her. It was the devil of a coil, but one that would, that must, come about.

Annabelle and Mr. Holden did decide to count the stones and to be particularly careful not to miss any. This process was deliciously difficult and called for wandering all about the field, arguing gracefully with one another as to whether they had counted any twice. And since, inevitably, they decided they had, it was necessary to begin all over again.

In short, it was evident to anyone with the least trace of the romantic in his character, why Long Meg's Circle was such a popular destination for courting couples for a full forty miles around.

"Miss Mayfield," Basingstoke began haltingly when their conversation had faltered.

"Yes?" She smiled up at him, forgetting in that moment to guard her heart.

"Miss Mayfield, will you marry me?" Basingstoke blurted out the words. Then, cursing himself for a clumsiness none of his acquaintances would have recognized, he pressed on, taking her hand in his, "I know we have not known each other long, but it is long enough that I know my own heart and have reason, I think, to believe you know yours."

Elizabeth looked at him in dismay. Of all the things she had imagined might happen today, a proposal of marriage from Mr. Wythe was not one of them. But he was looking at her, waiting for an answer. What was she to say? If only she did know her own heart! "Have you spoken with my father yet, Mr. Wythe?" she asked a trifle breathlessly.

Basingstoke hesitated. It was, he knew, the weak point of his plan. "Not yet. I thought to wait until I had some notion of how you felt."

It was as though a cloud suddenly passed in front of the sun and a chill stole over Elizabeth's heart. Slowly she pulled her hand free and turned a little away. Again all the doubts crowded in, relentlessly repeating themselves. She could not forget his manner the day they had met, nor her certainty that he meant to pursue her sister. Then, of a sudden, he had turned to her, pursuing her with a dedication that argued a warmth, a depth of feeling she must have sworn was not there, not at first. Too clearly the words echoed in her mind of how his pockets were to let and Annabelle innocently proclaiming that she was an heiress. She did not wish to believe he cared only for her supposed fortune, but if there were not something havey-cavey about the business, why had he not spoken with her father first? She thought she read a warmth in his eyes, and yet what if that, too, were feigned? Elizabeth had long since lost her heart to Mr. Wythe, but she could not, would not, lose her head as well.

Elizabeth took a deep breath and turned back to Mr. Wythe. "Will you speak with my father first? Before I give you my answer?" she asked.

"I should rather have your answer first," he answered gently.

A hand seemed to tighten about Elizabeth's heart. With a mock curtsy she said, "Then I am very honored, Mr. Wythe, but I cannot accept your kind offer."

"Kind offer!" he repeated explosively. "I am offering you marriage, not a sugared plum or a trip to the theater!" He paused and in that moment his temper got the better of him. His eyes glittered and his voice was dangerously cold as he said, "You are afraid I have not sufficient fortune, perhaps? Or you regret that I lack even the title of 'sir'? Perhaps you are hoping that if I speak to your father I will disclose that I am not as poor to pass as you fear?"

"It is not a question of title or fortune," Elizabeth replied from between clenched teeth. "It is a question of honesty and forthrightness."

The blow struck home, and Basingstoke winced. Then he recovered himself and tried again. "Can you not simply trust me?" he asked coaxingly.

Elizabeth longed to do so. Indeed, she could not help but recall that she was about to deceive him as well as her family. Who was she to demand more honesty than she could give in return? But she did. And while there was that in her heart which bade her to throw caution to the winds and give her hand to this man whom she already loved, she could not do so. Not with so many questions unanswered. Far worse to agree to marry Mr. Wythe and then learn that he cared nothing for her, that her suspicions were right and he was in some way using her, than to remain a spinster all her life. Even as she felt her heart tearing, Elizabeth knew this was the quarrel she had been seeking. She backed away and said coldly, "I am very sorry, Mr. Wythe, but I cannot."

Then she turned, and with a quaking heart, walked slowly,

deliberately to where Leala and Giles stood waiting for her. Basingstoke joined Trahern, and a moment later those three came over to the carriages, and with unspoken consent, all six pretended that nothing of interest had occurred and that eating the luncheon the cook had prepared was the only thing on their minds.

In spite of all the pretense, however, it was evident to everyone that a damper had been cast on the outing, and as soon as the luncheon had been finished, it was agreed that they should return to Ravenstonedale.

"I think I should like to ride with Giles and Leala," Elizabeth said, her voice not altogether steady.

"Of course," Basingstoke agreed with a bow.

He wouldn't have agreed, of course, had it not been for his injured pride, but agree he did. It was a decision he would shortly bitterly regret, but at the moment it seemed quite the best thing.

Indeed, so hurt was Basingstoke's pride that he did not wait for Pickworth's carriage to take the lead. He prided himself on his eye for landmarks and his sense of direction and so he set off determined to show everyone he was not dependent on that . . . that puppy to find his way home. Trahern, all too well accustomed to the look on his friend's face, hastened to hand Annabelle into their carriage and follow as swiftly as he was able.

Pickworth watched with a grim smile as he handed Leala and Elizabeth into his carriage. He had meant to find an excuse to fall behind, but now he needed none.

"Will they notice, do you think?" Leala asked anxiously.

Elizabeth took her friend's hand in hers. "I think they will notice nothing for some time. If we lag behind, they will only think it because we are three in the carriage and the horses cannot travel so fast as theirs. Even when they know we are late, they will only think one of our horses has thrown a shoe or the carriage has lost a wheel or something. By the time anyone is truly anxious, it will be too late to set out to find us. They will be sure we have taken shelter some-where for the night, and since there are two of us with Giles, they will not worry about the scandal. And even should they guess that you and Giles are running away together, they will assume we have gone north to the border and never dream we are headed south to Inglewhite.''

''But with luck, Elizabeth will be home before anyone realizes something is truly wrong,'' Giles said with satisfaction, ''and she can answer all their questions.''

''How grateful I am to you for that,'' Elizabeth retorted dryly.

''Then stay with us,'' Leala urged. ''Surely Giles's aunt and uncle won't mind. Not if they don't mind him appearing with me, that is,'' she added doubtfully.

''They won't,'' Giles told her stoutly, ''not once they have seen you. And even if they did, I have told you I will simply take you on to London and marry you there. And Elizabeth is welcome to join us, as I have told her before.''

Elizabeth did not answer. She had agreed to come today, and laid her plans well, but not by any means did she intend to be swayed from her determined notion to return to Ravenstonedale as soon as she had seen the pair safely placed in his aunt and uncle's care. It was no part of her plan to cause a scandal for her father, and with luck there would be none. She was not so sanguine as to believe that Captain Pickworth and his wife would greet the sudden appearance of Giles and Leala and herself with joy. She was also certain, however, that faced with the knowledge that if they did not countenance the match, Giles and Leala would do something far more imprudent, the captain and his wife would agree to help. And then she could safely be on her way home.

12

BASINGSTOKE stood in Sir Edmund's library at Mayfield Manor. He was neatly attired but with a trifle less care than usual, for he had dressed with some haste when Sir Edmund's note had been brought round to him. Until this morning, he had not known that Elizabeth had not returned to her home the night before. Now, his face set in grim lines, he spoke with Sir Edmund, voicing hesitantly the thoughts that had occurred to him.

"An elopement? Surely you must be mistaken. What reason would Elizabeth have for eloping with Giles Pickworth? She must have known we would have approved the match," Sir Edmund replied incredulously. "Nonsense! What can make you think such a thing? Did she tell you something you have not told me?"

Basingstoke hesitated. "No. She said nothing certain," he admitted. "It is just that three days ago we were talking, jesting really, about the subject, and your daughter said some things that made me think she had given the subject a great deal of thought. I said as much, and her manner led me to believe she had indeed been thinking about running off with someone."

Sir Edmund grunted. "Well, I still cannot think it likely. None of her things are missing, and she left no note. No, I think it far more probable that their carriage overturned somewhere on the road between Long Meg's Circle and here."

"If you think that," Basingstoke countered reasonably, "then why did you send for me?"

Sir Edmund looked down at the papers on his desk for a

moment before he answered. "To discover why my daughter refused to return in your carriage," he said at last. "Annabelle will say only that you and Elizabeth quarreled. May I ask why? And whether she said anything to you that might indicate another reason she would not have returned?"

"I am afraid it was my fault," Basingstoke said unhappily. He turned and strode to the window. Over his shoulder he tried to explain. "I pressed her to marry me. Upset her greatly."

"Without my permission?" Sir Edmund demanded angrily. "How dared you do so?"

There was a tight, angry smile on the earl's face as he replied, "You would have asked me questions, sir, that I could not have answered. And I was vain enough to hope your daughter would have me in spite of that. I realize that I contradict myself by saying that your daughter may have been planning her escape three days ago, while I only proposed to her yesterday." He paused, then went on, "But I think it possible that what only was a thought before then became reality at Long Meg's Circle and she—they—acted on impulse. An impulse they must regret."

"I need hardly say, Mr. Wythe," Sir Edmund said grimly, "that you are barred from this house. I only pray you may be mistaken about Elizabeth and Giles Pickworth. If it were a match she wanted, that would have been different. I should have been delighted, as well she knew. But if what you conjecture is true, that she ran away with him to escape your attentions, then that is unconscionable. I shall leave for the north at once. No doubt I shall meet them along the way somewhere and discover that there is a harmless explanation for all this. But if not, well, they have a day's start on me, but perhaps I shall be fortunate and find them before—"

Sir Edmund broke off, his voice full of anger and hurt. Basingstoke whirled around. "Let me go after her, sir," he said. At Mayfield's look of astonished outrage, he went on implacably, "If the trouble is indeed no more than a broken-down carriage, I shall render them what assistance I may and return with them. If not, well, I can ride faster than you could drive, I think, and if you stay, you can cover her absence with some plausible story. If they have eloped and it is seen that you ride north after her, there will be no hope of keeping all this secret or preventing a scandal.''

Mayfield sat down. ''You have a point,'' he agreed unhappily. ''But I cannot like sending you. You are not family. Worse! By your own words, it may be your fault Elizabeth has fled, *if* she has fled. And if she has fled, what makes you think my daughter would consent to return with you? And even if she did, what then? Either she has already married Pickworth or the tale is bound to leak and she is ruined. Don't forget, sir, that she has already spent a night in his company.''

''If your daughter has already married Pickworth, then of course there is nothing to be done,'' Basingstoke said heavily. ''But if she has not, I swear to you that I shall bring her back to you safe and sound. The tale must not be told, that must be your part. In any event, recollect that there was another female of the party. Surely that will stand warrant for her honor?''

Sir Edmund nodded slowly. ''Perhaps. Though if your fears of a flight to the border are correct, I cannot think there are many men who would marry Elizabeth after such an escapade.''

There was no mistaking the torment on Basingstoke's face as he replied, ''I would. But she will not have me.''

For the first time, Mayfield felt a glimmer of sympathy for the man before him. Then he said, more harshly than he meant, ''Well, you'd best be going, hadn't you? And if she were willing to marry you, she might do so and be damned!'' he added as a parting shot.

Captain Pickworth and his wife, Amanda, had a snug house very close to Inglewhite. He was Sir John's younger brother and he had inherited the estate from an uncle who felt that someone ought to provide for him. And since the uncle had also been named Matthew, he had taken it upon himself to do so. He had made his will in the boy's favor and purchased colors for him when he voiced an ambition to enter the military. Captain Pickworth had served with distinction in

India and been retired for medical reasons some ten or twelve years before. He had never ceased to mourn the injury that had forced him to sell out before he had a chance to pit himself against Bonaparte's armies.

Giles had visited the house near Inglewhite often, and now he greeted its appearance with a relief that might have seemed all out of proportion to the event, had the journey thus far not been such a horror. First the carriage had overturned and then the three had been forced to take refuge in a wholly unsuitable inn overnight until the damaged wheel could be fixed. Fortunately, that had occurred south of Ravenstone-dale, so that even if they were pursued, it was unlikely that anyone would get wind of them or their accident. In the past hour it had begun to rain, and all the evils attendant upon traveling in an open carriage had been borne in upon Giles, making him extremely unhappy with himself for not fore-seeing the possibility that such a thing would occur. Now he pulled up in front of the house and made an attempt to brush the worst of the mud off his pants before handing the reins to Elizabeth and descending from the carriage. It was still raining, and Giles mounted the steps two at a time to reach the portico, where he would at least be afforded some shelter. He sounded the knocker on the door, but it seemed a long time before anyone answered, and Elizabeth and Leala both decided to climb down from the carriage as well.

"I hope someone is home," Elizabeth said doubtfully as they reached Pickworth's side. "It will be dark soon."

"Hope someone is home?" Giles repeated impatiently. "Of course someone will be home. My aunt and uncle never go anywhere."

At last the door was opened by a woman who looked at Giles and the two ladies with the liveliest astonishment. "Why, Master Giles! Whatever are you doing here?" she demanded.

"Hello, Mrs. Goods! How are you? You look as wonderful as ever. Are my aunt and uncle in? I've come to visit and brought a couple of friends with me," Giles answered with a friendly grin.

At this a worried frown appeared on Mrs. Goods's face. "Come to stay for a visit?" she asked. "I can't think why the captain didn't tell me. But surely there must be a mistake in the dates, for they've been in London the past three weeks or more. They're simply not here."

Elizabeth, Leala, and Giles stared at the housekeeper in dismay. "N-not here?" he stammered helplessly.

"No, Master Giles, I told you, they've gone to London," the housekeeper repeated patiently. "But you and your friends are welcome to stay the night and decide in the morning what it is you wish to do."

Pickworth scarcely knew what to say, but Elizabeth's hand was on his sleeve before he could speak. "Leala is all done up," she said softly, "and I confess I'm tired as well. I cannot think you want to drive back to the main road in the rain and at this hour, do you?"

"No, of course not," he said at once. Then, to the housekeeper he added, "Thank you, Mrs. Goods. We shall need three bedchambers."

"Two would be sufficient," Elizabeth corrected him quickly. "I am sure I should sleep better with Leala nearby."

"Oh, yes," Leala agreed swiftly.

The housekeeper approved of the arrangement, for it settled some of her fears as to the oddness of Pickworth's extraordinary behavior and sudden appearance on the door-step. She rang for the upstairs maid and gave orders for the rooms to be prepared while a footman took their cloaks. "No doubt your luggage is on the way," she said, not bothering to hide the doubt in her voice.

"If that carriage has not overturned again," Elizabeth said with a sigh. "Everything is in it, as well as Giles' valet and our maids. After the trouble they have had, I shouldn't be surprised if they give us their notices to quit. I vow I have never been on a journey more plagued with troubles."

The housekeeper nodded, and it could be seen that her shoulders relaxed a trifle as she said, "Well, anyone hereabouts can direct them to this house, if they do manage to get here tonight. Now, you'll all be hungry, I'll be bound. I remember Master Giles's appetite, right enough, from all the times he's visited before. Come sit in the parlor and I'll see what Cook can prepare on short notice.''

As soon as she was gone, both Giles and Leala turned to Elizabeth. ''Our baggage carriage has overturned?'' he echoed grimly.

Elizabeth shrugged. ''I had to say something. Surely you could see her doubts? We are disreputable enough as it is, appearing unannounced as we have. You cannot say it is implausible when that is precisely what happened to us.''

''And when no baggage or servants appear?'' Giles persisted.

Elizabeth was thoughtful a moment. ''We shall have to leave for London tomorrow anyway, shan't we?'' she asked. ''We must simply say that we expect to meet it on the road and that if we do not and it appears here, she is to send it back to Ravenstonedale after us.''

Giles gawked at her in disbelief, then laughed. ''Lord, Elizabeth, you never grow up, do you? Why, you've been inventing fantastic tales for us ever since we were children together.''

''Yes, and they've always worked, haven't they?'' she pointed out.

''I think Elizabeth is extremely clever, and I, for one, am grateful for her quick thinking,'' Leala said firmly. ''I quite see why you ought to be a writer, Elizabeth,'' she went on pensively. ''Indeed, it is your destiny.''

''After this, I shan't have a choice,'' Elizabeth said gloomily. ''I shall have to make my fortune with my pen. It is already too late for me to return home without my absence being too well-noted. And I don't mean to desert you. You will still need a chaperone going to London.''

Giles came and took her hands. ''I am sorry, Elizabeth. I never meant this to happen.''

''I know,'' she agreed, but there was a grimness to her mouth that belied the calmness of her words.

''You will go home tomorrow,'' Leala said quietly. ''Giles will see to that. In a post chaise with postilions.'' Two pairs of eyes stared at her, and after a moment she went on, ''I've thought about it, you see. With or without Elizabeth, there will be a great deal of talk about our journey to London, Giles. There is bound to be such gossip. I think it best if we find someone who will marry us by special license. There must be a bishop in Lancaster, if nowhere else. Then Elizabeth can go home. There is no need for her to be tarred by our flight.''

"But, Leala," Elizabeth said, troubled, "surely you cannot wish to be married in such a slapdash way?''

Leala met her friend's eyes squarely. "No," she agreed, "I cannot. But you know the reasons that led to this flight and you well know they were good and sufficient for such a step. Can you say they were not also good and sufficient for us to choose to be married by special license, if need be? And I would rather do that than keep you from your home any longer.''

Elizabeth shook her head. "No. Very well, if that is your wish, so be it.''

Leala held out her hand to Giles, who took it. "It is," she said simply.

And then the housekeeper, Mrs. Goods, was back and there was no more time to talk.

Things might have been very different were it not for the weather. The rain which had begun an hour before Giles and the ladies reached Captain Pickworth's home near Inglewhite continued unabated for almost two days. It was not to be expected that Leala, Giles, or Elizabeth would look with favor upon such a setback. And indeed they did not. At Captain Pickworth's house, some two mornings later, Elizabeth looked at Giles in dismay. Leala looked at Elizabeth. Giles looked out at the rain. "We cannot leave today either," he said quietly. "The carriage will get stuck in the mud.''

It could be seen that Elizabeth was a trifle pale, but her voice was steady as she said, "If there is no help for it, then there is no help for it. I must suppose my family to have long since given up on me.''

"What are you going to do?" Leala asked unhappily.

"By the time there is something I can do," Elizabeth answered dryly, "I hope I shall have an answer for you.''

She paused, then added, ''I begin to wish I had left a note for my family.''

''I did not leave one for my mama either,'' Leala said softly. ''I was afraid that something might go wrong if I did. But I cannot believe she will much care. She has said often that she wishes I were off her hands.''

Both young ladies looked expectantly to Giles, who shrugged impatiently. ''Oh, I left no note. To have done that would have been to defeat the purpose of having our families believe some sort of accident delayed our return. But I own that I thought that by now I should have been able to send them some sort of message to reassure them.'' He smiled ruefully as he added, ''Had I guessed what would happen, I would have contrived to bring a change of clothing for each of us. I cannot like to borrow my uncle's shirts, nor you my aunt's things either.''

''Well, it is fortunate you did not, for if we had brought anything with us, people would have been bound to guess at once that we'd run off,'' Elizabeth replied impatiently.

Realizing that Elizabeth had the headache, Giles and Leala wisely decided to leave her in peace until later.

The Earl of Basingstoke also cursed the rain. He had been riding in it for the better part of two days now and was returning to Ravenstonedale in defeat. In spite of the money he had taken care to spread about lavishly to jog memories all along the road north, he had been able to discover no word about Miss Mayfield, Giles Pickworth, or the young woman with them. Sir Edmund had not been pleased to hear there had been no trace of his daughter and had sent Mr. Wythe packing with a few choice curses.

Worse, when Basingstoke had returned to the Black Swan, Trahern informed him that Pickworth's disappearance with Elizabeth had already become common knowledge, thanks to Lady Mayfield's indiscreet tongue. Basingstoke cursed the woman roundly, much to Trahern's amusement, then said harshly, ''Pack. We leave within the hour.''

''Now?'' Trahern demanded, taken aback. ''But it's

raining. And it will be dark soon. And what about Anna-belle?''

"Somehow I doubt that either of us will be welcome in that house," Basingstoke retorted grimly. "As for the dark and the rain, better that than stay in this town one more night." He paused, then added more kindly, "I am leaving, but there is no need for you to, I suppose. Call on me when you return to London and I shall have a draft for one thousand pounds for you. It seems you've won the bet, after all."

It was this bleak capitulation, perhaps more than anything else, that alarmed Trahern. "Here!" he said too quickly. "You don't think I'd let you return to London alone, do you? How do I know you won't take a powder and I'll be out my thousand pounds?"

Basingstoke was not in the least deceived. "I shall see if we can hire a closed carriage while you write a note for Anna-belle, if you like."

Trahern nodded. But when the earl left the room, it was several moments before he could bring himself to begin to write. What, after all, was there to say? At last he settled upon a short few lines telling her he had been called back to London on urgent business. And that, he reflected, was the truth.

13

ELIZABETH TURNED to Mr. Wythe and looked up at him expectantly. He frowned. "Why the devil are you here?" he demanded impatiently.

Elizabeth blinked in surprise. Speaking slowly, as though to one who lacked some of his wits, she replied, "Why, Mr. Wythe, I live here. Ravenstonedale is my home. One might better ask: Why are *you* here?"

A bleak expression crossed Mr. Wythe's face and when he did not at once reply, Elizabeth placed a hand on his arm as she said gently, "Forgive me, I had not meant to pry."

Immediately his hand closed over hers, warmly, and there was a rough apology in his voice as he said, "It is my place to ask pardon! I meant only that you deserve better than to be here, lost in this wretched village, unappreciated by a step-mother who has no more sense than a goose to keep you here. You ought to be in London, feted, courted, toasted by a host of suitors, dancing until dawn every night!"

To his surprise, Elizabeth laughed and withdrew her hand from beneath his. Tilting back her head to look up at him, she said, her voice brimming with amusement, "Have done, Mr. Wythe. As though I do not know very well that I should be cast in the shade by all the beauties there. I need only look at Annabelle to know how easily that could occur."

Again he frowned. "Annabelle is a diamond of the first water," he agreed, "and I cannot deny that some would say she is the prettier. But you! You are the more taking one."

Elizabeth curtsied. "That is no doubt why you were so pleased to be saddled with my company instead of Anna-belle's the first day we met," she said with heavy irony.

A hit. It was a perceptible hit and Mr. Wythe winced. Then, abruptly, chagrin changed to something else and a gleam of warning lit his eyes. "Oh, no, Miss Mayfield," he said advancing on her, "I have already apologized for being sadly shatterbrained in not recognizing my good fortune that day. This is the last time you will lay that charge at my door, for I have already answered it."

As he advanced, Elizabeth hastily retreated, but now she found herself backed into a corner of the garden. "Mr. Wythe," she said a trifle breathlessly, "I must see to something inside."

But he ignored her protests and ruthlessly swept her up into a harsh embrace. Or rather, it started harsh and softened as his lips closed on hers alternately demanding and caressing, asking and promising. Without her consent, Elizabeth's own arms crept up and fastened on Mr. Wythe's lapels, holding him to her rather than thrusting him away.

When, eventually, Mr. Wythe set her free, they were both breathing hard. Mortified, Elizabeth colored a fiery red but still stood frozen to the spot. Wythe made no attempt to evade her eyes or even to apologize. Instead he explained quietly, "I could think of no other way to convince you that I meant what I said when I told you I preferred you to your sister. Or that I was content—more than content—to be in your company." He paused. But before Elizabeth could find her voice, he went on, "Miss Mayfield, will you marry me?"

Miss Mayfield stared at him in blank surprise. "I am not," she said at last, her voice not entirely steady, "in the habit of fainting, but at the moment, I feel distinctly light-headed. I thought I heard you ask me to marry you."

"You did," Mr. Wythe replied promptly, and with a hint of a smile in his voice.

"Surely you are jesting?" Elizabeth protested. "We have known each other such a short time."

"Why must I be jesting?" he asked with a frown. "Does it take so long to know one's own heart?"

Unbidden, the words echoed in Elizabeth's mind that Giles Pickworth had spoken, that one could know one's own heart in a day or an hour or a moment, and she knew it was true.

Of her own heart, she had no doubt. But his heart? That was
the rub. Something was amiss. No embrace, no cry of her
own heart, could shake the certainty she felt that something
was amiss about this courtship. And so, with elaborate
courtesy, Elizabeth smiled and said, ''I am very sorry, but
I cannot agree to marry you, Mr. Wythe.''

''Ever?'' he asked anxiously.

Doubt warred with desire and shook Elizabeth. Finally in
a low voice she replied, ''I don't know.''

It was so little and yet enough for Mr. Wythe to sweep
her into his arms again. Enough that for the briefest of
moments Elizabeth allowed herself to answer his kiss with
her own. Immediately Wythe lifted his face and looked down
at her, certainty and triumph evident there as he said fiercely,
''You will marry me, you know. In the end, you will!''

And then he was kissing her again, ruthlessly, and she was
responding in kind. Indeed, as his hands roamed, caressing
first her breasts and then lower still, her own treacherous
hands stole around his back, clutching him tightly. This was
against all propriety, against everything Elizabeth had ever
been taught, but she could not help herself, she wanted his
touch, wanted him to hold her even closer, wanted him to—

Abruptly Elizabeth came awake, her breath coming in
gasps as she clutched the sheet to her breast. A dream. It
had only been a dream. But a dream that now brought the
color to her cheeks as she remembered what it had been
about. Hastily she tried to thrust away the memory. But it
would not go. The feel of Mr. Wythe's hands on her breasts,
on all of her body, still seemed unbearably real. As did her
desire for them. This would not do! she told herself fiercely.

Silently, so as not to wake Leala, she got out of bed and
sat in the stiff-backed chair by the window. What on earth
was she going to do? Even if she had been wrong to spurn
Mr. Wythe's proposal of marriage at Long Meg's Circle,
it was a chance long gone. Surely he would be aware, by
now, of her disappearance, and if she were to return to
Ravenstonedale, he would not renew his suit. And if he did,
the reasons for her refusal had not changed. What point to

these constant dreams of him? Dreams in which he proposed to her, as though for the first time, as though she had had no expectation of him doing so? Dreams in which he took liberties with her body that she ought never to permit, but which, instead, she welcomed, looked for, had even begun to ache for? What on earth was she to do?

And because Elizabeth had no answer, she sat in the chair until morning, afraid to sleep again and dream. When she heard sounds below, she dressed quietly, still not wanting to wake Leala, and silently opened the door. Perhaps some-one could give her breakfast in the parlor. Giles would wish to make an early start, in any event, for they had traveled so short a distance the day before.

As she started down the stairs, Elizabeth heard a com-motion in the yard, and she paused, unwilling to face other travelers just yet. In the next moment she was very grateful for her caution, because Mr. Wythe's angry voice reached her where she stood.

"Breakfast! Now!" he commanded. "I'll not stop more than half the hour!"

Elizabeth could hear the landlord bowing and saying in his most obsequious voice, "Yes, your lordship. Right away, your lordship."

Before she could sort that one out in her mind, she heard Mr. Holden's voice saying, "So we are back to being the Viscount Trahern and the Earl of Basingstoke? Good, I, for one, am tired of the discomfort of being a mere Mr. Holden. But still, don't you think it the outside of enough to try to wake the entire inn at this infernal hour? We might be mad enough to travel through the night, but must everyone else suffer for it?"

In utter fascination, Elizabeth sat slowly down on the steps and listened to Mr. Wythe's reply. "I do as I choose," he said roughly. "Recollect that I told you you need not come."

"Aye, and recollect I told you I meant to have my thousand pounds straightaway," Mr. Holden's amused voice replied. "I doubt you mean to go to London, you know. Far more likely you will retreat to your country home, and it would be months before I could collect upon the wager."

"Liar," Mr. Wythe retorted amiably. "You know I have never dodged paying off on a wager, though you are right to say I do not mean to stay in London. You mean to shepherd me to my home estates and stay with me because you are afraid that I am in such a temper I shall come to some sort of harm."

"Well, yes, frankly I am," Holden admitted, unabashed. "Recollect that I know your dark moods, and this is decidedly one of them."

"Oh, decidedly," Wythe agreed, and Elizabeth could easily picture him waving a hand carelessly. "I never thought to be bested by such a chit. I was certain she would accept when I tossed her the handkerchief. I never dreamt she would hare off with Pickworth to escape my attention."

"Is it certain she did so?" Holden asked, and Elizabeth could all but see him frowning. "Perhaps they had some sort of accident? Or perhaps there is some other explanation?"

"No!" The flat of a hand smacked a table. "I asked at every conceivable point where their carriage could have come to grief. And while Sir Edmund swore she took nothing with her, her own maid admitted some of her things were missing."

"A toothbrush, a comb, a few gewgaws," Trahern protested, "nothing more."

"Perhaps she was afraid we would notice if she took a trunk or even just a bandbox," Basingstoke suggested acidly. "Good God, man! What else could she or would she take if she wanted to be sure no one would guess what she was about?"

Trahern did not at once answer. Finally he said, with a puzzled frown, "Wait a minute, if some of her things were missing, how could she have run away to escape your attentions? You said you didn't propose to her until you were at Long Meg's Circle. This argues she made her plans well ahead of that."

Silence. Then Elizabeth heard Wythe's voice, bleaker than before, "Perhaps you are right. But by God, I would have sworn she did not love the Pickworth boy."

"No," the man she knew as Holden agreed, "but the

gossip was that she had no choice, that she had to marry, and quickly. They say it was her own stepmother who said so.''

In spite of herself, Elizabeth gasped in dismay. If that indeed was what Beatrix had said, then she could not return to Ravenstonedale. It must be London, after all, though what hope she had there with these two men who knew her story to tell it, she did not know. So stunned was she that Elizabeth almost missed Wythe's next few words.

''I would not trust a word that woman said,'' he told Trahern curtly. ''But whatever the reason for her flight, it is enough for me to know that she chose Pickworth. And that your wager is won. You will, I trust, be discreet. I should not like anyone to know that the Earl of Basingstoke could not convince a mere provincial chit to wed him.''

Elizabeth shivered at the ice in his voice. Holden was not, however, so easily abashed. ''Tell me,'' he said quietly. ''If she had agreed to marry you, would you have wedded Miss Mayfield after all?''

And then the voice came, more icy and deep and dangerous than before. ''Do I look mad?'' was all he said.

Silently Elizabeth crept back up the stairs and into the room she shared with Leala. Silently she began to cry. And to write the letter she would ask Giles to have sent to her parents, for she had no desire to return there ever again. It was better this way, anyway, for then Leala and Giles need not be married by special license. She would accompany them to London. And perhaps in London her Aunt Elizabeth could advise her what to do next. After all, the Earl of . . . of Basingstoke, she thought he had said, had vowed he would not go there himself.

It wasn't difficult to convince Leala and Giles to continue to London to find his aunt and uncle. Not after Elizabeth told them what Basingstoke had said was being said back in Ravenstonedale. They quite saw she couldn't return there. And after all, there was no risk of encountering Mr. Wythe and Mr. Holden on the road if they were indeed traveling in such a hurry. To herself Elizabeth kept the knowledge of the wager. It was no part of her plan to have that become common knowledge. And yet . . . and yet a thought began to form in Elizabeth's mind, and when they stopped at the next night's inn, she pulled out the notebook she persuaded Giles to stop and let her purchase and began to write: "*The Reckless Wager*, A Romance by Mrs. Bethfrey."

By the time they reached London, Elizabeth thought grimly, she would have quite a few chapters ready to show Mr. Collier and Mr. Linley. It would not be the novel they had been expecting, of course. Thanks to Willoughby, there was no chance of that. And yet somehow Elizabeth thought they would not be disappointed by this new tale of an evil duke and his friend, the sinister marquess, and their attempt to spin a web of deceit about the innocent young heroine. All she had to do, she thought dryly, was create a plausible hero. Not so very difficult, her treacherous heart replied, if she used the one she had been dreaming about ever since Mr. Wythe had come to Ravenstonedale.

At every stop along the way to London, Leala and Giles could be certain of discovering Elizabeth at her notebook, her pen flying across the page as she wrote out the story in her neat, copperplate hand. For once she did not spend hours hesitating and finally tearing out the pages she had written. No, this time every word she wrote stayed, as her clever mind thought of the words and her angry, hurt heart supplied the pain.

Fortunately, Captain Pickworth and his lady were at their hired London town house, and however unhappy they were at this odd start, they were unwilling to shut their door to Giles. When he had seen Leala settled there, Giles escorted Elizabeth to her aunt's house. The footman who opened the door betrayed by not a flicker of an eyelash that he considered it in the least unusual for a young lady to appear on the doorstep, claim kinship with Lady Salvage, and announce that she had come to visit carrying not even a bandbox. But then, neither did Aunt Elizabeth. Lady Salvage was a large woman, though not as tall as her niece, and dressed in the latest fashion in a dress of dark green silk. She was, as anyone could have told her young guests, noted for her shrewdness and had a reputation for never being put out of countenance. As it was, Lady Salvage greeted her niece warmly, thanked Giles for escorting her all the way from Ravenstonedale, accepted his refusal to dine with them, and informed her majordomo that her niece was to be given the blue room next to her own. Then she swept Elizabeth upstairs to her dressing room, which had been furnished in the conceit of a silver-and-pink-striped tent. Elizabeth paused at the doorway and gazed in awe at the folds of material which had been hung from a central point in the room.

"Absurd, isn't it?" Lady Salvage asked with a laugh. "But it was something my dear Henri wanted for me. He had it done just before he died, the same year as your mother, and I have never wished to take it down, for every time I enter this room, it makes me think of him."

"It's extraordinary," Elizabeth replied honestly.

"Yes, but you've not come to see how I decorate my house," Lady Salvage retorted shrewdly. "You're in some sort of scrape, aren't you?"

It was, Elizabeth reflected later, fortunate that her aunt was not the sort of woman to be disconcerted by tears, for that was what she had promptly burst into. Lady Salvage merely waited until Elizabeth cried herself out and then said calmly, "I expect you'd best tell me all about it. There is a solution, I assure you, even if it takes us a little while to discover what that may be."

And that made Elizabeth chuckle. Why, oh, why had her father cut off his sister when it would have made all the difference in the world to Elizabeth to have had such an aunt to turn to after her mother died?

So she told Lady Salvage all about it, including the wager she had overheard. She even, after explaining the need for absolute discretion, told her about Giles Pickworth and Leala Comfrey. Lady Salvage understood perfectly. Far from being dismayed, she said approvingly, "I like a girl who can keep her wits about her. Very clever of you to discover what Basingstoke was about, and very kind of you to tell me. All of London, or the *ton*, at any rate, has been atwitter trying to discover where he had gone and what he was about. You see, he was supposed to offer for the Marquess of Wey's daughter and he didn't. Even more astonishing, he is said to have given his mistress her *congé*. A pity he didn't fall in love with you. It would have been the making of Hugh.''

''Do you know the Earl of Basingstoke?'' Elizabeth asked in amazement.

''Yes, I do. I knew his father even better,'' her aunt replied. ''I had good cause to be grateful to the man, in fact. He was a shockingly poor father, however.'' She paused, then added dryly, ''Now that I know what Hugh was doing, I am really very angry with myself for not guessing that that was whom Beatrix meant when she wrote to ask if I knew of a Percival Wythe. Wythe is his family name, you see, but everyone has always called him Basingstoke or Hugh, and that is why I didn't think of it. Mr. Holden, I suppose, is Viscount Trahern. Family name again. It quite sinks my vanity to realize that your stepmother wrote both names and I didn't recognize either of them. I must be entering my dotage.''

This was said with a sigh, but such a prospect seemed so entirely unlikely that Elizabeth was surprised into laughing. ''Much better,'' Lady Salvage said approvingly.

After a moment, however, Elizabeth sobered. ''Yes, but what shall I do, Aunt Elizabeth?'' she asked quietly. ''I cannot return to Ravenstonedale. Not after what Beatrix has said about me.''

''You will stay with me, of course,'' her aunt replied, as though the question were absurd. ''I shall bring you out and enjoy doing so.''

''Yes, but even I have heard of the Earl of Basingstoke and his doings. I can place no reliance on his discretion, and recollect that he knows the supposed tale of my flight with Giles Pickworth.'' She paused and looked down at the hands clenched tightly in her lap before she went on. ''I believe, indeed I am certain, that he took my flight as a . . . a direct affront and that he has reason to be very angry with me. I cannot believe he would refrain from such a convenient way to hurt me.''

Elizabeth Salvage looked at her niece, a thoughtful

expression on her face, as she said, "I do not think Hugh will tell people about your flight, since it must inevitably lead to public knowledge of what he did. Still, if it seems likely that he will so far forget his own interests, I shall speak to Hugh. He would, I think, keep silence if I were the one who asked him to do so. He would even, if I asked it, allow you to explain the truth to him."

Elizabeth looked at Lady Salvage beseechingly. "Please, Aunt Elizabeth," she said, "I don't think I could bear to speak with him again."

"You must, at some time, if you remain in London," Lady Salvage pointed out reasonably. "You are bound to encounter one another sooner or later."

Elizabeth shivered. "I pray it is later," she said.

Her aunt frowned. "I know that Hugh can be—has been, in fact—horrid at times. Have you taken him, then, in such deep dislike?"

Yes! her mind cried. But a deeper part of her answered differently, and Elizabeth met her aunt's eyes squarely as she replied, "I have fallen in love with him, Aunt Elizabeth. I know it is hopeless and foolish and that he courted me only as part of a horrid wager. I even know that he would call it mad to marry me if I had accepted his proposal. I call it mad to love him, under the circumstances, and that is why I cannot bear to meet him again."

This time even Lady Salvage was troubled. "There is some sense to what you say, for ten to one, he would know you care, and that would only prove a source of jests for Hugh. Dear as he is to me, I cannot deny that he has a troublesome streak to his nature, and I should not like to see you hurt. Very well, if need be, I shall see him myself to ask his discretion. He will not refuse it to me, I think. I was used to feed him milk and cookies, after his mother died, and listen to his troubles. He was such a promising boy. I have often thought that if his father had ever shown an interest in him, ever taken the trouble to know his son, Hugh might have turned out very differently." She leaned forward and patted Elizabeth's hand. "Leave it to me, my dear," she said. "I shall make sure he does not trouble you. And perhaps, as you say, he will not come back to London straightaway and we need not worry about the matter. Meanwhile,'' she added more briskly, ''we must arrange for you to acquire a suitable wardrobe, and you must write your father that you are safely here.''

''Aunt Elizabeth,'' her niece said hesitantly, ''there is one more thing.''

With foreboding, Lady Salvage asked, ''What, my dear?''

Elizabeth hesitated, not certain how to begin. ''Have you ever heard of Mrs. Bethfrey?'' she blurted out at last.

Somewhat taken aback, Lady Salvage stared at her niece. ''Of course,'' she replied. ''Everyone has heard of Mrs. Bethfrey. Her books are all the crack. But what has that to do with you? Never say you know her?''

Again Elizabeth hesitated. ''Aunt Elizabeth, I *am* Mrs. Bethfrey. I wrote *The Trials of Magdalena, Miss Sarabelle's Folly*, and *The Horrid Horatio*.''

Lady Salvage's first reaction was that her niece had gone mad. She found herself reaching for a vinaigrette that she had never used in her life. Carefully, because one ought not to argue with those who have lost their wits, she said faintly, ''My dear, what an amazing surprise!''

''Yes, and I can see you don't believe me,'' Elizabeth retorted with a good-natured chuckle. ''Infamous of me to have sprung it on you this way.''

Well, that certainly didn't sound mad. Cautiously Lady Salvage essayed another comment. ''But, my dear, tell me how this all came about.''

''You know, perhaps, that my mama was positively addicted to romances?'' Elizabeth asked hesitantly. Lady Salvage nodded and Elizabeth went on. ''Well, so, too, was I. Mama and I used to make a game of making up our own stories. After she died, I gave it up, for it hurt too much to do alone what we had once shared. Do you understand that?'' she asked anxiously.

''Perfectly,'' Lady Salvage assured her niece.

''Later, after Papa remarried, I went back to that game. I wasn't precisely happy, and it was an escape for me. I even began to write down the stories I made up and read them to my friends. They thought the stories were wonderful, and when Beatrix, my stepmama, began breeding, I gathered up my courage to send one off to Mr. Linley and Mr. Collier, the publishers. I was astonished when they wrote back to say they wanted the book,'' Elizabeth said, her voice still tinged with awe.

"*The Trials of Magdalena*, I collect,'' Lady Salvage replied. Elizabeth nodded, and she said, a puzzled frown on her face, ''Never tell me your father approved?''

"Oh, no,'' Elizabeth said quickly. ''Indeed, my stepmama strictly forbade me ever to tell anyone I scribbled stories, as she put it. Neither she nor Papa know that I am Mrs. Bethfrey. With the help of my friends Leala and Giles, I managed to send off the manuscript in secret and arranged to have my correspondence sent to another spot, where Giles retrieved it for me. He also handled the drafts that were sent me in payment for my books. I have almost four hundred pounds from my writing, which seems,'' Elizabeth said candidly, ''a great deal of money to me, but I know it is not enough to set up a household of my own.''

"I should think not!'' Lady Salvage said, aghast. ''And even if it were, such a thing is not to be thought of! Why, people would say you were eccentric at the very least, and you would shatter any chances you might have of being creditably married.''

"I must suppose I have already done so,'' Elizabeth said in so mournful a tone that Lady Salvage patted her hand in sympathy.

"Nonsense,'' her ladyship said bracingly. ''We shall come about. Depend upon it, dressed as you ought to be, you will be all the rage.''

Elizabeth smiled but shook her head. She could not allow it. She also made one last attempt to return to the subject of her writing. ''I have my next book that I am working on, Aunt Elizabeth,'' she said. ''I am sorry if you dislike it, but I mean to keep publishing as Mrs. Bethfrey.''

Lady Salvage was known throughout the *ton* for her good sense. She knew that to be considered a bluestocking would be fatal to Elizabeth's chances to form an eligible connection.

And yet it would be wrong to deny that she was tempted to let her niece finish the book and have it published. For one thing, like many ladies of the *ton*, Lady Salvage enjoyed Mrs. Bethfrey's work. For another, she was shrewd enough to know that the distraction of writing might serve to raise Elizabeth's spirits and keep her from dwelling on what had happened with Hugh. More, in her own youth, Lady Salvage had written. In her case, the scribblings had been poetry and one attempt at a play, begun after her first visit to the theater, for that experience had at once enchanted and inspired her. That attempt now lay at the bottom of a trunk somewhere in this very house, abandoned after the ball at which she had met the Comte de Salvage. Elizabeth thought it very likely that something of the sort would happen to her niece once she, too, became caught up in the round of balls and routs and parties. Finally to be discovered to be Mrs. Bethfrey would not be as horrid as if she had, say, written a satire of the *ton* or some scholarly or educational text. So for once Lady Salvage allowed the promptings of her heart to override her common sense, and replied kindly, "By all means, finish your novel, my dear. The first order of business, however, is for you to write your parents that you are safe with me, then for us to go shopping and procure you a wardrobe. And now I shall show you to your room, for you have had a long trip and I am sure you will wish to tidy up."

Happily, Elizabeth agreed.

14

IT IS NOT to be expected that any young lady, particularly a young lady raised in the north of England, could fail to enjoy the novel experience of shopping in the smartest shops in London, looking for bargains in the Pantheon Bazaar, taking in a show at Astley's Amphitheater, an evening at the opera, or watching a farce at the theater. Nor did Elizabeth disdain such topics of conversation as the relative merits of lace, ribbons, and rosettes, or crepe, muslin, and silk. Then there was the matter of gloves and stockings and shawls and reticules, not to mention hats, all of which became one to perfection. And since Lady Salvage answered every objection, as to expense, by saying that as Elizabeth was to be her heir, it was ridiculous to cavil at spending some of it on her now when she could benefit so greatly by doing so. For Elizabeth it was as though she moved about in a dream, afraid that an unwary step would cause her to awaken.

One of the things that brought Elizabeth particular pleasure was the Pickworths' acceptance of Leala. Now that matters had all worked out, she allowed herself to admit that she had been worried. It was not to be expected, after all, that Captain Pickworth or his wife would look with favor on the arrival on their doorstep of Giles and an unknown young female. Indeed, Captain Pickworth's first words, once Leala was out of earshot, were, "You've got to take her back! That's all there is to it, you've got to take her back. A more ramshackle business I've never seen, and I don't thank you for bringing it onto my doorstep. What your father is going to say when he knows that you've come to me is beyond my imagining. What the devil made you think I'd approve?"

"I didn't," Giles answered frankly. "But I also didn't think I had any other choice."

That admission had been followed by a complete explanation of Leala's circumstances and Giles's plans for her future. Captain Pickworth had argued with him, and when that didn't serve, had rung a rare peal over his head. Giles had remained unswayed. The captain's wife had no better luck, and, if the truth be told, found it difficult not to pity the pair. So, in the end, Captain Pickworth found himself faced with the choice of either casting the pair out into the street, knowing that Giles meant to marry Leala, by hedge or by stile, or of aiding him with what passed, at least, for an air of complacency. And since Leala was a taking thing with a gentle sweetness that could not fail to please such high sticklers as Captain Pickworth and his wife, by the time the marriage was performed, they had come round to accepting her into the family. "I don't deny I have reservations, my dear," Captain Pickworth had told his wife as they dressed for the ceremony, "but what will be will be, and there's no sense in fighting the inevitable. Besides, the girl will do. Particularly as Giles seems to think he can keep her mother and stepfather-to-be from encroaching. As for her father's disgrace, well, the less said the better, and most people will not blame her for what he did."

Then, having accepted the marriage, Captain Pickworth and his wife made every effort to help establish them socially. Relieved of worry over her friends' future, Elizabeth was free to take pleasure in her own come-out, for that was what it was. The social affairs she had seen in Cumbria counted for nothing next to the smallest of London events. And the smartest of beaux in the north, with the exception of Mr. Wythe and Mr. Holden, could not hold a candle to those who now begged the pleasure of dances with Elizabeth or the honor of driving her in their carriages or calling at Lady Salvage's town house of an afternoon.

Lady Salvage watched her niece's patent enjoyment of these new experiences with satisfaction. The first Lady Mayfield, she knew, had been a kind mother, but even the most generous of mamas would not have bought for a daughter as young as Elizabeth had then been, the sort of toilette she could now wear. And while the second Lady Mayfield had not been so cruel or foolish as to dress her stepdaughters in rags, neither had she been liberal with the purse strings. This combined with a natural desire to wear dark colors that showed she still mourned her mother had led Elizabeth to dress modestly for the past several years. Lady Salvage watched as the handsome niece who had arrived on her doorstep blossomed into a very pretty young lady, one who would, she felt sure, prove a credit to her sponsorship.

As she had predicted, Lady Salvage was enjoying her unusual role as chaperone. It had not proved in the least difficult to coax vouchers for Almack's out of Lady Jersey, one of her bosom bows. Nor had other invitations been backward in arriving, once word of Lady Salvage's charming young niece got about. Several ladies of her acquaintance had called to meet Elizabeth and taken away the news that she was a well-behaved girl with no affectations, and if she was a trifle more intelligent than might be seemly, well, that was only to be expected in a niece of so clever a woman as Lady Salvage. The verdict was that Elizabeth would take, and so the invitations continued to arrive.

Meanwhile, still writing at her headlong pace, Elizabeth finished her manuscript. Indeed, if there was any flaw in her situation, it was that every time she asked her aunt to take her to the publishers to show them her book, Lady Salvage recollected some errand or other that required her immediate attention. And Elizabeth began to wonder if her aunt meant her to publish the story at all.

If the truth be told, Lady Salvage did not. She had read the manuscript as soon as Elizabeth had finished it, and, to her dismay, discovered it to be witty and delightful and something she was unable to put down until she had finished reading it. It was borne in upon her, long before she did finish, that it was Mrs. Bethfrey's best effort yet and that her publisher would be a fool not to take it. And that was the rub. Even though it would be published under Mrs. Bethfrey's name, Lady Salvage could not help but feel that sooner or later someone would be bound to guess her identity, and that would not do. Elizabeth had neatly skewered both Basingstoke and Trahern, something which the *ton* would enjoy but not forgive her for. Hugh would certainly never forgive her. Worse, in spite of having made Basingstoke's character the villain of the piece, it was evident to the reader that the author was not entirely indifferent to him. That could only further serve to make Elizabeth a laughingstock and prove fatal to her chances to form an eligible connection. And however eccentric Lady Salvage might be, that eccentricity did not extend to wishing her niece to set herself up as an odd one at the age of four-and-twenty. She did not dare to tell Elizabeth, however, what her thoughts might be, for her one attempt to gently hint to the girl the wisdom of not publishing the book had sent her into the boughs, vowing that she did not care in the least what anyone might say or think. So Lady Salvage had been treading carefully, merely finding excuses not to take Elizabeth and her manuscript to the publishers. That was why, one fine morning a couple of weeks after her arrival in London, Elizabeth slipped out of the house before Lady Salvage was up and about. She had managed, several days before in a similar maneuver to drop her manuscript off at the publishers, and today was the day appointed for her to return for an answer.

A short time later she was ushered into the office of Linley and Collier's Publishing House and found herself speaking with Mr. Linley, who apologized for the absence of Mr. Collier.

"Well, Mr. Linley, what do you think?" Elizabeth asked eagerly.

Mr. Linley eyed the young woman on the other side of the desk nervously. To say that her appearance had come as a shock to him was an understatement. Both he and Mr. Collier had speculated, of course, on the identity of their most popular author. Between them they had fixed it that she was either a widow or a spinster of middle age living on some sort of jointure up north, in Cumbria. They had never expected her to appear in their offices, much less considered the possibility that she was a young lady of quality. Indeed, it had taken some persuading for Elizabeth to convince him that she was Mrs. Bethfrey. Eventually, however, she had. But Mr. Linley might have been pardoned for feeling at a distinct disadvantage now, in facing her, and he said the first thing that came to mind, "Is this story pure fiction?" he asked.

"Do you seriously believe such a tale could be true?" Elizabeth countered easily.

He did. He also thought that that would make it all the more salable, for the *ton* would be eager to discover the identity of the miscreants. Aloud, however, he merely said repressively, "I think it will take extremely well, as all of Mrs. Bethfrey's books have done. We are overdue for one of her books, and therefore I think we shall endeavor to shorten the time it normally takes between the arrival of one of your manuscripts and the publication of the same. I shall take steps to see to it myself. And, naturally, I shall keep you informed of the progress of your book."

He rose to his feet and Elizabeth did so as well. She positively glowed with happiness. "I hope to have another for you quite soon," she said.

"And we shall be delighted to publish it, Mrs. Bethfrey," he replied with a gallant bow and a smile over the use of her pseudonym.

And with that Elizabeth left quite satisfied.

After she was gone, Mr. Linley sat back down at his desk, staring at the manuscript, lost in thought for some time. Finally he stood again. There were discreet inquiries to be made and certain steps to be taken to advertise the select edition he intended to publish. Mr. Linley believed in his instincts and, just now, they urged him to publish this novel as quickly as possible. The real Mrs. Bethfrey was a lovely young lady, and now that she had come to London, Mr. Linley had no doubt she would soon find a husband and he had no doubt that if she did so, her husband-to-be would have something to say about her writing. It was quite likely, in his opinion, that Miss Mayfield's marriage would signal the end of Mrs. Bethfrey, and he intended to have her book published before such an event occurred, in case the gentleman should take it into his head to object. Indeed, Mr. Linley intended to bring the book out with a speed that his competitors would have soundly denounced as impossible.

As for Elizabeth, she had no notion of the repercussions that would occur from this event. She returned to Lady Salvage's town house after conveniently providing herself with an excuse for her absence, in the form of a book from Hookham's lending library. It was a wise precaution, for Lady Salvage was just rising from the breakfast table when Elizabeth returned.

When the letter from Lady Salvage finally arrived at his estate some weeks later, Basingstoke roused from his black mood to seize upon it, hoping it would carry word of the whereabouts of Elizabeth Mayfield. Or Elizabeth Pickworth, as she was no doubt called by now. Instead he discovered it was merely a plea from Lady Salvage for his discretion concerning any information he might have about the girl, and a request that he come and call upon Lady Salvage in London. No word of where the girl might be, no word as to whether she might be wedded.

For some time after he read the note, Basingstoke stared into the empty fireplace. That was where Trahern found him. "Well?" Trahern asked impatiently. "Do you mean to come out riding with me, or not?"

"Not, I think," Basingstoke replied curtly, without looking away from the fireplace.

Trahern tossed his riding crop onto a table and flung himself into a chair. "What's put you in such a temper now?" he asked amiably.

Basingstoke turned about. He was tempted to deny the charge, but realized, ruefully, that Trahern would never accept such an obvious lie. "This," he admitted, holding up the note where the viscount could see it. "Lady Salvage writes to ask my discretion on Miss Mayfield's behalf. Lady Salvage also asks me to call upon her at my earliest convenience. She writes that she has an important matter to discuss with me."

"How the devil did she know to send it here?" Trahern

asked with a frown. "And how the devil did she know we were in Ravenstonedale?"

Basingstoke shrugged. "Recollect that I warned you that sooner or later she would remember that my family name was Wythe. I presume that she finally did so, and that when Miss Mayfield's family wrote to tell her what had occurred, she felt it best to ask me to be discreet. I can only hope she will be equally discreet in not informing the family of my identity."

"Well, what word has she of Miss Elizabeth?" Trahern asked cheerfully. "Did she marry that young whelp after all? Or did she return to Ravenstonedale in disgrace?"

"Lady Salvage does not say," the earl replied heavily.

"What impertinence!" Trahern exclaimed. "Telling you to be discreet. I suppose you will spread the tale of Miss Mayfield's romp just to punish her?"

A ghost of a smile crossed Basingstoke's face. "No, I think not," he said. "As I told you up north, I live in lively dread of Lady Salvage and her wrath. If I did so, I have no doubt she would still sally forth to box my ears as she did when I was a boy and vexed her sadly. Though to be fair to her, she was far more patient than I had any right to expect," the earl added wryly. "No, I shall be discreet, and so shall you," he told his friend pointedly.

Trahern held up his hands. "Oh, never fear, I have no wish to draw attention to our trip north." He paused, then asked hesitantly, "Do you mean to write and ask about Miss Mayfield?"

Basingstoke turned back to stare at the empty fireplace again, and for a long moment he did not answer. Finally he said, "It would undoubtedly be foolish beyond permission for me to do so, would it not?"

"Undoubtedly," Trahern agreed cheerfully.

Basingstoke eyed his friend sharply, then said smoothly, "That is why I think I shall pay a courtesy call on Lady Salvage instead, as she asks me to."

"What?" Trahern gave a startled squawk.

"Never fear, I shan't make you come up to London with me," Basingstoke said with an amused gleam in his eye.

"You are perfectly free to remain here until I return." He paused, then added deliberately, "Since you already have your thousand pounds, you can't give that as an excuse this time, can you?"

"That has nothing to say to the matter," Trahern replied, rising to his feet. "I mean to come with you because it promises to be amusing, that's why. What I mean to say is that if it's moon madness with you over the girl, then I want to be there to see it."

"Then I suggest you go upstairs and warn your man to pack your things and be ready to leave in the morning," Basingstoke said mildly.

"The morning?" Trahern said, startled again. "Don't you mean to leave right away?"

"Right away?" Basingstoke repeated, a look of haughty surprise in his face. "When there is a promising bottle of port to be opened tonight? Don't be absurd."

"Don't you be absurd," Trahern countered wrathfully. "I know you too well for you to lord it over me like that. If you want to leave in the morning, that's fine with me. Indeed, I should prefer it. But after the headlong way you dashed about up north, you can hardly be surprised that I expected you to do so again." Then, in an altogether different tone Trahern added, "Do you mean to come out riding or not?"

Basingstoke hesitated; then his eyes sparkled grimly as he said, "Why the devil not?"

15

LADY SALVAGE sat at her writing desk, looking over her correspondence with no little satisfaction. London might have begun to be thin of company, but no one would have known it from the pile of invitations before her. Already Lady Salvage had taken Elizabeth to any number of small parties and been pleased with the girl's deportment. Elizabeth was amiable, yet not insipid, she could dance without a fault, and the gentlemen had seemed to find her taking. She had made her appearance at Almack's, and while the hostesses had not yet given her their permission to waltz, they had smiled on her benignly. And now Lady Salvage was looking through her invitations to see where this week would take them. Lady Sefton's ball? Perhaps the party at Holland House, two days after that?

It was in the midst of just such delicious considerations that a visitor was announced. "The Earl of Basingstoke, ma'am."

Lady Salvage rose at once to greet him. "Hugh!" she said with delight. "How good of you to come so quickly in reply to my letter. I was afraid you might take a pet and not come at all."

Something in the sight of this woman, who had once been a sort of second mother to him, altered Basingstoke's dark mood, and his frown turned to a swift smile. He came forward and took her hands as he kissed her cheek. "It's wonderful to see you again," he said. "How are you?"

"Happy and busy," Lady Salvage replied easily. Then, with something of a twinkle in her eyes she added, "And how do you go on? Or shouldn't I ask?"

"Well enough, though I'm not certain you really want to know what I've been up to," Basingstoke answered, not troubling to hide the laughter in his voice.

"As usual," Lady Salvage retorted dryly. She eyed him speculatively and said, "Now, I wonder why you were so prompt in answering my letter."

"Why? Because you are the dearest woman in my life and I couldn't wait to see you again," he answered, placing a hand over his heart.

"Rubbish!" Lady Salvage told him roundly, though she smiled. "Never mind. Come sit down. It's almost time for tea. I'll ring for it to be brought in now, and we can have a comfortable coze. It's been far too long since I have seen you."

"Let me ring for you," he said instantly.

But Lady Salvage would have none of it. She looked up at him and tilted her head charmingly as she said, "A fine thing that would be. Or do you mean to take over my house, Hugh?"

Basingstoke laughed, reassured by the sharpness of her tone. "How well I remember you taking me to task," he said. "Do you mean to do so now? Is that why you asked me to call?"

"Perhaps. That depends upon you," she replied dryly. "Is there any reason I should take you to task? What have you been up to of late?"

Uneasily Basingstoke avoided her eyes, well aware that it was he who had started the conversation down this dangerous path. "Oh, this and that," he said with a shrug, fiddling with the set of his cravat.

"This and that?" Lady Salvage echoed in a tone he knew far too well.

To his relief the door to the morning room opened and a maid appeared with the tea tray. They waited until she was gone and Lady Salvage seated herself behind the tea tray and began to pour before she spoke again. Then it was to ask if the earl still liked milk in his tea. When that matter was settled to her satisfaction and she was leaning back against the cushions of her chair with a cup in her own hand, she asked gently, "Why did you answer my summons so promptly, Hugh?"

"I dared not refuse to do so," he retorted with a laugh. And yet he avoided her eyes as he went on, "I received your letter and thought I would reassure you myself about Miss Mayfield. I have no intention of causing her distress by spreading about the tale of her disappearance from Ravenstonedale." He paused, then added, "I collect that is why you wished to see me?"

"I am very reassured to hear you say you mean to be discreet," Lady Salvage agreed calmly.

"Good." He paused; then his voice turned serious as he said, "What did happen to Miss Mayfield? Is she married to young Pickworth now?"

"No."

The reply was so brief as to puzzle the earl. "Has she returned to Ravenstonedale, then?" he asked with a frown.

"I cannot think it would have been comfortable for her to do so. Her stepmother lost no time in spreading the tale there of Miss Mayfield's disappearance."

"Most uncomfortable," Lady Salvage agreed equably.

Suddenly Basingstoke's neckcloth felt far too tight for him. "May I ask where she is, then?" he said warily.

Lady Salvage set down her teacup gently and took her time in replying. "That depends," she said. "May I ask why you introduced yourself to her as Mr. Wythe? And your friend, the Viscount Trahern, I presume, was introduced as Mr. Holden?"

"Actually, it was Trahern who chose to introduce us that way," Basingstoke said uneasily.

"But you didn't correct him," Lady Salvage pointed out reasonably.

"No," the earl agreed.

"No doubt you had a good reason?" she suggested helpfully.

The earl set down his own cup and rose to his feet. He paced the room a few times before he replied, and then it was with honesty that he said, "We did so for the most damnable of reasons! For a wager that depended upon no one knowing our identities."

"A wager involving my niece?" Lady Salvage asked.

He looked at her unhappily. "Yes. And I fear she may have been hurt by it. That is why I have asked you where she is. Perhaps her disappearance had nothing to do with me, but if it did, then . . ." He hesitated a moment before he went on, ". . . then I am concerned and wish to be certain she is all right."

Lady Salvage watched his face, seeing the distress visible there just as it had always been when he had done something wrong as a child and wanted to make amends. Amends his father had never allowed him to make. Compassion softened her heart and she started to answer him. But before she could speak, however, the door to the morning room opened again, blocking the earl from the view of the person who stood there.

"Aunt Elizabeth, the proof sheets are here!" Elizabeth Mayfield crowed excitedly. "And Mr. Linley has written that if all goes well, it will be published in no time."

"How delightful for you," an icy voice replied.

Elizabeth Mayfield froze. Her mouth gaped open and she stood there as though rooted to the spot, dismay etched across her face and the color drained away. Basingstoke was just as stunned, however better he might be at concealing his emotions. In Ravenstonedale he had thought Elizabeth Mayfield an entertaining young woman, well-bred, with an intelligent, well-informed mind. He had even thought her attractive. But he had by no means thought her a beauty or fashionable. Now he stared at a young woman dressed in the first stare of fashion, in colors and fabrics that suited her, and with her hair dressed by Lady Salvage's own hairdresser. And Elizabeth Mayfield was beautiful.

Perhaps because he was so disconcerted, Basingstoke came away from the side of the room and stood in front of Elizabeth, his eyes sparkling with anger as his words lashed out at her. "Miss Mayfield?" he asked. "Or is it Mrs.

Pickworth by now? Whichever it is, you seem amazingly unperturbed by your extraordinary situation.''

Elizabeth looked to her aunt. "Haven't you told him?'' she whispered in dismay.

"Your aunt has had time to tell me nothing,'' Basingstoke replied, taking her wrist in an iron grip and drawing her into the room. With his foot he sent the door shut, and his other hand prized the papers she held from her grasp. "Why don't you tell me everything yourself?'' he suggested with a grim smile as he forced her to sit down.

Basingstoke stood over her chair, giving Elizabeth no chance for escape. For a moment she didn't speak. Then a grim smile stole over her own face. "What shall I tell you . . .'' She paused, then said, ". . . Mr. Wythe?''

"Why you left Long Meg's Circle with Pickworth and never returned to Ravenstonedale. Whether you are married. How you come to be here, in this house,'' he said, gazing down at her coolly. "Did Pickworth abandon you? I see no ring upon your finger.''

But Elizabeth had herself well in hand now. She looked back at Basingstoke and replied calmly, "Won't you be seated first, Mr. Wythe? I assure you I shan't run away today.''

He nodded curtly, sat opposite her, and waited. After a moment she began. "I accompanied Giles Pickworth and his bride-to-be to London to be married. To lend propriety. We had intended to go only as far as Inglewhite, where his aunt and uncle lived. They were not there, Captain Pickworth having removed to London for the Season, and we followed. Then Giles brought me here, to Aunt Elizabeth's house,'' Elizabeth concluded.

"Do you expect me to believe this . . . this Banbury tale?'' Basingstoke demanded with a frown.

Elizabeth's eyes opened wider. "Banbury tale?'' she said softly.

"What else would you call it?'' he demanded. "You can scarcely expect me to believe that anyone would consider it proper for you to take part in such a romp?''

Elizabeth rose slowly to her feet. "It is a matter of complete indifference to me what you believe. Particularly as you appear to be quite a creator of Banbury tales yourself. Lord *Basingstoke*!"

At this, Basingstoke started. He was on his feet before she had finished speaking. "Elizabeth," he said, holding out a hand to her.

She turned on her heel and fled from the room, leaving Basingstoke to watch in dismay. He turned to Lady Salvage, who was regarding him with a distinctly speculative gleam in her eye. "What shall I do?" he asked her curtly.

"That depends, I should think, on what it is you would like to occur," Lady Salvage replied with her usual good sense. When he didn't at once answer, she repeated gently, "What is it you do want to happen, Hugh?"

"I want her to marry me," he said wrathfully.

"Ah," Lady Salvage said wisely, "she has piqued your pride. The first female to deny your charms and show herself indifferent to you!"

Again Basingstoke paced the room, thinking through his reply. At last he said, pausing to look at Lady Salvage. "No, it is not my pride. Not entirely, at any rate. I look at that exasperating chit and I see the first woman to whom I could imagine myself wedded for the rest of my life. I cannot explain it to you, I cannot even explain it to myself. I only know that I went north to carry out a silly wager, fully expecting to return to London with my heart untouched. Instead I have returned captive to a girl who will not even speak to me."

"And after you have treated her with such tender address!" Lady Salvage said, clucking her tongue in mock amazement.

That drew a shaky laugh from the earl, and she nodded her approval. "Yes, but how do I make amends for my roughshod treatment of her?" he asked.

Lady Salvage regarded him with raised eyebrows and faint astonishment as she said, "Do I take you to say that you have forgotten how to charm a lady?"

That drew another, firmer laugh. "No, but rarely have I had to do so after giving the lady a marked distaste for me.

Tell me, is she well? Is she happy here in London?'' Basingstoke asked. ''Does she wish it were possible to return to
Ravenstonedale? Is there any way I can ease her path?''

Lady Salvage was silent a moment. Finally she said,
''Hugh, have you ever heard of Mrs. Bethfrey?''

''No, who is she?'' he demanded impatiently.

''Elizabeth,'' was the curt reply.

Basingstoke was stunned. He turned very pale and, after
a moment, he presented his back to Lady Salvage. Over his
shoulder he said in a colorless voice, ''You should have told
me before, so that I might have wished Miss Mayfield—that
is, Mrs. Bethfrey—happy. I collect Mr. Bethfrey is someone
she met here in London?''

''There is no Mr. Bethfrey,'' was the dry reply.

That startled Basingstoke into looking at his hostess again,
this time with hard, shrewd eyes. ''Surely you advised her
that pretending to be married when she is not will bring her
to grass faster than almost anything else I can think of?''

''You misunderstand me,'' Lady Salvage said smoothly.
''Elizabeth has no intention of introducing herself to the *ton*
as Mrs. Bethfrey. In fact, she, we, hope to keep her identity
a secret!''

Thoroughly bewildered now, Basingstoke sat down
opposite Lady Salvage and said, ''I think you had better
explain. If there is no Mr. Bethfrey, how can there be a Mrs.
Bethfrey? Unless you mean to say she is a widow?''

Lady Salvage shook her head. Then, taking pity on the
earl, she explained, ''I am astonished you have never heard
of Mrs. Bethfrey, but then, perhaps you don't read novels.
Not lurid romances, at any rate.''

''I don't,'' he agreed curtly.

''Perhaps you should. Mrs. Bethfrey is all the rage with
her tales of scandalous deeds and lovely heroines and horrid
villains.''

''Mrs. Bethfrey,'' Basingstoke repeated absently. Then,
with feeling he demanded, ''You don't mean to tell me Miss
Mayfield is a published author?''

''That is precisely what I do mean to tell you,'' Lady
Salvage replied gently. ''And why I sent for you. I think

you had better read the proof sheets of her latest novel. She has entitled it *The Reckless Wager*.''

"What?" he thundered.

"I knew she was writing it," Lady Salvage continued calmly, ignoring the interruption, "but up until a few days ago I had no notion the girl had managed to sneak out and show it to her publisher. I had hoped to dissuade her from doing so, you see. But nothing I can say will sway Elizabeth from her determination to have it published. Worse, I spoke to the publishers and they absolutely refuse to refrain from publishing it. I thought you might have better luck in persuading them not to do so." She paused, then added, "Mind you, though, Elizabeth is not to know I have told you all this. She would never forgive me for this betrayal." She paused again. "The devil of it is," she said gloomily, "I do sympathize with Elizabeth. She is a remarkable girl. The trouble is that I also foresee disaster if the *ton* were to discover that she was the author and that it was based on a true story. At any rate, read the proof sheets. The publisher is Linley and Collier."

"I shall read this most carefully," he promised her grimly, rising to his feet and taking the proof sheets from the table where he had set them.

"Oh, and, Hugh," she said as he turned to leave, "we attend Lady Sefton's ball the night after next. I shall look for you."

"I shall be there," he answered curtly, and then he was gone. Lady Salvage sat for a few minutes, deep in thought, before she went upstairs to see her niece. Elizabeth was, as her aunt suspected, crying in her room. Hastily the girl tried to wipe away her tears as the older woman entered. "He's made a sad muddle of it, hasn't he?" Lady Salvage said wisely.

"He despises me!" her niece replied in tragic tones.

"Does he?" she asked with raised eyebrows. "That is scarcely the impression he gave me, after you left the room. Indeed, he seemed quite convinced that it was you who had taken him in dislike."

"Well, I have," the younger Elizabeth said with a distinct sniff.

"A pity, then, that he means to attend Lady Sefton's ball," Lady Salvage replied, avoiding her niece's eyes. "Particularly as I think he means to stand up with you for a dance or two. Which would be a great help in launching you, for it would raise your credit considerably to be seen to please the Earl of Basingstoke."

"Aunt Elizabeth, you are roasting me," Elizabeth said severely.

Now the aunt met her niece's eyes with a limpid gaze as she said innocently, "Oh, but I am not. It truly would raise your credit to dance with Basingstoke. If the two of you could avoid a quarrel on the dance floor, that is."

Elizabeth got to her feet and went to stand staring out the window. "Well, you can place no dependence upon that," she said gloomily. "You have seen how we quarreled downstairs."

Her aunt was silent a moment before she said, "Did you quarrel a great deal in Ravenstonedale?"

"Only the day I left," her niece conceded, "and that was because I needed to find a cause to ride in Pickworth's carriage."

"I see. So you had not taken him in dislike then?" Lady Salvage pressed the point.

"No." The answer came so softly her aunt could scarcely hear it. "I just distrusted him because I thought perhaps he was courting me because he thought I was an heiress."

"I see." Lady Salvage managed to control the smile that trembled at the corners of her mouth as she said, "Well, at any rate, you can acquit the Earl of Basingstoke of pursuing you for your expectations. He is one of the wealthiest men in England."

"Yes, but that makes it all the more difficult for me," her niece replied seriously. "If I tell him now that I . . . I do not dislike him, he will think it is because I have discovered who he is. He will never believe that I fell in love with Mr. Wythe in Ravenstonedale." Then, just before she burst into tears in her aunt's arms, Elizabeth demanded, "How could he make such a dreadful wager?"

When her niece's sobs had subsided a trifle, Lady Salvage tried to reply to the question. "I suppose Hugh came to do such an outrageous thing because he is, like most men, remarkably foolish. I suppose someone told him that he was acceptable to the fairer sex only because of his title and wealth. Which, unfortunately, is at least partly true. And I do see that it makes your position difficult. However much he may say that he does not care by what means you come to accept his suit, in time he will wonder if it was his title and wealth. And that he would find hard to forgive."

"You are not helping my spirits, Aunt Elizabeth," she said reprovingly.

Her aunt looked at her in surprise. "I am not trying to lift your spirits, my dear, I am trying to help you ensnare a husband."

A laugh escaped the girl. "Yes, but for all that I love Basingstoke, I am not certain I want a husband capable of carrying through such a wager. He didn't care a fig that the girl he pursued might be hurt, indeed ruined, by such a prank."

"No, he didn't," Lady Salvage admitted sadly. "And I can no more pardon such behavior than you. But recollect what I have told you of his childhood. I cannot think that he would act as he had if he had someone by his side whom he loved. Now, come dry your tears and let us decide what dress you will wear for Lady Sefton's ball. The blue jaconet, I think, with silver edging. For whether you are to reconcile with Basingstoke or not, it is of the greatest importance that we launch you properly." When her niece started to protest, Elizabeth leveled a look at her and said repressively, "Let me tell you, my girl, that I have the liveliest dread of anyone saying that I have dared to bring out a girl who is dowdy! If you will not think of yourself, think of my reputation."

And with that, Elizabeth Mayfield sighed and began to enter into the discussion with what her aunt could not help but feel was the proper enthusiasm.

Elizabeth also, however, promised herself that she would send round a note warning Leala and Giles that Basingstoke and no doubt Trahern were back in town.

16

BASINGSTOKE wasted no time in reading the proof sheets Lady Salvage had give him. He was alternatively entertained and outraged by what Miss Mayfield had written. Like Lady Salvage, he recognized and applauded the talent which guided her pen, even as he cursed her choice of plot. Involved as he was, Basingstoke could not believe that anyone could read the book without recognizing himself as its chief villain. Nor did he fail to realize the mixture of emotions that had sped the hand that wrote these words. It was a mixture, he thought with heavy irony, that mirrored his own for reading the proof sheets left him with a strong desire to thrash Miss Mayfield for her impertinence, at the same time that it reawakened in him all the delight he had enjoyed in her company in Ravenstonedale.

The proof sheets were read in one sitting that lasted well into early evening. Then he made an ample if silently thoughtful dinner and went out to visit his clubs, where he spent a few hours at cards and conversing with friends. If a few of the high sticklers seemed inclined to snub him, particularly those who were friends of the Marquess of Wey, others were perfectly willing to share a glass of wine, a hand of cards, or the latest *on-dits*. Trahern appeared midway through the evening and they finished it out together, Basingstoke keeping his own counsel, however, about his visit to Lady Salvage.

The worst shock of the evening, for Basingstoke, was the unpalatable discovery that he had become the subject of one of the latest *on-dits*. Indeed, he had not been in his club more than half an hour before he had been informed of the Lady Sophia's betrothal to the Earl of Andover.

"Seems she found one earl as suitable as another," Grantham had added dryly. "But come, when are we to wish you happy, eh? Heard you gave the *congé* to your bird of paradise. Must mean something. Or did you mean to offer for the Lady Sophia after all and Andover stole a march on you?"

"Oh, no, I wish the pair joy of each other," Basingstoke said coolly.

Basingstoke depressed the fellow's pretensions easily enough, but he soon discovered that Grantham had been stating only what a great many others were thinking. No one, it appeared, believed his and Trahern's tale of leaving town to look at horses. One school of thought was that he had put his luck to the test in the matter of Lady Sophia and been rejected in favor of Andover. That group held that Basingstoke had gone into hiding to lick his wounds. The other school of thought was that Basingstoke had had no intention of coming up to scratch with her ladyship and had left London to pay his addresses to another, as yet unknown, young lady.

Basingstoke, of course, was not the only interested person to hear all of these conjectures. The Lady Sophia and the Earl of Andover had heard them as well. Indeed, Andover had called upon his fiancée and asked her with brutal directness, "Well, my dear? Did Basingstoke put his luck to the test? Or was your decision to marry me intended to cover up the fact that he did not?"

"You are not very flattering," Sophia retorted crossly.

Andover took her hands and kissed them. "Ah," he said with laughing eyes, "but that is why we are so particularly well-suited! Neither you nor I was made for missish games. We may be perfectly honest with each other. I shall not think the less of you, whatever your answer."

"Oh, very well," she said with a pettish shrug of her shoulders, "Basingstoke did not come up to scratch. Indeed he sent a most insulting note to me saying he would not. So of course I turned to you, my best of fellows."

This last was said with an arch look and a charming smile. Andover was not in the least offended. Instead he laughed and said, "I told you we are well-suited! I shall not complain over the result. But do you know, I have a fancy to punish Basingstoke for insulting you?''

"Will you?" Sophia asked with a cry of delight. "How?"

Andover shrugged easily. "I don't know yet," he admitted. "Have you any ideas?"

Lady Sophia all but purred as she replied, "No, but I have no doubt you will think of something perfectly horrible, and I can't wait to see what it is!"

In spite of his having sought his bed that night at a remarkably advanced hour, Basingstoke presented himself at Linley and Collier's Publishing House well before noon the next morning. Puzzled as to what the Earl of Basingstoke could possibly wish with him, Mr. Linley directed his clerk to admit his lordship immediately. After declining an offer of tea or even something stronger, Basingstoke came right to the point. "You are not," he said evenly, "going to publish Mrs. Bethfrey's latest work: *The Reckless Wager*."

"How can you possibly know about Mrs. Bethfrey's next work?" Mr. Linley asked with some astonishment. "And in any event," he added, suddenly recollecting his responsibility to the firm, "what can it possibly have to do with you?"

Basingstoke proceeded to answer the question in great depth. Mr. Linley argued valiantly but fruitlessly that the work had already reached too definite a point to be stopped. Basingstoke countered with a smile that did not reach his eyes but which did alarm Mr. Linley. He mentioned lawyers. Mr. Linley mentioned contracts. Basingstoke mentioned the Prince of Wales.

By the time the Earl of Basingstoke was bowed out of the offices of Linley and Collier's, some thirty minutes later, Mrs. Bethfrey's book was no more. And that, Mr. Linley thought bitterly, was as he had been afraid it would be. Somewhere, in the midst of threats and counterthreats and cajoling, the word "betrothal" had been breathed. It was not simply this Mrs. Bethfrey book that had been stopped, Mr. Linley thought sourly, but in all probability, all future Mrs. Bethfrey books as well. That's what came of having a lovely young lady as one's authoress. She inevitably got married. Now, why couldn't Mrs. Bethfrey have been a widow, as he and Mr. Collier had first thought? Or if she must have been a young lady of quality, why couldn't she have been butter-toothed or squinty-eyed or a drab angular sort of a thing? An antidote who might have gone on writing for the firm forever?

But it was no use. Things were as they were. With a sigh Mr. Linley turned back to his desk. At least, he thought gratefully, it would not be his task to break the news to the young lady in question that the firm would not be able to publish Mrs. Bethfrey's latest book. The earl had promised to undertake that task himself, and it was the only handsome thing he had done, Mr. Linley thought irritably. Although he had, it was important to acknowledge, promised to re-imburse the firm for expenses already undertaken for the purpose of printing *The Reckless Wager*. And it must, Mr. Linley thought acidly, be very nice to be rich enough to be able to do that.

Basingstoke was in scarcely a better mood than Mr. Linley. He did not relish the notion of telling Miss Mayfield that her book was not going to be published, but neither did he relish the notion of running shy and leaving it to poor Mr. Linley. His second stop, therefore, was at Lady Salvage's town house, where he suffered a setback.

"The ladies have gone out, m'lord," the porter informed him, "and I cannot say when they will be back."

"May I leave a message for Miss Mayfield?" Basingstoke asked, turning his most charming smile on the fellow and slipping a coin into his hand at the same time.

The porter bowed. "Certainly, m'lord. If you would care to step inside, you will find everything you need over here," he said, his fingers having unmistakably detected the feel of gold.

A few minutes later Basingstoke emerged from Lady Salvage's town house and headed for the Viscount Trahern's London abode, knowing his friend would only now be finished dressing.

* * *

Elizabeth, returning much later in the day, was surprised to be given a package and the note from Basingstoke. Lady Salvage, who was glancing through her own correspondence, which included a number of invitations hand-delivered that very afternoon, was startled to hear her niece exclaim, "No! He can't do that to me! I must see Mr. Linley at once!"

"My dear, what is it?" Lady Salvage asked in astonishment.

"See for yourself," Elizabeth said, thrusting the note at her aunt. Then, as the poor lady read it, Elizabeth paced about the room, hands clenched at her sides. "He thinks he has stopped my book? Well, he shall not! I must see Mr. Linley." She glanced at the clock on the mantelpiece. "It is too late to see him today, but tomorrow morning I must, and I shall see him. What right has Basingstoke to interfere? It is my book, not his! He must have stolen the proof sheets out of this house. I wonder he dares return them. Oh, what I shall say when I see him! Perhaps I should go see him now. He will be at home. No doubt he will be dressing to go out for dinner or something. Well, I shall make him sorry he dared to interfere with my work!"

"Elizabeth!" Lady Salvage remonstrated in alarm. "You must not! You cannot go to a gentleman's house, and certainly not alone!"

"Will you come with me, Aunt Elizabeth?" her niece asked evenly.

"Elizabeth, it will not do! Write him a note. Ask him to call on you. Anything of the sort, but do not, I beg you, be so shatterbrained as to think it will do for you—or even for you and me—to call on Basingstoke at his town house," Lady Salvage implored her niece. "Besides, you do not even know for certain that he can stop the book," she added desperately.

Elizabeth paused at that, and an arrested look came into her eyes. "To be sure," she said slowly, "I don't know it. And there's no sense upsetting myself if he can't. I shall call upon Mr. Linley tomorrow morning and see what he may have to say. I think you may be right, that it is all wishful thinking on Basingstoke's part, for surely if he had spoken to Mr. Linley and arranged to stop the book, then either Mr.

Linley or Mr. Collier must have written to tell me so.''

Much calmer, Elizabeth kissed her aunt on the cheek and went upstairs to change her dress. Lady Salvage kept her agitated reflections to herself. Let the girl have her optimism; it would, she suspected, be dashed soon enough. There were a dozen reasons why Mr. Linley or Mr. Collier might not have written, the chief of which was that they might not have had time. The other was that it would have been just like Hugh to say that he would tell Elizabeth himself, for, whatever other faults he might have, Hugh was not a coward. But since she did not want Elizabeth cutting up her peace more than need be, Lady Salvage said nothing, but went upstairs herself to change. They were due at the theater tonight, and she would not dress in a rush. No, nor keep dinner waiting either.

Meanwhile, Trahern, upon learning that Basingstoke meant to drag him to Lady Sefton's ball, was inclined to be indignant. ''Why the devil are we going there, Hugh?'' he demanded. ''It's precisely the sort of thing you are always telling me you abominate!''

Basingstoke hesitated. ''Lady Salvage tells me to go,'' he said with a queer smile.

''Why?'' Tarhern asked with the liveliest astonishment. Then, more severely, he added, ''You've been acting dashed queerly since you visited her, and I've been patient far too long. I think you'd better tell me what happened.''

Basingstoke did so, putting him in possession of the facts as succinctly as possible, including the story of the book. ''She calls it *The Reckless Wager*,'' Basingstoke concluded, ''and you may well guess what it is about.''

''A novel? Miss Mayfield? But how did she know?'' Trahern demanded, not altogether coherently, the color drained from his face.

''I collect she overheard us talking somewhere,'' Basingstoke replied coolly. ''Or so I deduce from what she has written.''

''You've managed to steal the manuscript?'' Trahern asked

hopefully. "Then destroy it, man, and we are saved."

"Unfortunately, I acquired only the proof sheets," Basingstoke replied as he flicked an imaginary speck of dust from his sleeve. "And the name of the publisher. I was able, I think, to convince the fellow that he did not wish to bring out the book, after all," he added meditatively.

Trahern shivered, quite certain the earl was correct. "What do you mean to do about it?" he asked irritably. "Or perhaps I should say, what do you think Miss Mayfield means to do? Dash it all, Hugh, if she was willing to publish a book about us, what's to stop her crying the truth to the rooftops?"

Basingstoke raised his eyebrows in surprise. "Why, I shall charm Miss Mayfield, of course, and convince her not to publicize our wager."

"That's all very well to say," Trahern retorted sharply, "but I don't recall that you parted on the best of terms at Long Meg's Circle. Nor do I find it credible that any authoress is going to be charmed by you after you've kept her work from seeing print."

"Perhaps. But I shall try my touch, nevertheless, and we shall see," Basingstoke said calmly. "And that is why we are going to Lady Sefton's ball."

"Very well," Trahern said, grumbling, "though I fail to see how you are supposed to turn Miss Mayfield up sweet at a ball."

"Care to make a wager on the matter?" Basingstoke asked with a quizzing grin.

Trahern visibly recoiled. "Oh, no! I'm dashed if I'll ever make a wager with you again, Hugh. At least, any wager that doesn't have to do with horses or something equally safe. And I hope you can charm Miss Mayfield, for the last thing I want is for anyone to discover our wager." He paused, and a thought struck him. "She's going to tell her sister, Annabelle, isn't she?" he said gloomily.

"I think it very likely she already has," Basingstoke answered grimly. "You'd best put all thought of that girl out of your head."

"You know, Hugh, being your friend can be deuced unpleasant sometimes!" Trahern told him hotly.

With a lift of his eyebrows Basingstoke retorted, "Only sometimes?"

In spite of himself, Trahern grinned and slapped his friend on the shoulder. "Oh, come on, you gudgeon! We're promised to meet Alvanley for dinner." As they went out the door, he shook his head and said, "I just hope you're wrong about Miss Mayfield telling Annabelle."

Unfortunately, Basingstoke was not mistaken, at least not entirely. Annabelle had not yet received the letter from Elizabeth, but she was about to do so the next morning.

17

THE BREAKFAST ROOM at Mayfield Manor had recently been redone in the Egyptian mode, which the second Lady Mayfield had seen somewhere and greatly admired. Some people might have felt that to have animal heads staring at one from the furniture might inhibit one's appetite, but the Mayfield family had soon grown accustomed not only to that conceit but also to the hieroglyphs painted on the walls as well. Only Elizabeth had never ceased to mourn the mauve paper and rosewood furniture that had been replaced, and her humorous comments on the current style of the room had been one of the many sore points between Beatrix and her stepdaughter.

Just now, however, Sir Edmund was not concerned with the modish nature of the room. Instead he stared at the letter Lady Mayfield had just handed him. "She wrote to you and not to me?" he demanded. "How dare she? I'm her brother!"

"She has always done just as she wished, or so you have told me more than once," Lady Mayfield reminded him calmly. "In any event, I cannot see what it is you are in such a taking about. Your sister writes that Elizabeth is safe and sound in London, having traveled there well-chaperoned by the Comfrey girl."

Sir Edmund snorted. "Well, she has taken her time writing to tell us so! And don't remind me that we already had a note from Elizabeth herself, for that is not the same thing at all. My sister ought to have written at once to ask our permission for Elizabeth to stay with her, not assumed we would agree. For all she knew, we wanted Elizabeth back here to avert a scandal. As for that Comfrey girl, don't tell me her presence makes everything all right. As if that isn't a scandal in itself, running away with Giles Pickworth! Sir John and Lady Pickworth are in quite a taking, I can tell you. How that whelp of a boy had the audacity to run off with Comfrey's daughter and think his family would accept a *fait accompli* is beyond me!''

Lady Mayfield might have said that perhaps the boy didn't care what they thought, but the look on her husband's face told her that such a suggestion would not have been propitious. Instead she made some soothing sort of sound and, after a moment, he relented a trifle and said grudgingly, ''I must admit the boy has done what he could to put a good face upon the matter. At least he didn't run north and marry her over the anvil as the Barnett boy did, bringing scandal on *his* whole family. I understand from Sir John that he has arranged to be married from his aunt and uncle's house in London and that the banns have been posted quite properly after all.''

''What about Leala Comfrey's mother?'' Beatrix asked mildly.

Again Sir Edmund snorted. ''As though she wouldn't be delighted to see their daughter so well-settled! Mind, it's her own fault things came to such a pass. If she hadn't been thinking of marrying that fellow from Kendal, her daughter might not have run away. Havey-cavey sort of fellow, even if he were quality. Which he's not. Do you know he's a damned merchant?'' Sir Edmund demanded, as though they had not all been party to this information for some time.

''Do Sir John and Lady Pickworth go to London for the wedding, Papa?'' Annabelle asked hastily.

''No,'' Sir Edmund said roundly, ''for that would be the outside of enough, encouraging every young couple who met the slightest opposition to do the same. Besides, I must suppose that by now the ceremony has already taken place.'' To his wife he added, ''Sir John has told me privately, however, that he does mean to accept the pair home again after they are wed. And, to be sure, what else can he do?''

''Particularly when Giles has threatened to go and work

in his future stepfather-in-law's shop if Sir John should cast him off,'' Beatrix added tranquilly.

Sir Edmund stared at his wife in astonishment. ''How the devil do you know that?'' he demanded.

''Cook's daughter is second parlormaid and she had just brought in the tea tray as Sir John was reading the letter from Giles. I believe Cook said he bellowed out the news before Lady Pickworth could stop him,'' she explained thoughtfully.

''Good God! Do our servants gossip about us like that?'' Sir Edmund demanded warily.

''I expect so,'' she answered with a smile. ''And that, Annabelle, is why your father and I tell you to always be discreet in front of the servants.''

There was nothing more to be said to that, particularly as the butler chose that moment to enter the room with another rack of toast. Lady Mayfield pointedly turned her attention once more to the London paper that had also arrived in the post. As usual, her eyes scanned avidly for mention of members of the *ton*. Secretly she could not help but wish that Sir Edmund would decide to pursue his wayward daughter to London and take her with him. She had had a London Season and still remembered wistfully the gaiety and endless round of parties. She had not taken, however, and it had only been after she returned to Cumbria that she had married Sir Edmund. Long after she had returned.

Lady Mayfield was lonely here. To be sure, Sir Edmund had many acquaintances and they entertained often. But Beatrix was between in age. That is to say, she was younger than the wives of Sir Edmund's friends and older than their daughters. Her face and figure still aroused jealousy in the breasts of those wives, and her age aroused disdain in the daughters. Gradually Lady Mayfield began to turn over in her mind ways she might persuade Sir Edmund to venture to London after this baby was born, if not before.

Annabelle sat and watched her father and stepmother in silence. It was a measure of the shock they felt that they had spoken so frankly in front of her. Or perhaps, she thought gloomily, they had simply forgotten she was there. Her own

long-awaited letter from Elizabeth did nothing to raise her
spirits. To have been taken in by Mr. Holden! And to hear
how poor Elizabeth was in no dire straits but rather being
brought out by Aunt Elizabeth and enjoying herself was the
outside of enough. It simply wasn't fair. If Elizabeth was
able to go to London, then so should she. Instead it looked
as if she were to find herself confined to Ravenstonedale
forever!

When the butler had left the room, Sir Edmund cleared
his throat noisily. Lady Mayfield looked at him expectantly.
"I wonder," he said offhandly, "if Elizabeth will meet Mr.
Wythe again while she is in London."

"We must hope she does not," Beatrix countered with a
shudder. "Recollect that he knows of her flight with Giles
and the Comfrey girl."

"Yes, but he told me before he left here that he had
proposed marriage to her. In fact, he thought that was the
reason she had run away," Sir Edmund pointed out mildly.

"Never say so!" Beatrix marveled.

"Well, I didn't because I thought it wouldn't come to anything, what with Elizabeth marrying Giles Pickworth and all.
But now that we know she did not, I did think that perhaps
if she encounters Mr. Wythe in London, he may renew his
suit," Sir Edmund said apologetically.

"Basingstoke," Annabelle said in a queer voice.

"What?" her father and stepmother said in unison.

"Basingstoke. Mr. Wythe is really the Earl of Basing-
stoke," Annabelle repeated in the same queer voice.
"Elizabeth finally decided to write to me, and she says Mr.
Wythe is the Earl of Basingstoke and Mr. Holden is the
Viscount Trahern."

Lady Mayfield looked as though she would faint. "My
stepdaughter to wed the Earl of Basingstoke?" she demanded
weakly.

Annabelle slowly rose to her feet and drew the letter
Elizabeth had written her out of her pocket. "I don't think
so," she said. "Elizabeth has written that she overheard Mr.
Wythe and Mr. Holden talking at an inn along the road to
London. It was all a hum. A wager, in fact. Between Mr.

Wythe and Mr. Holden. Basingstoke didn't really want to marry Elizabeth, it was all part of the wager. He just wanted her to say yes and then he meant to cry off and disappear.''

Now Sir Edmund rose to his feet, hands clenched at his sides. "My daughter? To be jilted by such a man? For a wager? How dare he? I shall write to my sister at once that our Elizabeth is to have nothing to do with that man. I won't have it.''

"But you said you hoped Mr. Wythe would renew his suit,'' Lady Mayfield said, confused.

"Never mind that,'' Sir Edmund said grimly, "that was before I knew who Mr. Wythe was. I should rather see her dead than married to Basingstoke! His father ruined my sister's life, but he shall not ruin my daughter's. If Basingstoke's father hadn't rescued that damned French jackanapes and then thrown him at my sister's head, she would never have married the fellow. Well, he won't take my daughter away from me as well. My dear, I am going to London at once!''

In London, Elizabeth was up with the sun, pacing about her room, making and discarding plans for revenge against Basingstoke as she waited until it was late enough for her to set out to call upon Messrs. Linley and Collier. She could not believe he had succeeded in suppressing the book when Lady Salvage had not, but neither could she imagine Basingstoke allowing himself to be balked. Nor, she discovered when she was ushered into Mr. Linley's office, had he been.

Nothing could have been more courteous than Mr. Linley's manner, or more affable. Neither could anything have been more implacable than his refusal to publish *The Reckless Wager*. Miss Mayfield protested. Mr. Linley spoke of lawsuits and libel. Miss Mayfield stamped her foot. Mr. Linley shook his head, called it a bad business, and invited Mrs. Bethfrey to submit another novel of whatever sort she chose, provided it did not include a portrait, in any form, of the Earl of Basingstoke. Miss Mayfield vowed that she would, though not necessarily to Linley and Collier's; her eyes sparkling with a dangerous faraway look. Mr. Linley

begged her to remember their past amicable partnership. Miss
Mayfield, very much upon her dignity, rose to her feet and
said she would think the matter over. Mr. Linley bowed her
out of the office and then mopped his brow, congratulating
himself for having brushed through the encounter tolerably
well. Miss Mayfield returned to Lady Salvage's town house
seething with anger and not in the least gratified that the Earl
of Basingstoke must have risen at an uncharacteristically early
hour to call upon her while she was out.

Nor was Basingstoke happy. He had not expected to discover that Miss Mayfield had gone out, and he had been
nonplussed as to what to do. The porter, recognizing, as he
thought, a gentleman in love, kindly advised Basingstoke to
return that afternoon, when he confidently predicted Miss
Mayfield would be found at home and Lady Salvage would
be prepared to receive visitors. Nettled, the earl retorted,
"I shall, but pray don't tell Miss Mayfield that, for I don't
want her to have any warning!"

If the porter could not engage himself to go that far, he
did, at least, restrain himself from doing more than informing
Lady Salvage. "He's quite right," she said. "Don't tell my
niece. I want Basingstoke to see her, and ten to one she'd
take a pet and refuse if she had time to think about it."

In this Lady Salvage was mistaken, but as there was no
way of knowing so for certain, it was perhaps as well that
Elizabeth was in ignorance of Basingstoke's projected visit.
And of the orders Lady Salvage gave that no one but
Baskingstoke should be admitted, for Lady Salvage wanted
no one present if the two young people should come to cuffs
over the matter of Elizabeth's book.

So it was that a few hours later Elizabeth sat in the drawing
room attempting to set stitches in a tambour frame as she
waited for afternoon callers. It was an occupation which
bored her to tears but which Lady Salvage assured her was
a necessary accomplishment for a young lady. To which
Elizabeth replied tartly that if she had not yet acquired the
skill, she was unlikely to do so now. Lady Salvage had
replied, hiding a smile, that Elizabeth need not actually
acquire the skill, merely cultivate the appearance of it. And

while she could not help but be scornful of such hypocrisy, Elizabeth had done so to please an aunt who had been more than kind to her. Basingstoke was ushered into the drawing room just as she pricked her finger, and he could not help but laugh at the sight of her vexed expression. "My poor dear Miss Mayfield, is that what you have been doing since you arrived in London?" he asked sympathetically as he came forward.

"It's all very amusing to you, I suppose," she retorted crossly.

"Well, yes," he confessed, "I do find it amusing to see you engaged in such an absurd occupation. Could you find nothing better to do?"

At this, remembering her grievance with the earl, Elizabeth rose to her feet, a martial gleam in her eyes as she said, "Why, yes, I did find something better to do. I wrote a book. A book that I understand you have persuaded the publisher not to publish, and I should like to know what right you think you had to meddle in my affairs?"

Now a certain angry sparkle was evident in Basingstoke's eyes. "Didn't you think I might have some interest in what you had written?" he demanded in reply.

"It's only a novel," Elizabeth said, avoiding his eyes.

"Merely a novel! Well, I should dearly love to know how you came about the notion of such a wager as you wrote about," Basingstoke told her as he reached out and seized her arm in a strong grip.

"Hugh!" Lady Salvage said warningly.

Basingstoke ignored her. Instead, his eyes were fixed on Elizabeth's face as he said, "Well? A guess, perhaps? A vivid imagination? A desire to hurt you or myself with such a game? Or perhaps you were listening at doors? Where? In Ravenstonedale? Was that why you ran away?"

Elizabeth could bear it no longer, and pulled her arm free. "No!" she flung up at him. "I did not run away because of you. Nor did I suspect just how fickle your pursuit of me was. I had no notion of listening at doors. But on the road to London you made a present of this knowledge to the entire inn where you stopped to breakfast. Foolish as I was, I had begun to believe that perhaps you did care, a little, for me. I meant to return to Ravenstonedale and hoped you would understand what I did to help Giles and Leala. But after what I overheard, there seemed no point.''

"So you followed me to London?" Basingstoke asked, a speculative gleam in his eye.

"No. You also made me a present of the knowledge that you meant to retire to your country estate," Elizabeth answered sweetly. "I knew I should be safe from encountering you in London.''

Basingstoke meant to answer coldly. Instead he found himself taking a step toward her. "Elizabeth!" he said, and there was anguish in his voice.

Elizabeth meant to move away, out of his reach, but she did not, and when Basingstoke took her in his arms and kissed her, oblivious of Lady Salvage's presence, Elizabeth could not protest. It was as though she were dreaming again, and did not want the dream to end. Finally Basingstoke lifted his lips from hers, and his words were a dash of cold water flung in her face as he said coaxingly, "Come, Elizabeth, admit that it's not such a tragedy not to publish your book. You may always write another, one that will not reflect badly on us both if the truth came out.''

Elizabeth fought to be free, pummeling his breast, kicking at his feet, and when he let her go she backed away, hissing in anger, "Now we have the truth of it! You only want to make sure my book is never read by the *ton* because you fear for your reputation! Nothing is beyond the line in convincing me to forget about my book, not even going so far as to pretend to make love to me. Well, you shan't stop the book, you shan't! I'll find another publisher if I must! Or pay for a private printing myself. Anything to see it in print!''

She would have run from the room then, but her aunt's quiet voice stopped her. "To be sure, Basingstoke has been something of a fool, but I see no reason to let him ensure your discomfort by having the servants see you with your hair falling free from its pins and your breath coming in ragged gasps. Wait a moment until you can repair the damage and then you may leave the room if you wish. Neither Hugh nor I will stop you, will we, Hugh?" Lady Salvage asked, her voice brooking no refusal.

With as good grace as he could muster, Basingstoke nodded. Indeed, after a moment, and before Elizabeth had regained her composure, he said seriously, "Your aunt is quite right to say that I have muddled things, Miss Mayfield. I think I have done nothing else since the day I first met you."

He paused, and Elizabeth looked up at him uncertainly. "Why?" she asked quietly. "Why did you make such a wager?"

Gently the earl possessed himself of her hand and kissed it. Only then did he answer. "Foolishness. Fear. Fear that I was the worthless knave everyone said me to be. A knave that only my rank and fortune made acceptable to women. I wanted to prove that fear wrong."

"And you were no doubt foxed," Lady Salvage offered dryly.

"Oh, undoubtedly. I was dipping rather deeply the night the wager was made," Basingstoke said over his shoulder, his eyes not leaving Miss Mayfield's bemused face. "The difficulty is," he went on, "that I gave no thought beforehand to what the young lady involved might feel. And once I did, I had no wish to pull away, for I had lost my heart to her."

Miss Mayfield was not generally a foolish creature, but her pride had been badly hurt by all that had occurred. And she could not forget the matter of her book. It was all of these things that made her take her hand from his and say, more churlishly than she intended, "Ah, but you did pull away. Decamped for London, in fact."

Basingstoke repossessed himself of her hand as he said with a chuckle that startled Elizabeth into looking up at him again, "Yes, but recollect that you had already decamped, permanently, or so it seemed. I tell you frankly, it was a heavy blow to my pride to think that you preferred Pickworth's suit to mine. Particularly as I knew you had not found it to your liking before my arrival in Ravenstonedale."

Elizabeth Mayfield meant to give the earl a setdown. A

severe setdown. But the hurt in his eyes was so real that somehow she found her treacherous lips smiling at him instead. "I am sorry for that," she said softly.

Basingstoke's grip on her hand tightened and he started to pull her toward him, when Lady Salvage's sharp voice stopped him. "None of that, now!" she warned. "Good heavens, Elizabeth, what were your mother and stepmother about not to teach you that a lady does not allow a gentleman to embrace her in such a way unless she is betrothed to him?"

Elizabeth colored a fiery red and moved away from the earl as she said with some constraint, "They did tell me so."

"Well, see that you don't forget yourself again," she said reprovingly. Lady Salvage paused and cast a speculative glance at Basingstoke, who stood with wooden countenance staring at her niece. "As for you, Hugh," she said sternly, "you undoubtedly ought to know better."

"I do," he replied, mortification evident in his voice.

"Well, don't let it happen again," Lady Salvage told the pair of them. Then, relenting a trifle, she said, "Do you still mean to attend Lady Sefton's ball, Hugh?"

"Of course," he said, forcing himself to answer lightly. "I hope, Miss Mayfield, that you will grant me a dance."

Mischievously Elizabeth looked at him then and said, "Aunt Elizabeth has told me it will add greatly to my credit to be seen dancing with you, but I cannot see why, since you are considered such a hardened rake."

Instead of being offended, Basingstoke turned laughing eyes on the girl. "Ah, but I am also considered to be a connoisseur of females, and to be seen to have drawn my interest is to be certified either a beauty or an original," he said without rancor. "Indeed, to be seen to have held my attention is to gain the approval of all the malicious persons in London who cannot wait to see me leg-shackled."

There was an edge to Basingstoke's voice, and Elizabeth looked at him with something akin to sympathy in her eyes as she said, "I quite see why you have been so anxious to avoid the parson's trap. It cannot be pleasant to know bets are being laid at White's as to whether you will toss someone the handkerchief this month or next."

Basingstoke frowned. "Now, what do you know of bets laid at White's?" he demanded severely.

"Only what I have heard," Elizabeth replied serenely. "You were to have offered for the Marquess of Wey's daughter and did not. That overset your nearest friends, who had all placed bets upon the matter."

"You are remarkably well-informed," Basingstoke said suspiciously.

"Giles told me. He is here in London, as well."

"Yes, and married to Leala Comfrey, I know. You told me the other day, remember?" Basingstoke replied grimly. "And I should dearly like to know what the devil made you take part in such an improper start! Surely you must have known it might ruin the pair of them?"

"That is my affair and you cannot claim to have the least right to interfere with that!" Elizabeth told him sharply.

Basingstoke looked as though he meant to come to cuffs with her again, and Lady Salvage intervened, saying tartly, "I wish the pair of you will tell me why you both seem determined to become the subject of servants' gossip! For if you keep yelling at each other I can assure you that you will. Now, Hugh, I think it time you left. We shall see you at the ball tonight. Elizabeth, see if you can't contrive to repair the damage to your hair, for I will not have you looking as if you've gone backward through a briar bush."

"Yes, Aunt Elizabeth," her niece said promptly.

"Yes, Aunt Elizabeth," Basingstoke echoed outrageously. Then, as he walked toward the doorway where Elizabeth stood, he told her under his breath, "I shall most assuredly call upon you again tomorrow, my dear!"

Elizabeth could not decide if it was a promise or a threat.

18

IN SPITE of the Season being all but at an end, no one would have had the least hesitation in describing Lady Sefton's ball as a shocking squeeze. Even Giles and Leala were there. How Captain Pickworth, or more likely his lady, managed to arrange an invitation for Giles and his new bride, neither of them dared to ask, but an invitation had been procured. And they accepted it gratefully, knowing that Leala's acceptance, here in London, would make matters immeasurably easier with Sir John and Lady Pickworth. For the ball, Leala wore a gown of pink muslin with white under-skirt that set off her coloring admirably. Giles was dressed in a newly purchased set of evening clothes and his aunt pronounced the pair of them complete to a shade.

Leala was understandably nervous, but the first hurdle was passed easily enough when Lady Sefton greeted the Pickworth party and they were able to continue on into the salon filled with flowers. Giles patted his young bride's hand and said, "There, my love, I told you there was nothing to fear."

Leala started to agree, but stopped as she spied someone. "Perhaps," she said, "but Mr. Wythe—that is, the Earl of Basingstoke—is here."

Giles looked in the direction of his wife's gaze and spied Basingstoke standing in a small circle of men, all of whom appeared to be eyeing and commenting upon the young ladies present. "According to Lady Salvage, we may count on his discretion," Giles said hopefully.

"Count upon whose discretion?" his aunt asked, trying to discover whom he was staring at.

"The Earl of Basingstoke. He is standing over there," Giles explained gravely.

"The Earl of Basingstoke?" his aunt echoed in astonishment. "Does he know your story? I devoutly pray you are mistaken, for the last thing he is known for is either kindness or discretion."

Leala moaned unhappily and Pickworth's aunt turned her attention to the girl. "I advise you most strongly to smile and appear as if nothing is amiss, my dear. Then if Basingstoke spreads the tale of your elopement, one may look the inquirer in the eye and say it is absurd. You must do so, for otherwise you are most certainly ruined."

Not unreasonably, the force of this argument had a powerful effect on Leala, and she smiled brightly then. Giles also smiled and accepted the congratulations of his aunt and uncle's acquaintances, all the while keeping an uneasy eye on Basingstoke. He was concerned, not simply for himself and Leala, but for Elizabeth as well.

The earl, in turn, noted the appearance of the Pickworth party. He had no more desire than they did to have the story of their acquaintance bruited about Lady Sefton's ballroom. He was far more concerned with the whereabouts of Miss Mayfield and Lady Salvage, for he had not yet seen them come in. Nor did he care to be too obvious in his search for her. Indeed, in a rare display of common sense, he spent some time dancing, for he had realized that to dance only with Elizabeth or only to begin to dance when he danced with her would attract the sort of attention neither he nor she could like. It was possible, therefore, that he might have missed the entrance of Lady Salvage and Miss Mayfield. Nevertheless, he was uneasy.

If Basingstoke was uneasy, Elizabeth Mayfield was distracted. She looked charming in a confection of pale blue that served as a perfect foil to her aunt's darker blue gown. And there was nothing to cavil at in her manner, for Elizabeth answered politely all the conversation directed to her, and no one would have guessed her distress. Nevertheless, as she accepted an invitation to dance from some gentlemen she had met a few days earlier, Elizabeth's mind was still upon *The Reckless Wager* and how she might manage to get it published without Basingstoke's discovering what she was about. This time she would take care not to tell Aunt Elizabeth until the volumes were actually in hand. Lord Basingstoke would discover she was not the sort of meek, helpless creature who would accept such high-handed treatment from him.

Finally Basingstoke spied Miss Mayfield. He watched her dance with mixed emotions. The sight of her took his breath away and yet he was too shrewd to immediately approach her. There would be much made of him dancing with her later, but if he sought her out the moment she arrived, it would be the outside of enough. Then there would be no hope of shielding her from malicious tongues, whatever care he took to dance with other young ladies as well. So Basingstoke watched as Elizabeth danced, and when he judged that enough time had passed, he made his way to Lady Salvage, where he bowed low and greeted her amiably. "How delightful to see you out and about again."

She, for her part, smiled back equally amiably. "Yes, I have a niece I have undertaken to introduce to the *ton*. I think you will find her quite delightful, Hugh," she said, as though he had never met her. "Here she is now. Elizabeth, I would like to make known to you the Earl of Basingstoke. He has desired to make your acquaintance."

Elizabeth hesitated. She knew that she ought to curtsy and pretend, as he was doing, that they were virtual strangers. She was to dance with Basingstoke and let the world see him charmed by her, for that would ensure her success. But she could not. The sense of grievance she felt toward the earl was still too strong. Her best effort could not prevent her from coloring up as she said, "M'lord."

Interested eyes noted all of this. The Lady Sophia was there, as well as the Earl of Andover, and while neither was close enough to know what was being said, both noted the air of constraint between Basingstoke and the unknown chit he was talking to.

Basingstoke felt his own temper rising. Stiffly he said, "I am charmed, Miss Mayfield." Then, making an effort, he asked, "May I have this dance?"

Elizabeth was about to reluctantly place her hand in his when the orchestra began to play a waltz. She pulled back sharply as she said, "I must not! I have not been given permission."

"By the patronesses of Almack's?" Basingstoke hazarded with a frown.

"Yes." When he did not draw back the hand he held out to her, Elizabeth looked up at him and said impatiently, "I daresay it seems absurd to you, but for someone in my position, it is no small thing to be banned from there."

For a moment, matters hung in the balance; then Basingstoke relented. "You are right, I hadn't thought. Shall I sit with you instead?"

If the earl's abrupt compliance surprised Elizabeth, it astounded almost everyone else party to the scene. Lady Salvage turned an appraising eye on Basingstoke and said dryly, "Very kind of you to have such consideration for my niece's reputation."

In spite of himself, Basingstoke laughed. "Yes, it was, wasn't it?"

That did it. Helpless to control her tongue, Elizabeth retorted, "Oh, I make no doubt you are generous with gestures that cost you nothing."

"Elizabeth!" Lady Salvage remonstrated in a shocked voice that she kept as quiet as she was able.

"It is of no consequence, ma'am," Basingstoke told Lady Salvage, a muscle quivering in his cheek. "Miss Mayfield's want of conduct does not distress me in the least."

Elizabeth gasped. "As though it is not all your own fault!" she said indignantly.

But this was too much for Lady Salvage. "Enough! It is evident that you have taken each other in dislike, but I will not listen to you quarrel in such a public place."

Stricken, the pair both went pale, for they had forgotten where they were. "I beg pardon, Lady Salvage," Basingstoke said at once.

"Yes, well, take yourself off," she retorted. "I won't have you upsetting my niece." Then, unbending a trifle, she added, "You may come to call tomorrow."

He did so while Elizabeth watched, stiff with mortification.

It was too much to hope that their quarrel would go unnoticed. And indeed it did not. But by dint of Basingstoke's ability to depress pretensions by the lift of an eyebrow and Lady Salvage's ability to shrug and laugh just so before confiding that her niece was the most ingenuous of creatures and had spoken without thinking, the matter was passed off tolerably well. Basingstoke did not offer to take Elizabeth in to dinner or ask her to stand up for another dance later in the evening. If Elizabeth was disappointed that the earl paid far more attention to a number of other young ladies than he did to her, she did not allow it to show. Instead, she displayed a flattering degree of attention toward the gentlemen who partnered her.

When they returned home that evening, Lady Salvage pronounced herself very well pleased with Basingstoke's discretion.

"Oh, did you think that was what it was?" Elizabeth asked anxiously.

The older woman eyed the younger one sharply. "I grant you, I was surprised to discover such a virtue in Hugh, but yes, I am quite certain it was the reason for his behavior. That or pique. What on earth possessed you to behave toward him in such an appalling manner?"

"I'm sorry," Elizabeth said remorsefully. "But when he said he knew his discretion was very kind, there was no bearing it."

"Well, it was kind," her aunt told her tartly. "And how you thought he would be so foolish as to put his luck to the test again with all those eyes on the both of you is beyond me. Basingstoke may be a scapegrace, but no one has ever been able to accuse him of having more hair than wit. Depend upon it, he wished to spare you the unpleasantness of either having people say you were a hoyden with no manners or, if you did stand up with him, that he was amusing himself with you and that you were foolish enough to be taken in."

"I suppose they would say that," Elizabeth said thoughtfully, tracing an intricate pattern on the back of a chair with one finger.

"Yes, they would," her aunt answered cheerfully. "Think, child! What else would one think to see a man known as a heartless rake who has received one setdown from a girl, pay marked attention to her again in the same evening?"

Slowly Elizabeth sat down. "If she snubbed him, they would say there must be something shocking behind it. If she did not, they would say he was piqued and wished to prove no girl could stand against him. It would cause a great deal of talk either way."

"Precisely," her aunt said with satisfaction.

"Then you think . . ."

Elizabeth broke off in confusion and her aunt eyed her shrewdly. "I think it is late and time for both of us to be abed. I also think that tomorrow or the next day Hugh will be on our doorstep and wanting to see you again."

It was not, perhaps, a perfect answer, but it was one that reassured the girl a great deal. Soon she was asleep, dreaming of the Earl of Basingstoke.

He didn't come, however, the next day or even the day after that. Nor did he send flowers or a note or any trinket such as other of Elizabeth's admirers had delivered the morning after the ball. So much did his silence distress Elizabeth that she was hard put not to let it show. She could not help remembering, after all, his grimly spoken promise to her before he left the house that he would assuredly see her the day after the ball.

Lady Salvage was also uneasy. Promise or not, she knew the look Basingstoke had had on his face well enough to be certain that he would come to call as soon as possible. His absence, therefore, puzzled and disturbed her almost as much as it did her niece.

As for Basingstoke, he had meant to keep his promise. Indeed, had he not been so lost in his attempt to resolve the problem of Miss Mayfield's grievance against him, he would assuredly have noticed that the hack that took him up lacked a lantern and that the driver was unusually taciturn. Trahern did notice and begged Basingstoke not to take it, but rather to come with him, in another hack, to a new gaming hell he had just heard about.

Basingstoke smiled his charming smile and shook his head. "No, you go and tell me tomorrow how it was. I've some matters to sort out tonight, and mean to return home."

"Well, at least choose a less-ramshackle hack than this one," Trahern protested.

The earl shrugged. "I don't care. What need have I of a lantern? And if the fellow is short of words, all the better. Come, don't be such a nodcock! I shall be fine."

With misgivings Trahern watched the hack drive away. Then, with a shake of his head, he left in his own hired carriage.

Basingstoke settled back on the seat, his chin almost against his chest. He fully intended to ask Miss Mayfield to marry him, but first there were a few steps he ought to take to recoup his reputation. While he might not care what people thought of him, it was another matter for his bride. He wished to be quite certain she would be accepted without reserve. And to that end, he thought grimly, he must both retrieve his own reputation and make certain that no one ever discovered Miss Mayfield's part in the Pickworths' marriage.

So lost in his own thoughts was the earl that he did not even notice the route the driver took until the hack drew to a stop. Then, looking out, Basingstoke was startled to see Hampstead Heath rather than the door of his own town house before him. "What the devil?" he exclaimed softly, letting his eyes droop disarmingly in a way that belied the alertness of his body.

In the next moment the door was wrenched open and a hand closed on his arm, pulling the earl out of the carriage. He let himself reach the ground, then threw a punch, feeling his hand connect with his assailant's nose. In the next moment a sack dropped over Basingstoke's head. He swung out in another direction and his hand connected with something else. But before he could do anything more, something struck the back of his head and knocked him unconscious.

"That'll teach you to thinks before you gets up to your bloody tricks again!" a harsh voice said.

Then there was a bustle of movement as the earl was dragged off to the side of the road and all traces of the struggle were covered up as well as possible. With curt orders, the driver of the hack was dispatched back to London with a warning not to speak of what he had seen. The other men disappeared as well, across the field, dragging the unconscious earl with them. At the first copse of trees, however, they halted and loaded his inert body onto a wagon waiting there. Then it was a jolting ride across the heath to another carriage and a sardonic gentleman who watched the body being transferred once again with patent satisfaction. Beside him a lady laughed, and her eyes sparkled dangerously. "Pleased?" the gentleman asked her idly.

"Tolerably, Andover," she retorted. "Though I wish I might see his face when he wakes and discovers his condition."

The gentleman chuckled. "Bloodthirsty, aren't you, Sophia? Well, you shall not. You must be content with knowing he is my prisoner and with the tales I tell you of what he says."

She pouted prettily, and the gentleman took her gloved hand and kissed it. "Come, my pet," he said coaxingly. "Surely you must know that you could not pass anywhere unnoticed, and we do not wish to draw attention to his hiding place."

"No, I suppose not," she reluctantly agreed as she watched the men finish loading Basingstoke's body into the carriage.

When the job was done, the gentleman told his men, "You know where to take him. Keep him hidden and quiet. I shall come by in the morning to speak with him." He paused and smiled in a way that Basingstoke would have recognized very well as he said, "I have a great deal to say to him, and I fancy that, for once, his lordship will listen."

"Ain't you coming with us?" one of the men asked.

"Of course not!" the other retorted sharply. "His nibs has got to show up back at some party nor other. You don't want nobody suspecting him nor us."

"Quite right, Reems," the gentleman agreed, not altogether pleased by this display of acumen. Too smart a tool might look for ways to better his lot by using the knowledge he possessed and had puzzled out. Reems would have to be dealt with, if that occurred. But meanwhile he was necessary. None of this, however, showed on the face of the gentleman as he said, "Just carry out your part and I shall do mine."

And with that he and the lady walked back to where their own carriage was hidden in the trees. A few moments sufficed for the coachman to turn it about and head back to Lady Sefton's ball, to, as Reems had so aptly put it, prevent suspicion from falling on their heads once Basingstoke's disappearance was noticed. Not that either greatly feared suspicion. For that Basingstoke had himself to thank. After his sudden disappearance weeks earlier, no one would be surprised to see it happen again. In the most cheerful of moods, the Earl of Andover smiled as he and his lady went back to Lady Sefton's ball.

19

BASINGSTOKE came awake slowly, the throbbing pain in his head outweighing the pain of his bound wrists and ankles, though that was by no means negligible. His first thought was that he must have been imbibing too freely of remarkably poor-quality brandy. His second thought was that while doing so had caused his head to ache and swim just like this in the past, it had never caused him to forget what he had been about. Or to make him unable to use his hands or feet. And it was then that the pain of his bound ankles and wrists made itself felt. "What the devil?" he murmured to himself, trying to make his eyes focus clearly in the dark.

Unfortunately, or perhaps fortunately since his captors had been given orders to keep him quiet, no one was nearby to answer the earl. Even now it took several moments before the true nature of his situation penetrated Basingstoke's usually sharp mind. And then his eyes narrowed in an ugly way as he tried, with grim care, the tightness of his bonds. They would not give an inch. Nor could he discover, in the darkness around him, anything to help cut or saw through the ropes.

With a great effort Basingstoke managed to get into a sitting position and survey the room from a somewhat better vantage point as his eyes tried to accustom themselves to the dark. The room was damp and evidently without windows, for no source of light penetrated. Unless, of course, it was still night, Basingstoke acknowledged. But even then there ought to have been a hint of something where there were windows. More than that Basingstoke was unable to determine. Whether the room was large or small, empty or full of one thing or another, was something he could not tell without the advantage of a candle or the freedom to move about.

Basingstoke's head throbbed, but he thrust the knowledge of the pain aside as he tried to figure a way out of his predicament. After several moments he had to allow that the situation did not seem promising. His first thought was that he had been set upon by common highwaymen who had robbed him and then kidnapped him in hopes of holding him for ransom. After all, the Earl of Basingstoke was known to be quite warm in the pocket. But a very brief reflection pointed out the folly of this notion. The purse of sovereigns he always carried with him was pressed uncomfortably against him and it was evident that whoever had brought him here had not robbed him of that, nor of his gold signet ring nor of the diamond pin set into his cravat. No, whatever the motive, it had not been robbery. What, then? Ransom? Too risky, by half, to be likely. Revenge? Now, that rang more true. Basingstoke tried to decide who among his acquaintances might have reason to play such a trick on him. To his chagrin, he realized that the list was distressingly long. It would no doubt have pleased Miss Mayfield to know that Basingstoke even briefly considered the possibility that, in light of her highly inventive novel, she somehow had had a hand in the arranging of this imprisonment. But although he credited her with sufficient imagination and resourcefulness, Basingstoke could not believe she would have sufficient reason to do so. That left the aforementioned long list of possibilities headed by the Duke of Devon and the Marquess of Wey, Sophia, and the Earl of Andover.

Grimly Basingstoke wondered what form of revenge he faced. He also found himself wondering what Miss Mayfield would think when he failed to keep his promise to wait upon her in the morning. Not that it signified. Just let him get free and he was certain he could straighten out matters with her. He had read her book with a jaundiced eye, recognizing the portrait of himself to be one written in anger. An anger he could not deny was justified. And yet, through the anger had been evident a creeping affection and finally love, even though the villain (himself!) had ended upon the gallows. The devil was that she had described the fellow's appearance in such a way that no one could fail to recognize in him the Earl of Basingstoke. Thank God he had managed to suppress the dratted thing. It was a mistake to think about Miss Mayfield, however, for it softened the earl's own angry edge and so he almost missed the sound of his captor approaching the other side of the door.

Hastily Basingstoke threw himself back down on the floor in what he hoped was a semblance of the position he had been in before. He had no wish for his jailer to realize he had yet regained consciousness. The weaker they judged him to be, the less careful they might become.

As it was, the man, or rather the two men, who came into the room moved with the greatest caution. One stood by the door, holding a lantern high so that the other one could see. And he stopped a foot or more away from the earl. "And howsomever might yer lordship be feeling?" he demanded sarcastically.

Basingstoke lay motionless, not answering. After a moment, in a louder voice the fellow said, "Come on, quit yer shamming, yer lordship. We know yer awake."

Still Basingstoke did not move. The other man, the one by the door, said in an anxious voice, "Do you think he might be done for? We did hit him pretty hard."

"Him?" the first man said scornfully. "Not likely. Unaccountably hard heads, these lords be. Couldn't kill 'em if you was wanting to."

"Happens you might be right," the man by the door said doubtfully. "I wouldn't want to be here if you was wrong."

For a long, thoughtful moment, the closer man was silent. Finally, carefully, he crept closer, thrusting the earl with his boot. Basingstoke allowed himself to be rolled over, keeping his body as limp as possible, though it was almost more than he could manage when the fellow's boot connected again with his sore ribs. "Musta done him more hurt than we thought," the man said with a frown.

"Is he dead?" the man by the door asked worriedly.

"No. Happens he's still breathing," the closer man answered after bending down to check. "Just out cold still. Must be weaker than he looked."

"Oh, aye, terrible weak," the man by the door agreed sarcastically. "That's why I've a lump the size of a rock coming up on my head and why he was able to darken your daylights."

The first man didn't at once answer. Finally he said sharply, "You'd best fetch me a basin of cold water to throw over his lordship. We've got to bring him around."

"Why?" the man by the door demanded. "Let's wait until his nibs arrives, then bring him around. If he ain't awake, he can't cause us no trouble."

"Oh, aye, and what if we can't bring him around, then? What are we going to say? Do you mean to tell his lordship that we didn't try sooner for fear of *trouble*?" the closer fellow retorted incredulously. "I wouldn't want to do it, not by a long chalk, I wouldn't!"

The man by the door shivered but remained adamant. "Well, what are we going to say if we can't bring him around now?" he demanded.

"It'll at least give us time to think on that, won't it?" the first man replied. "Now, go and fetch me that water!"

"What about the lantern?" the man by the door asked reasonably.

"Oh, give it here. I'll hold the bloody thing."

Basingstoke waited, listening to the retreating footsteps of the one man and the angry mutterings of the other. Now was his chance, if he could have taken it, to overpower the man left behind. But trussed up as he was, it was impossible. Slowly he forced himself to act as though he were just coming out of a daze, timing matters so that he only just preceded the other's return, having no desire to have a basin of cold water thrown over him. At his first groan, the man nearby was down on his knee beside the earl, the lantern set well out of reach. "Here, yer lordship, don't try to struggle now. We've got you tied up right and tight. But no need to fear you'll be murdered, either. We've orders to keep you alive."

Basingstoke pretended he had heard nothing, and groaned

again, still not opening his eyes. Only when the second man appeared and said, "Here's the basin of water. Shall I throw it on him?" did the earl open his eyes and whisper, "Where am I?"

This simple question was greeted with great happiness by his captors. "Here, your lordship, don't try to sit up yet. As I was trying to tell you, but I misdoubt you was awake enough to hear me, you're in our power, but we've no desire to murder you. No, we're just to keep you right and tight until his nibs can get here."

"His . . . his nibs?" Basingstoke echoed with just the right note of confusion.

"Now, look, you've addled his wits," the second man said in disgust.

"I?" the first demanded. "You're the one struck him with the board."

"What else was I to do when it looked as if he was going to get away?" the other demanded indignantly.

Basingstoke, while finding this account of his abduction extremely gratifying, decided it was time to put an end to the argument. "Where . . . where am I?" he asked again in the same failing voice as before.

"You're where you ought to be," the man beside him said decisively. "And not another word on that head you'll get from us."

"How . . . how long?" Basingstoke managed to ask weakly.

"How long you been here or how long you'll stay?" the other asked critically.

"Both."

"A couple of hours you've been out. It's not daylight yet. As to how long you'll be here, I reckon that's something you'd best ask his nibs," was the reply.

"His nibs?" Basingstoke echoed.

"You'll see him when he comes," the closer man said hastily when he saw that his partner might say something more. "And any more questions you'll have to address to him. We'll be going now. We just wanted to be sure you was all right."

"No, I've not shot my bolt yet," Basingstoke managed
to answer with a wry smile.

"That's the spirit," the man next to him said approvingly.
"And if you was reasonable, there's no reason you should
be done for. No reason at all."

Then he got to his feet with a curt toss of his head at the
other man. They left the room together, taking the lantern
with them and locking the door once they were on the other
side.

20

MISS MAYFIELD stared out the window at the rain. She was attired in a modish dress of green figured muslin that exactly matched the ribbon threaded through her curls. Had Lady Mayfield been privileged to see her stepdaughter, Elizabeth would have aroused a jealous rage in that poor lady's breast. But not even that thought, suggested by Giles Pickworth as he surveyed her, could bring a smile to Elizabeth's face. Instead she turned to him with a woebegone expression and said, "Why hasn't Basingstoke come?"

Giles, who had already been favored with a description of both of Elizabeth's encounters with the earl here in London, could only shrug helplessly and say, "Lord, Elizabeth, I don't know! Of course I don't move in quite the same circles, but I have heard word that he has gone out of London. He is said to have missed more than one appointment with friends." Giles paused, then added gently, "I collect it is something quite to be expected with his lordship."

"What? That he goes off on wild fits and starts?" Elizabeth cried out in protest.

"He has that reputation," Lady Salvage said quietly from the corner of the drawing room where she had been talking with Leala.

"No, I cannot believe it. Not when he promised to call," Miss Mayfield persisted.

"He was to have called on the Marquess of Wey concerning his daughter, and came, instead, to Ravenstonedale to cool his heels for a few weeks," Giles pointed out bravely. "And don't tell me that the case is quite different, for I shouldn't believe you." He paused and then in a different tone altogether said, "Elizabeth, you must give over this pining for Basingstoke. Do you mean to go into a decline over a fellow so false or so wild that he can never be depended upon?"

"A decline?" That drew a smile from her. "No, he would think very poorly of me if I were to do so. Not for Mr. Wythe the frail damsels with the die-away airs. He would quite expect the woman he loved to do something about it."

Giles eyed Elizabeth with distinct misgivings. He knew that smile of old, and it always boded ill for any friend foolish enough to be drawn into her schemes. "What do you mean to do?" he asked warily. "You cannot go jauntering about the countryside looking for Basingstoke."

"Not jauntering about," she retorted instantly. "I should go with definite purpose. After all, he might be at his estate."

"You cannot go there," Giles told her firmly. "Not by yourself."

"Of course not by myself," Elizabeth said, looking up at him, faintly surprised. "That would be improper."

"Yes, but—"

Pickworth got no further, for the door opened and a footman announced the Viscount Trahern. Lady Salvage regarded him with some interest, while her niece regarded him with some anxiety and young Pickworth said in disgust, "Hello, Mr. Holden. Or, rather, Lord Trahern."

Trahern bowed to the ladies first, and greeted them politely. Afterward he turned to Pickworth. With an insulting carelessness he studied the boy through his quizzing glass, then let it fall. His voice was kind, however, as he replied, "Hugh would say I ought to give you a setdown, but I cannot help feeling that in your shoes I should be as angry as you are. I do beg, however, you will refrain from offering to draw my cork or darken my daylights."

"Then I wish you will cease trying to provoke him," Lady Salvage said tartly. "And come to the point. Why are you here?" She saw him glance toward her niece and added, "Don't try to gammon us into thinking you came to fix your interest with Elizabeth. You were at the ball a few nights ago and made no attempt to stand up with her for even one dance.''

"Perhaps he came to ask about Annabelle, Aunt Elizabeth,'' her niece suggested gently.

Trahern flushed. "Well, no,'' he said. Then, as three pairs of eyes looked at him in patent disapproval, he added hastily, "That is to say, of course I should like word of your sister, Miss Mayfield, but the matter upon which I came concerns Basingstoke.''

"I collect Hugh chose not to come himself and sent you in his stead,'' Lady Salvage said icily. "You may tell him that such ramshackle manners will not do. If he has something he wishes Elizabeth to know, Basingstoke must tell her himself. My niece has far too much pride to listen to anything you or anyone else may have to say on his behalf.''

"Well, no, that's not it either,'' Trahern said unhappily. Finally he said grimly, "In fact, the problem is Basingstoke himself. He's disappeared!''

The reaction was not in the least what Trahern expected. Pickworth gave a crack of laughter and said gleefully, "Left you in the lurch, has he?''

Lady Salvage merely regarded Trahern a moment, then said dryly, "Hugh appears to be making quite a habit of such behavior. When you see Basingstoke, you may tell him that I do not approve.''

Only Miss Mayfield seemed to comprehend what Trahern was trying to tell them. "When did you last see him?'' she asked quietly but urgently.

"The night of Lady Sefton's ball,'' Trahern told her gratefully. "I left him planning to return home. To sort some matters out, he said. Even refused to come with me to a new gaming club I'd offered to take him to.''

"Oh, a high treat, in fact,'' Lady Salvage said sarcastically.

Pickworth, however, was more impressed. "Basingstoke did not come?'' he said. "What then?''

Trahern shrugged. "I don't know. I saw him off in a hack and went on my way. If it weren't for his valet and his secretary both asking me if *I* knew where he'd gone, I'd think the same as you, that he'd just decided to shy away from everyone for a while.''

''But I don't understand. He didn't bring his valet to Ravenstonedale either,'' Elizabeth said slowly, ''for it was the talk of the servants at the house. My father's valet was particularly appalled that neither of you brought your gentlemen.''

''Yes, well, there's nothing new in that,'' Trahern said with a shrug. ''Hugh is forever haring off without servants. But he's never yet done so without telling them what to do in his absence. Or that he would be gone.''

''Maybe he has and they've orders not to tell anyone, including you,'' Lady Salvage said with some satisfaction.

''I've thought of that,'' Trahern said swiftly. ''But I spoke with Hugh's man myself, and I'll swear he's fretting over this. And his secretary would know better than to ask me if I knew where Hugh was if he did. Neither of them can understand why Hugh didn't tell them he would be gone. They say he never even came home that night.''

''Ten to one it's all a hum,'' Pickworth said impatiently. ''Tomorrow or next week you'll find he's back with some story to tell.''

''I wish that were so, but I fear not,'' Trahern told him grimly.

Lady Salvage eyed the viscount thoughtfully. ''I agree with young Pickworth,'' she said, ''but it is evident that you do not. What do you mean to do? And why come to call here? How do you imagine we can help?''

''I thought perhaps I was wrong,'' Trahern answered, looking away from both of them and toward Elizabeth. ''I thought perhaps Miss Mayfield had heard from Hugh.''

She shook her head. ''No, I have not. Indeed, I was telling Giles, just before you came, that I was worried and thought perhaps to visit his estate to see if he had gone there.''

Trahern looked at her. ''His man has already sent word to see if he had. He had not.''

''What, then, do you suspect?'' Elizabeth asked quickly.

"If I knew, I should be less concerned," Trahern told her frankly.

"Go to the Bow Street Runners?" Lady Salvage hazarded.

Trahern shook his head. "Hugh is of age, and without proof that something untoward has occurred, they will not act."

To everyone's surprise, it was Leala who spoke next. Her voice was quiet and thoughtful as she asked, "Lord Basingstoke was to have offered for the Marquess of Wey's daughter, wasn't he?"

"Yes," Lady Salvage said baldly. "The girl made no secret of her desire to marry Hugh. But if you're thinking Hugh had a *tendre* for Lady Sophia and is off somewhere nursing a broken heart, you're out," she said roundly. "I'd wager a fortune that Hugh meant to offer for her because he thought her as wild as himself and that therefore neither would chide the other for amorous activities outside the marriage."

Elizabeth shivered. "It sounds like a dreadful prospect," she said.

"Yes, and so I should have told Hugh had he deigned to ask my advice," her aunt retorted tartly. "But he did not. We may only thank heaven he changed his mind in time."

Trahern, who had been ignoring this diatribe, spoke to Leala. "Why did you ask about Lady Sophia?" he asked her kindly.

Leala blushed becomingly as she said in her quiet voice, "I can't help remembering that Lord Basingstoke left Lady Sefton's ball soon after Elizabeth and Lady Salvage, and I noticed that the Marquess of Wey's daughter and her fiancé, the Earl of Andover, left as soon as he did. Indeed, they appeared to have been watching him." As three pairs of eyes stared at her, Leala went on, "I know it sounds absurd, and even more so when I tell you that I tore the flounce of my skirt and I had just gone into one of the anterooms to repair the damage when I heard two people talking. They said they would need to make haste if they were to make a certain rendezvous in time, and they addressed each other as Sophia and Andover."

For a moment there was shocked silence and then Giles said testily, "Yes, well, I daresay ten or twenty people left the ball directly after Basingstoke. And they may have had a rendezvous anywhere, for I collect a number of people went on from Lady Sefton's ball to some other entertainment."

"Yes, but they didn't," Leala replied slowly. "For I saw Andover and Lady Sophia later, back at Lady Sefton's ball. And the hem of her dress was slightly muddy."

"No doubt she went for a walk in the gardens with Andover," Giles retorted impatiently. "A great many other couples did so, not all of them betrothed, either. Tell her that she's being foolish, Trahern."

The viscount hesitated. "I wish I could," he said uneasily. "Unfortunately, I have been thinking that if anyone wished to do Hugh harm, it would be Andover. They have been rivals for some time, and Andover is rumored to have done some very horrible things. I cannot help but own, Mrs. Pickworth, that what you say makes me extremely uneasy."

"What should we do?" Elizabeth asked. "Go to the Bow Street Runners with this?"

Lady Salvage snorted. "I think you would find they believed you to be a fanciful idiot, Elizabeth," she said bluntly. "And even if they did believe you, the man has a powerful protector in the Prince of Wales, for whom he is said to have performed various favors, none to his credit, has he not, Trahern?" The viscount nodded. Lady Salvage paused for several moments while the younger Elizabeth watched her, fists clenched tightly together in her lap. At last she said meditatively, "I do recollect a rumor that Andover had inherited a small estate from an elderly aunt and that it lay south of London. Near Dorking, in fact. Not so far as to be impossible for Andover to travel down to visit his prisoner, and yet still a wooded, sufficiently isolated region."

Trahern nodded again. "You're right. He did."

"But whom could he trust to carry out his orders? If, that is, you mean for me to believe he kidnapped Basingstoke and had him taken there," Giles said sensibly. "Surely his aunt's servants would not do so."

Trahern cocked his head thoughtfully. "It was said at the time, when Andover inherited the property, that he turned off most of the servants without a character and brought in the most appalling ruffians in their place. It was also said that he intended to use the place for his more shocking revels."

"He sounds a monster!" Elizabeth exclaimed. "I wonder the Marquess of Wey allowed his daughter's betrothal to the man."

Her aunt grimaced. "I should doubt he had a great deal of choice in the matter. The girl is dreadfully spoiled and Andover, when he chooses, has extraordinary charm and address. I make no doubt the chit threatened to run away if her father refused the match. Hugh is well out of her pocket."

"Perhaps she could tell us where Basingstoke might be," Elizabeth suggested hopefully. "If Lady Sophia once had a *tendre* for him, she might wish to help."

Trahern stifled a laugh. Lady Salvage made a derisive sound. "Her! Lady Sophia would be more likely to have abducted him herself, for revenge. She hasn't any heart."

"Oh." Elizabeth was silent a moment; then she straightened her shoulders as she said, "Then I suppose we must do something ourselves."

Pickworth gave a short, sharp laugh. "Beware, Trahern! If we listen to Elizabeth, we shall shortly find ourselves in the suds. She's never yet had a scheme that didn't land someone there."

"I have no intention of allowing Miss Mayfield to embroil herself in such an enterprise, particularly one that might prove hazardous," Trahern said stiffly. "I only meant to ask her for information. Now that I have done so, I will be on my way."

A martial glint kindled in Elizabeth's eyes as she listened to this pretty speech. "I see what it is. The pair of you mean to have an adventure and keep me out of it."

"Not me," Pickworth said hastily. "I've no intention of joining in anyone's adventure."

"This is scarcely a game, Miss Mayfield," Trahern said

curtly. "Hugh has powerful enemies, and even if you would, there is nothing you could do to help him." Then, taking pity on the distress evident on her face, Trahern took Elizabeth's hands in his and said gently, "I shall do my best to discover what has befallen Hugh. And I promise I shall tell you the moment I have definite news, Miss Mayfield. But there truly is nothing you can do to help me in this matter."

Elizabeth appeared to accept his answer complacently. Giles, however, mistrusted the look in her eyes and was careful to be out the door with his bride and with Trahern before Elizabeth could try to hatch some plot and embroil them in it with her.

When they were gone, Miss Mayfield turned to her aunt. "What shall I do?" she asked bluntly.

"Go to all the events you are meant to attend," her aunt advised sagely.

"But I cannot simply pretend nothing has occurred or forget that Lord Basingstoke is missing," Elizabeth protested.

Lady Salvage set down the piece of needlework that had occupied her attention for the past hour. "I do not mean you to forget," she replied briskly. "But there is much to be heard in gossip if one knows what to listen for, and at the moment there is nothing else I can think of for us to accomplish."

With that, Elizabeth appeared to be satisfied.

21

"I AM FLATTERED that you choose to honor me with your confidence, but I confess I am puzzled as to why you have done so," Lady Sophia, daughter of the Marquess of Wey, said, almost purring.

Miss Elizabeth Mayfield regarded her calmly, a sheaf of papers clutched tightly in one hand, as she said, also almost purring, "Why, I thought I might beg the indulgence of your opinion of my work, shortly to be published."

"Indeed?" Lady Sophia said frigidly. "If it is to be published, I cannot see why you need anyone's opinion."

"Ah, but I think you would find the story very interesting," Miss Mayfield replied thoughtfully, her eyes fixed on the small table between them. "It is, after all, about a rake, one who delights in jilting females. The sort of fellow both of us have reason to dislike."

The bored expression on Lady Sophia's face was arrested and her own voice was thoughtful as she said, "You begin to interest me, my dear. May I see what you have written?"

Elizabeth handed over the chapter she had chosen, knowing that its lurid pages would be the most likely to bear out what she had next to say. She waited in silence as the Marquess of Wey's daughter read. Finally that lady raised her head, her eyes narrow and piercing as they rested on Miss Mayfield. "Very interesting," she agreed coolly. "Dare I ask if the wronged heroine is you?"

"Yes," Elizabeth declared. She paused, took a deep breath, then said, "And I wish there were some way I might be revenged upon him."

Lady Sophia lowered her eyelids. "But why do you come to me?" she asked gently.

For a moment Miss Mayfield hesitated. Then, as though unsure of how far to go, she said diffidently, "I am told you know his lordship well and have reason to feel wronged by him. I thought perhaps you might be able to advise me how best to go about the matter. That is to say, I have been told you are a most resourceful woman and I thought you might help me. If, that is, we can find Lord Basingstoke," Elizabeth said gloomily. "I'm afraid he's gone into hiding somewhere."

Lady Sophia hesitated. It was not in her nature to trust another woman easily. Indeed, she much preferred the company of men to that of her own sex. And yet she was drawn to Miss Mayfield. Here was a resolution to match her own. And admiration from another female, something which in her experience was rare, for she was far more accustomed to envy from her rivals. But perhaps the deciding factor was curiosity. She did not entirely trust Miss Mayfield. The look on Basingstoke's face when he had talked to her at Lady Sefton's ball had been too marked to deny. And yet they had unmistakably quarreled. It would be interesting to see what Basingstoke's face would reveal if Miss Mayfield were to appear there. If the chit was in earnest, it would only add to the delicious revenge Lady Sophia plotted. If she were bamming it, hoping to discover Basingstoke's whereabouts, then she might join him in his prison. The trick would be to have the chit go with her and none the wiser, for if she were to disappear, Lady Sophia had no intention of the occurrence being laid at her door. Nor would Andover be pleased that she had taken the girl to see Basingstoke.

It was several moments, therefore, before Lady Sophia spoke. Then she said carefully as she handed back the manuscript to Miss Mayfield. "Be at the Three Magpies Inn at a quarter past ten tomorrow morning, and perhaps I may have a surprise for you. And, mind, no one must know what you are about."

"The Three Magpies?" Elizabeth repeated hesitantly.

"Yes, it is a quiet place toward the south of town, and

you are to come without a maid or footman or abigail. Don't fail me! I shall look for you at a quarter after the hour of ten,'' Lady Sophia said sternly.

Elizabeth's chin came up and her back stiffened as she rose to her feet. "I shall be there," she said. Then, with a swift smile Elizabeth added, "And I do truly thank you, Lady Sophia. It is a harsh world and we women must help one another.''

And with that she left. Lady Sophia pondered her words, not at all displeased by the sentiment they conveyed.

The earl waited, alert for the sound of footsteps. Grimly he pondered his alternatives. Already he had searched every inch of the walls for a way out, but without success. If he left this room, it would be by the door. He had no way of measuring, in the dark, how long he had been here. His watch had long since ceased to work, damaged, no doubt, in the struggle when he was abducted. Still, judging by how often his captors had brought him food, Basingstoke placed his captivity at several days now. During that time he had seen his tormentor only once, which argued that the fellow did not like to be absent from town. Basingstoke knew him; how could he not? The *ton* was not so large that those of its members who lived in London would be entirely unacquainted. Indeed, he had once moved in the same circle, shared in some of the pranks that had led Andover to be dubbed the Mad Earl. They had been rivals and friends until Andover's excesses had appalled even Basingstoke and he had moved to distance himself from the earl. But Andover had never forgiven him for that desertion, nor ceased to consider himself Basingstoke's chief rival. That they shared the same rank only made matters worse. Thus it had come as no great surprise that Andover proposed marriage to the Marquess of Wey's daughter in his absence.

This knowledge, however, provided Basingstoke with no comfort. Nor did Andover's refusal to tell Basingstoke what he meant to do with him. If Basingstoke was judged wild to a fault, this man was called utterly heartless. And now it seemed he was determined to be revenged upon Basing-

stoke for the discovery that instead of outmaneuvering his
rival, Andover had allowed himself to be tricked into offering
for Sophia after Basingstoke decided he didn't want her. With
any other member of the *ton*, it would have been absurd to
imagine his abductor meant him any real harm. With Andover, it was impossible to believe he did not.

One might have supposed that these past few days would
more than have sufficed for a resourceful gentleman like
Basingstoke to escape his prison. Unfortunately, that was
precisely Andover's opinion and he had given strict orders
to his henchmen never to visit Basingstoke alone. Instead
they were always to descend to the room in a pair, one
covering the earl with a pistol in case he should try to escape.
So thoroughly had Andover impressed upon them Basingstoke's resourcefulness that he felt as though they regarded
him somewhat in the light of an unknown fiend and would
not relax their vigilance. To be sure, Basingstoke could have
freed his hands before now, but he had no sure notion what
good it would do him. And to do so would have been to warn
his jailers as to his intentions if he failed to win free. Only
the measured certainty that no other recourse save to rush
the two men lay before him had led Basingstoke to prepare
for that step. So now he waited. And wondered what Elizabeth might be thinking about his continued absence from
London. Had he known what she intended, he would have
been appalled.

But no one knew what Elizabeth intended to do. Giles,
Leala, and even the Viscount Trahern would have stopped
her if they had discovered her plans, and she knew it. Nor
did Elizabeth doubt that her aunt would pack her off back
to Ravenstonedale, if need be, to stop her. For however much
Lady Salvage might talk about the resolution shown by
females in her day and however much she might bemoan the
insipidness of today's young ladies, she would never
countenance so mad an undertaking as this one. Elizabeth
laid her plans accordingly, and on the morning in question,
she was up early, long before her aunt would emerge from
her bedroom.

"I am going out, Finley," Elizabeth told the butler when he brought a pot of tea and a tray of scones into the breakfast room. "I am pledged to meet Mrs. Pickworth at Hookham's library this morning and we are to go on from there to a luncheon with one of her cousins. Pray tell my aunt I shall not return before dinner."

"Very good, miss," he answered with a fatherly smile, for Finley, like most of the staff, had taken a definite fancy to the mistress's niece. "I shall have the carriage brought around as soon as you have finished your breakfast."

"Thank you, Finley."

Not by a flicker of her eyes did Elizabeth betray either impatience or second thoughts. When the footman handed her into the carriage, and again, later, when he handed her down at the lending library, she thanked him in a cool, sweet voice. "You need not wait for me," she added kindly to the coachman, "for I shall be going in Mrs. Pickworth's carriage a little later."

"Very good, miss."

Elizabeth made herself enter Hookham's library and spent several desultory minutes looking at books before she allowed herself to yawn, as though bored, and leave. Fortunately the hour was too early for her to fear encountering anyone she knew. Then, glancing impatiently at the timepiece pinned to her blue corded pelisse, she left the lending library and walked round the corner before summoning a hack. If the driver was taken aback at being directed to go to the Three Magpies Inn, he did not betray it, and Elizabeth allowed herself to reflect that had the establishment been a disreputable one, he would most certainly have done so. Whatever Lady Sophia intended, it was not, then, to lead her to some shabby place where she could be robbed or assaulted.

And indeed, when the hack pulled up in the courtyard of the Three Magpies, Elizabeth could see that the place had a definite air of respectability. Oh, it was certainly not of the first stare, and Elizabeth doubted that it often saw clientele of the quality of Lady Sophia, but the customers would be genteel, if of modest means. It was without trepidation, therefore, that Elizabeth entered the establishment and

allowed herself to be shown to a private parlor that over-
looked the courtyard to wait for Lady Sophia. She ordered
coffee so that it would not seem odd to the innkeeper, but
she had no expectation of swallowing more than a sip or two.
If he thought her presence here odd, the fellow was a master
of discretion and did not betray the slightest curiosity or ask
any questions, for which she was grateful.

Elizabeth had not long to wait. No more than Miss
Mayfield did Lady Sophia wish to draw attention to their
visit here. She alighted from her coach and entered the inn.
Upon asking if her cousin had yet arrived, Lady Sophia was
informed that she had just been served a pot of coffee, and
would my lady care to join her? Lady Sophia graciously
consented to be shown into the private parlor, where the
proprietor immediately left them alone. Lady Sophia con-
gratulated Miss Mayfield upon her admirable discretion and
then informed her that nevertheless they must be off at once
if they had any wish of being able to return home before
dinner.

Within a short time Lady Sophia's coach was free of the
city, but the two ladies were not free of the constraint between
them. At last Elizabeth said coolly, "I admire your
resolution, Lady Sophia. I should not have thought it possible
to catch Basingstoke unawares and therefore abduct him."

Her ladyship gave a sharp trill of laughter. "My dear Miss
Mayfield," she said, her glowing eyes fixed on the girl's
face, "nothing is more simple than to catch men unawares.
They are in general such trusting creatures. Though why they
should be when they are so villainous themselves is a matter
quite beyond my comprehension. But as for admiring my
resolution, why, it is nothing to yours. A novel about Basingstoke! It is a masterstroke, my dear. He would positively
abhor such a thing. To be the subject of such gossip as will
certainly arise is something he detests."

"I thought he cared very little for his reputation,"
Elizabeth countered with a puzzled frown. "I am told he has
always behaved in a way that has given rise to gossip."

Lady Sophia shrugged. "He doesn't care for people
knowing he has done something outrageous. It is different

to be made a fool of by some young lady such as yourself. *That* he will dislike.''

"Perhaps people will not guess he is the person I based the character on in my book," Elizabeth suggested meekly.

Again Lady Sophia laughed. "Oh, you need have no fear. I shall undertake to vouchsafe that everyone will know the source of your inspiration within the first week your book is out and about. You shall have an instant success, Miss Mayfield. Yes, and an instant fame as well.''

"I thought to remain anonymous," Elizabeth said diffidently.

"Anonymous? Impossible, child. Do but consider! The tale takes place in the north of England, and you are known to have come from there. The book is published shortly after you arrive in London. (And someday, my dear, you must tell me how you contrived that miracle.) You were seen to quarrel with Basingstoke the first time you met here in London. What would be more natural than that people should guess? Particularly with a little help from me.''

"Must you tell them?" Elizabeth asked uncertainly.

"Yes," her ladyship answered with great firmness. "How else will they know to believe me unless I can furnish them with the particulars? Oh, don't pull such a face! It cannot signify to you. After all, you've nothing to blush for, it is Basingstoke who comes off the villain. He is the one who raised expectations which he never meant to fulfill. He is the one who deserted you the moment you accepted his proposal of marriage. He is the one who ought to be made to see he must make amends. You may rest assured no one will blame you. Oh, how uncomfortable it will be for Hugh to be everywhere laughed at and snubbed because of your book!''

She had nothing to blush for. The words echoed hollowly in Elizabeth's head but she could not contradict them, nor tell Lady Sophia that the tale she had written had gone far beyond what had, in truth, transpired. For these words were the basis of her claim for a desire for revenge against Basingstoke. She could not deny them now without arousing Lady Sophia's suspicions. Elizabeth began to perceive, finally, that perhaps there had been some justice in Basingstoke's desire to prevent her book from being published, and if she succeeded in rescuing him, she would tell him so. Still, there would be time to think about that later. Now Elizabeth leaned back against the squabs and said dryly, "Do I take you to mean, then, that Basingstoke will have his freedom by the time my book is published?"

Lady Sophia's eyes narrowed as she replied, "Oh, I think his release might be arranged the day after your book arrives among the *ton*. Then the question will naturally arise as to where he has been, and after reading your illuminating tale, the *ton* will draw its own conclusions as to the answer."

"Won't Basingstoke tell everyone the truth?" Elizabeth asked cautiously.

Her ladyship shrugged. "Even if he could bear to be made ridiculous by admitting to the world that he was bested by Andover and myself, and I don't think he could, who would believe him? Can a more improbable tale be conceived? Particularly when another explanation will be so convenient to hand? There will not be a household in London that will receive him after this." The picture so skillfully drawn by Lady Sophia caused Elizabeth to turn pale. Her ladyship saw this and patted Elizabeth's hand. "You needn't worry," she purred, "you will be everywhere received and, no doubt, accounted something of a heroine."

Elizabeth felt there might be some doubt about that, but even were it true, it would have provided her with no consolation. What had seemed a lark, something to amuse herself and a way to be privately revenged upon Basingstoke, now began to assume monstrous proportions. She could only be grateful that he had succeeded in convincing Messrs. Linley and Collier not to publish the book. All her anger was fled as she realized that he had indeed known the world far better than she. The only difficulty was what to do if she did not succeed in freeing Basingstoke. Even now Lady Sophia was regarding her thoughtfully, and Elizabeth forced herself to smile. "How delightful to contemplate such sweet revenge," she said coolly. "But that is not for a few weeks yet. What shall we do to Basingstoke in the meantime? And what if he escapes?''

Lady Sophia had plenty of time to tell her. It was a two-hour drive to where Basingstoke was held prisoner, and her ladyship had no difficulty in filling that time with descriptions of the many possible torments she and Andover had thought up for her erstwhile suitor. She described with relish, moreover, the precautions Andover had taken to prevent Basingstoke escaping their clutches. Elizabeth listened carefully, storing up the information.

22

BASINGSTOKE did not hear the coach rumble into the yard outside. The room that held him had obviously been chosen with an eye to its imperviousness to sound. Still, the footsteps on the stairs so soon after the last meal had been taken away warned him that his tormentor was back, and Basingstoke was ready, his hands clenched behind his back as though they were still tied there. If he could get Andover to send the guards away, as he had done the last time, while he taunted him, then Basingstoke thought he could win free. He would take some pleasure in giving Andover a dose of his own medicine and leaving him tied up to be found later. Basingstoke smiled grimly as he waited for the door to open.

A frown replaced the grin, however, as soon as he saw Elizabeth and Lady Sophia. "What the devil?" he muttered.

Lady Sophia looked at him from between narrowed eyes. "I could not let Andover have all the pleasure of seeing you like this," she purred. Then, looking from one to the other, she noted Basingstoke's consternation and Miss Mayfield's cold smile. "I've brought you another visitor as well," Lady Sophia added sweetly. "Your fiancée, I collect."

"She's no fiancée of mine," Basingstoke retorted grimly.

"No?" Lady Sophia countered. "How odd of me to be mistaken."

Now Elizabeth stepped forward. If she seemed a trifle pale, it might easily have been set down to anger, for her words were swift and sharp as she said, "I collect you've forgotten Ravenstonedale, my lord, and your proposal of marriage. But I have not forgotten. However lightly you took it, I did not. No, nor forgiven you for making me the object of your reckless wager. I mean to see that you pay for that!''

"In company with her ladyship and Andover, I suppose? You make a pretty trio," Basingstoke said derisively.

Elizabeth had been moving steadily closer to the earl, but now Lady Sophia made a move to forestall her. "No closer," she said sharply. At Miss Mayfield's look of surprise she added, "Even bound as he is, I do not trust Basingstoke."

"He looks helpless enough," Elizabeth said with a toss of her head. "And I do so enjoy seeing him helpless."

"So do I," Lady Sophia said dryly, "but nevertheless you will oblige me in this."

Elizabeth shrugged and moved closer to her ladyship. "What now?" she asked eagerly.

"What now, indeed?" Basingstoke echoed sardonically. "What is it to be this time? Recriminations? A demand for a show of penitence? Perhaps you expect me to beg for mercy from the pair of you jades? While the guards look on because you are afraid of me, even bound as I am?"

"I am not afraid of you," Elizabeth retorted fiercely. "I need no guards at my back."

"Nor do I," Lady Sophia said coldly as she signed to the guards to put their lantern on an overturned box and leave. Looking directly at Basingstoke, she said, "You see? We are not afraid to be here alone with you. And now we may talk more freely." She paused, then added playfully, "But come! You do not smile, Basingstoke, and I made sure you would be happy that I had brought a friend of yours with me."

"We are not friends," he retorted harshly.

"And yet Miss Mayfield was so eager to see you," Lady Sophia said pensively. "We cannot let such devotion go unrewarded. Indeed, I quite feel for her situation. I am almost persuaded that it would be worth it to set you free if I were certain you would marry Miss Mayfield. I think it would be quite amusing to see you leg-shackled. Particularly to someone so counter to your tastes."

"So that was why you went to her," Basingstoke said, looking at Elizabeth with a frown. "But it will not serve, you know.'' He looked again at Lady Sophia and said, ''I will not marry Miss Mayfield to please you or to secure my release. If that was her object in approaching you, it has failed.''

''No, that was not my object,'' Elizabeth said in an altogether different voice as she brought a pistol to a level with Basingstoke's chest.

Two pairs of startled eyes looked at Elizabeth and at the pistol she held in her hand. ''Do you hate me that much?'' Basingstoke demanded in astonishment.

''Good God! You must not shoot him,'' Lady Sophia exclaimed, appalled. ''Think of the scandal.''

''I do not mean to shoot him here,'' Elizabeth answered indifferently. ''I regret, Lady Sophia, that I must borrow your carriage and leave you stranded, but I shall send it back as soon as possible.''

Lady Sophia was torn between chagrin and wonder at what Miss Mayfield meant to do. ''Is it loaded?'' she demanded, gesturing toward the pistol.

''Of course it is loaded,'' Elizabeth replied contemptuously. ''Of what use would it be if it were not?''

''More to the point, do you know how to use it?'' Basingstoke asked, frowning.

Miss Mayfield met his gaze steadily. ''At this range I scarcely think I could miss,'' she replied.

Lady Sophia was betrayed into a laugh. ''You have gone your length this time, Basingstoke. I vow I almost forgive Miss Mayfield for this, diverting as it may prove to be. I wonder if your gilded tongue will be able to talk you out of trouble this time.''

Basingstoke ignored her. ''Where do you mean to take me?'' he asked Elizabeth.

''That you shall see, all in good time. For now it is enough for you to know you are leaving here in my power. Lady Sophia, I wonder if you would be good enough to call your guards in here and give them orders to have your coachman drive me where I will?''

Lady Sophia hesitated, but then shrugged and laughed. ''Why not? Whatever then occurs is not my fault, and

Andover cannot blame me, for how could I refuse when you possess a pistol?'' she said. ''I will no doubt see you stand trial for this, Miss Mayfield, but you may be right that it is worth it.''

True to her word, Lady Sophia called in the guards and gave the necessary orders. Five minutes later, Basingstoke clambered into Lady Sophia's coach and then waited as Elizabeth joined him. He kept his hands behind him, the rope wrapped around them as though he were still bound. Leaning back against the squabs, he said as the horses moved forward, ''It seems I am in your power, Miss Mayfield. Will you tell me what manner of revenge you plan?''

But this time Elizabeth was frowning. To Basingstoke she said, ''I ordered the coachman to drive back to London, but I am not altogether certain what to tell him when we get there. It will not do to drive round to my aunt's house or yours, for very likely Lady Sophia and the Earl of Andover will only have you kidnapped again.''

She did not expect an answer, but in an entirely different voice than before Basingstoke replied ironically, ''Don't trouble yourself about the matter, Miss Mayfield. You shan't be giving the orders to the coachman, I will.''

Startled, Elizabeth looked at Basingstoke, and before she had time to react, he had swiftly brought his hands round in front of him and seized the pistol she held loosely in her grasp. He hesitated only long enough to verify that it was indeed loaded and set it aside before he seized Elizabeth's wrists in his powerful hands and pulled her face to within inches of his own. Her pulse beat frantically and she colored under the relentless force of his gaze. Her voice was steady, however, as she said calmly, ''I came to rescue you, you know, though I realize it may be impossible for you to believe me.''

To her surprise, Basingstoke chuckled and the grip on her wrists loosened. A moment later he let her go. ''No, not impossible,'' he said, leaning back. ''You forget that I heard the Banbury tale you told Lady Sophia in my prison.''

''It might well have been true,'' Elizabeth said defensively, rubbing her sore wrists and moving as far away from him on the seat as possible. "You did play a horrid trick on me, making me the means in your wager."

"Ah, but that was Trahern's decision," he countered easily.

Elizabeth looked away. Her voice was small when she finally said, "I see. I collect I should have realized how unlikely it was that I might be the object of your fancy, even for so short a time and so absurd a reason as your wager."

"Elizabeth! Look at me," Basingstoke commanded peremptorily. When she did so, his face was stern as he said, "Come here." She moved an inch closer and he repeated the command, "Come here."

Only when Elizabeth was right beside Basingstoke did he relent. And then he took her hand in his and kissed it. A moment later he kissed her lips. "My lord?" she said unsteadily, when he released her.

"You cannot bamboozle me into thinking you hate me after that!" he told her roundly. Then, when she would not look at him, Basingstoke took her chin in one hand and tilted it up until she was forced to meet his eyes. Her pulse leapt at the warmth in them, and again at his words. "Foolish girl! You could not make me believe you hated me, even without the kiss. You forget that I have read the pages of your novel, and however hard you may have tried to make me your villain, too much of your heart shows through."

At these words Elizabeth jerked her chin free. Her eyes sparkled with anger as she said, "You know, I had not believed you were right or fair in suppressing my book. But an hour spent with Lady Sophia convinced me you were right. She meant to do the most dreadful damage with it."

"How did Sophia come to hear of it?" Basingstoke asked with a puzzled voice.

"I . . . I showed part of it to her," Elizabeth said in a small voice.

"You showed it to her? Why?" Basingstoke asked with the liveliest astonishment.

Elizabeth looked at him. "I couldn't think how else to

make her take me where you were," she said simply, "except by convincing her that I, too, had cause to desire revenge."

"Yes, and by the by, that reminds me," Basingstoke said, his voice turning severe once again. "Did you have to bring a loaded pistol?"

"What if I needed to use it to free you?" Elizabeth demanded hotly. "Of what use would an unloaded pistol have been, pray tell?"

"Very true," Basingstoke agreed soberly, but it could be seen that his lower lip quivered with suppressed laughter.

"Now you are roasting me," Elizabeth said angrily, "and that is most unfair, when I came to rescue you!"

"I meant to rescue myself today," Basingstoke said meekly. "As you saw, I managed to free my hands, and would have done the rest if you had not come."

"Well, I wish you had done so three days ago and then I might have been spared having to do all this and let Lady Sophia read part of my manuscript," Elizabeth retorted crossly.

"Yes, but then I should have missed hearing you tell such fibs and seeing you wave that pistol about," Basingstoke retorted innocently. "Indeed, I begin to regret that I showed you I was free so soon. Now I shall never know what you meant to do with me. Unless you mean to tell me, of course."

With a glint in her eye Elizabeth proceeded to tell the earl precisely what she would have liked to do with him. Then she went on to give him a rare trimming, complete with her opinion of his character, temperament, and the horridness of persons who allow one to think they are in the direst straits when they might very well have said at once that they were not. Basingstoke listened to all of this with great satisfaction. At these last words, however, he broke into say thoughtfully, "Do you know, I think it's a good thing I didn't let on that my hands were free. I hardly think Lady Sophia would have been so obliging in lending us this carriage if she had known the true situation. And then we might have needed your pistol after all."

That silenced Miss Mayfield. After several moments she said, "Yes, but what are we going to do? As soon as she discovers you are free, won't she begin planning your abduction all over again? And what about Andover? He won't be pleased."

"I could take care not to get abducted again," Basingstoke said innocently as he kissed the tip of her nose.

"Do be serious," Elizabeth told him, with only the slightest tremor in her voice. "We must do something to stop them from taking revenge."

Basingstoke once more pulled Elizabeth into his arms and kissed her full on the lips. "I do wish you could bring yourself to believe that I am capable of protecting myself and you as well. Lady Sophia and Andover will make no further attempts to abduct me, I promise you," he told her gently.

"How can you know that?" Elizabeth demanded hotly.

She would have said more, but Basingstoke once again silenced her with a thorough kiss. Then he said, his eyes twinkling, "I can promise you that because I am quite certain that when Lady Sophia hears that you have accomplished your revenge—by what means, we shall leave her to imagine—she will feel herself quite satisfied. Andover as well."

"What revenge?" Elizabeth asked warily.

"Why, that you forced me to marry you, quite against my will, I assure you!" he said innocently, a dancing gleam in his eyes. Then, even more outrageously he went on, "And they will believe it, for I intend to let the whole world know how thoroughly put upon I am, and how thoroughly under the cat's paw, as your husband."

Elizabeth wisely ignored this obvious provocation. "But you don't want to marry me," she protested. "It was all for a wager. Or is it still for a wager?" she demanded, her eyes beginning to kindle in anger.

With an exasperated sigh the earl proceeded to demonstrate to Miss Mayfield just how distasteful he found her charms. At the end of which, her bonnet was on the floor of the carriage and her hair much disarrayed. In a resolute voice, however, she said, "I cannot marry you, Hugh. What would everyone think?"

"That somehow Lady Sophia contrived to have her revenge on me. That you or she forced me into this marriage," Basingstoke said promptly. Then, setting aside his teasing tone, he said, "Frankly, my dear little goose, I don't care what people may think. And as for Lady Sophia and Andover, I am quite certain I shall be able to convince them not to attempt to abduct me or trouble us again."

There was something in Basingstoke's voice that made Elizabeth shiver and believe him. Still, however, she hesitated.

"What is it, my love?" he asked kindly. "Is it Mrs. Bethfrey?"

Elizabeth nodded. "I don't think I can stop writing, you see," she said earnestly.

Basingstoke kissed the tips of her fingers. "I don't want you to stop," he told her gently. "I know I stopped Linley and Collier's from publishing *The Reckless Wager*, but only because it could have hurt us both. Your other romances, now, I have no objection to," he ended virtuously.

"You haven't even read them," Elizabeth retorted roundly, "so how can you know if you approve of them or not?"

"Well," he said, appearing to take the question seriously, "Lady Salvage did not seem to think them objectionable, and I have a great deal of respect for her opinion. I shall want to read every manuscript beforehand, however, once you are my wife," he added provocatively.

Elizabeth sniffed and pretended to look away in disdain. Basingstoke took her chin in his hand and gently turned it so she faced him. "Well?" he said. "Will you marry me?" Then, when she did not instantly answer, he added, a twinkle again in his eyes, "You cannot, after the past half-hour, pretend indifference toward me. Not unless you wish me to believe you are the most shocking flirt! Even Lady Salvage told you that you ought not to kiss someone like that unless

you are betrothed to him. And since I already have your
father's permission to ask for your hand—''

"You what?'' she demanded incredulously.

"It's not polite to interrupt people,'' he told her with mock
severity as he gently tapped her mouth with his fingertip.
"Now, as I was saying, since I spoke with your father, and
he gave me his permission to marry you, before I left Ravenstonedale, you need have no qualms on that score.''

"You told him who you were?'' Elizabeth asked in
disbelief.

"Well, no,'' Basingstoke admitted apologetically, "but I
did say that I wanted to marry you.''

"What did he say?'' Elizabeth asked suspiciously.

"He said that as you seemed determined to ruin yourself,
I might as well marry you, if you would have me, which
we both gave leave to doubt.'' Basingstoke paused and
frowned, then said with genuine sternness this time, "I wish
you will tell me why you did leave Ravenstonedale. Yes,
I know you've said it was to play propriety, but as I've said
before, it won't fadge. Was it to escape me, my little love?
Because if you really don't wish to marry me, you needn't
fly. I promise I shan't harry you into it.''

He looked down at her with such an anxious expression
that in spite of herself Elizabeth reached up to stroke his
cheek, an action that immediately caused his arm to tighten
about her further. "I did not leave Ravenstonedale to escape
you,'' she answered him softly.

"Then why?'' he persisted. "Why accompany a pair of
fools determined to ruin themselves?''

"Because if she hadn't fled her future stepfather, Leala
would have been ruined anyway,'' Elizabeth replied roundly.
"He was little short of a monster, and matters were reaching
a desperate pass for Leala. And I could not leave her, in such
distress, to fly alone. Or without me to serve as chaperone
and . . . Yes, I know you will say I was too young to serve
such a purpose, but let me tell you, it answered very well.
No one suspected any impropriety, for what young man
would run off with two young ladies at the same time?''

"Very true," Basingstoke said, as though much struck by this thought. "It would require a young man with far more address and gumption than poor Pickworth. No, no, my love. You shan't come to cuffs with me. While I might deplore the bumblebroth your journey might have landed you in, I quite understand why you did it. After all, any young woman with sufficient resolution to set out to rescue me might be entrusted with any mission of mercy."

"Now you are roasting me again," Elizabeth countered in an aggrieved tone.

"Just a little," he agreed, dropping another kiss on the tip of her nose. "Will you forgive me?"

Sometime later, when she had proved to his satisfaction that she had indeed forgiven him, they were startled to have the coach draw to a halt and the driver open the door. "London, ma'am. What address shall I drive round to?" he asked expressionlessly.

Elizabeth glanced quickly at Basingstoke, but his hands were behind him again, as though still bound, and he stared resolutely at the far side of the coach. She made herself speak coolly as she replied, "You may drive me round to Lady Salvage's house in Berkeley Square."

When they arrived and she was handed out of the coach, Elizabeth told the driver, "You may return to Lady Sophia. Pray tell her that I said his lordship has proved to be most cooperative, after all."

Then, without a backward glance for Basingstoke, Elizabeth mounted the steps to her aunt's town house. A rather startled porter admitted them. "Your aunt is in the drawing room, Miss Mayfield," he said forebodingly, "with a number of persons."

Elizabeth raised her pretty eyebrows in surprise but answered prosaically, "Aunt Elizabeth will be pleased to see his lordship. I'll announce us." To Basingstoke, as they mounted the stairs, she said, "I suppose it must be someone he disapproves of, but that need not distress us."

On the threshold of the drawing room, however, Elizabeth stopped in dismay. Her father and stepmother were engaged in spirited argument with Lady Salvage. Willoughby was investigating a table and about to tip it over. Annabelle was deep in conversation in a far corner with Trahern. At the sight of Elizabeth and Basingstoke, all conversation stopped and five pairs of eyes turned in their direction. "There you are!" Sir Edmund said to his daughter with patent disapproval, "in the company of that man! Elizabeth, you are to have nothing more to do with Lord Basingstoke."

"That will be a trifle difficult, sir," Basingstoke said in his most daunting, drawling voice, "as your daughter is going to marry me."

"Impossible!" Sir Edmund retorted. "I refuse my permission! Elizabeth," he said, turning to his sister, "I lay this at your door and blame you."

"Papa, I am of age and you cannot refuse your consent," Elizabeth said hotly.

Basingstoke's hand on her arm silenced her when she would have said more. "As you have already given me permission to marry your daughter, Sir Edmund," he said in a bored voice, "I think it a trifle late for you to refuse my suit."

"I? Impossible!" Sir Edmund exclaimed.

"Well, you did say that I might marry her and be damned," Basingstoke replied deprecatingly.

"Had I known who you were, I would never have said so," Sir Edmund shot back.

Lady Mayfield, who up until now had been too thunderstruck to speak, said, in fury that threatened to overwhelm her, "You? To marry the Earl of Basingstoke? No! I will not believe it! I will not have it!"

Annabelle had moved to her sister's side and was asking eagerly, "Really and truly, Elizabeth? You are to be Lady Basingstoke? Will you bring me out next year? It's beyond everything wonderful," she concluded in awed accents.

Willoughby meanwhile was tugging at his half-sister's skirts as he said, looking up at her, "You will take me to the circus! You will!"

Trahern was greeting Basingstoke and saying, "Thank God you're back. I charge you to tell me all about it. Later, of course, when we are out of this madhouse."

Lady Salvage, the only one to remain unruffled throughout all of this, merely said with quiet humor, "I see that you have contrived to rescue Basingstoke, Elizabeth. Is this proposal in the nature of gratitude, Hugh?"

Basingstoke's arm, much to the alarm of Sir Edmund and Lady Mayfield, slipped around Elizabeth's waist and tightened there. "No, Lady Salvage, it is not in the nature of gratitude. I have decided that the only way to deal with your niece's termagant pen is to marry her and have a close eye over everything she tries to write." At which point Elizabeth brought her heel down on Basingstoke's foot as hard as she was able. "Termagant," he repeated appreciatively as he looked down at her with a warmth that caused her pulse to race in the most absurd manner.

"I repeat: I absolutely refuse to allow you to marry my daughter!" Sir Edmund thundered, his color rising alarmingly.

Basingstoke raised his quizzing glass and eyed Sir Edmund slowly from head to foot. "Indeed?" he said frostily. "Nevertheless, I mean to marry your daughter. As she has so aptly pointed out, she is of age. Lady Salvage, I assume you will permit us to be married from your house? I warn you, I do not mean to wait long to make Elizabeth my wife." Lady Salvage nodded, amused, and Basingstoke continued, "You may, of course, make public your disapproval of the proceedings, Sir Edmund, but I cannot think what purpose that will serve, save to make your name an object of the most ridiculous conjectures. You will be held to have attempted to whistle down a most eligible match for your daughter."

"Why, you impudent jackanapes!" Sir Edmund gasped.

"Yes, but perhaps he is right," Lady Mayfield ventured to say uneasily. "It is what people would say."

This roused Sir Edmund to new indignation and he told his wife sharply, "I knew I should come by myself. I should have left you all in Ravenstonedale, the way I wanted to. I'd have made better time traveling, too."

Basingstoke ignored the high-spirited discussion that then ensued between Sir Edmund and his wife. Instead he turned to Elizabeth and said gently, "Well my love? Shall we withdraw until they contrive to talk themselves out?"

She blushed in what he considered a most delightful manner and nodded. Lady Salvage nodded approvingly. "Yes, do take her out for a drive or to the park or something and come back in a couple of hours. By then I promise you my brother will have had time to come round."

Gratefully the pair slipped away and, as a much interested and thoroughly scandalized maidservant told the rest of the staff downstairs later, Miss Mayfield and his lordship paused halfway down the stairs, where his lordship clasped Miss Mayfield in the most shocking embrace and kissed her soundly, not caring in the least who might see. Lady Salvage's most superior majordomo condescended to explain that when the girl had been in service somewhat longer, she would learn that such behavior was sometimes to be seen in engaged couples, as he had no doubt Lord Basingstoke and Miss Mayfield were soon to be announced to be. And that it was not her place to criticize her betters.

Since, at that moment Lord Basingstoke was once more kissing Miss Mayfield in just such a shocking manner, it is to be inferred that he would have agreed.